The Governess Tales

Sweeping romances with fairytale endings!

Meet Joanna Radcliff, Rachel Talbot,
Isabel Morton and Grace Bertram.

These four friends grew up together in
Madame Dubois's school for young ladies,
where they indulged in midnight feasts, broke
the rules and shared their innermost secrets!

But now they are thrust into the real world,
and each must adapt to her new life
as a governess.

One will rise, one will travel,
one will run and one will find her real home…

And each will meet her soulmate,
who'll give her the happy-ever-after
she's always dreamt of!

Read Joanna's story in
The Cinderella Governess

Read Rachel's story in
Governess to the Sheikh

Read Isabel's story in
The Runaway Governess

And read Grace's story in
The Governess's Secret Baby

All available now!

Author Note

The Governess's Secret Baby is Book Four
in The Governess Tales series, but it is a
stand-alone story and can be enjoyed even
if you haven't read the previous three. If
you *have* read the others, however, you will
be pleased to know that the epilogue—an
absolute joy to write—brings back all three
couples from the other linked books to find
out what has happened since the end of their
stories.

I loved bringing to life the gothic Shiverstone
Hall, nestled below Shiver Crag in the
Yorkshire Dales, and Nathaniel, its reclusive,
scarred and taciturn owner. Only a feisty
heroine will do for Nathaniel, and Grace
is certainly that: bold, impulsive and
determined, but also rootless and plagued
with hidden self-doubt.

Enjoy the emotional ups and downs as Grace
helps Nathaniel find the courage to embrace
life again, and Nathaniel proves to Grace that
she is capable of being loved.

THE GOVERNESS'S SECRET BABY

Janice Preston

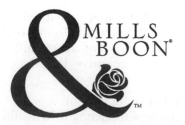

This is a work of fiction. Names, characters, places, locations
and incidents are purely fictional and bear no relationship
to any real life individuals, living or dead, or to any actual
places, business establishments, locations, events or
incidents. Any resemblance is entirely coincidental.

First published in Great Britain 2016
By Mills & Boon, an imprint of HarperCollins*Publishers*
1 London Bridge Street, London, SE1 9GF

Large Print edition 2017

© 2016 Harlequin Books S.A.

ISBN: 978-0-263-06759-0

Special thanks and acknowledgement are given to
Janice Preston for her contribution to The Governess Tales
series

Our policy is to use papers that are natural, renewable
and recyclable products and made from wood grown in
sustainable forests. The logging and manufacturing processes
conform to the legal environmental regulations of the
country of origin.

Printed and bound in Great Britain
by CPI Antony Rowe, Chippenham, Wiltshire

Janice Preston grew up in Wembley, North London, with a love of reading, writing stories and animals. In the past she has worked as a farmer, a police call-handler and a university administrator. She now lives in the West Midlands with her husband and two cats and has a part-time job with a weight management counsellor (vainly trying to control her own weight despite her love of chocolate!).

Books by Janice Preston

Mills & Boon Historical Romance

The Governess Tales

The Governess's Secret Baby

Men About Town

Return of Scandal's Son
Saved by Scandal's Heir

**Linked by Character
to *Men About Town* duet**

Mary and the Marquis
From Wallflower to Countess

Visit the Author Profile page
at millsandboon.co.uk.

To my fellow authors
Georgie Lee, Laura Martin and Liz Tyner:
it's been a pleasure collaborating with you, ladies,
and I hope I've done justice to your characters
in the epilogue.

Prologue

Early October 1811

Nathaniel Pembroke, Marquess of Ravenwell, threw a saddle on Zephyr's back, mounted up, and pointed the black stallion's head towards the fell, the words of the letter searing his brain and his heart. As Zephyr's hooves flashed across the ground the tears spilling from Nathaniel's eyes evaporated in the wind and his roar of rage was heard by no man. The fells above Shiverstone Hall were avoided by local villagers and farmers alike, and that was precisely how Nathaniel liked it.

The great black's pace flagged and, reluctantly, Nathaniel steadied him to a trot. The anger and the grief burning his chest had not eased—the hollow place where his shrivelled heart had struggled to survive this past nine years was still there, only now it was cavernous…a vast, stygian void. He should know by now grief could never be outrun. It cleaved to you like lichen clung to the rocks that strewed the dale below.

Hannah. Tears again clouded his vision and he blinked furiously, gazing hopelessly at the gunmetal grey of the sky. Dead. Never again to see his beloved sister's face, or to hear her laugh, or to feel the rare human contact of her arms around him, hugging, reassuring. And David, Hannah's husband of eight years and Nathaniel's loyal and steadfast friend…his only friend. Also gone.

The raw lump in Nathaniel's throat ached unbearably as the words of his mother's letter—delivered as he had broken his fast that morning—reverberated through his brain: a carriage accident; Hannah and David both killed outright; little Clara, their two-year-old daughter, the only survivor.

You are named as Guardian to the child, my son. If I can help you, you know that I will, but I cannot, at my age, shoulder all responsibility for her upbringing. Neither will I live in that God-forsaken place you please to call home in order to help you with the task.

I urge you to come home to Ravenwell and we shall raise Clara together. It is time you took your place in the world again.

If you choose not to, however, then you must come and collect your ward. It is your duty

*and you owe it to your poor, dear sister to take
charge of and care for the child she loved more
than life itself.
Your loving
Mother*

Nathaniel turned Zephyr for home, the realities
of his dilemma bearing down on him. He could not
deny the truth of Mother's words—she was getting
no younger and she would never be happy living at
Shiverstone Hall—his cadet estate near the border
between the North Riding of Yorkshire and West-
morland—nor would it be healthy for her. She lived
most of the year at Ravenwell Manor, his main estate
in the far more civilised countryside that surrounded
the town of Harrogate, on the far side of the Dales.

But…he considered those alternatives, neither of
which appealed. Go home to Ravenwell? He shook
his head in dumb denial. Never. He could tolerate
neither the memories nor the looks of sympathy from
those who had known him before. Still less could he
stomach the recoil of strangers at the sight of him.

By the time he rode into the yard behind Shiverstone Hall, his decision was made. He had one choice,
and one choice only. He must fetch Clara and bring
her to Shiverstone to live with him. His courage almost failed at the thought—what did he know about
children, particularly one as young as Clara?

* * *

'You have responsibilities, Nathaniel. You cannot continue to hide away. How are you ever to produce an heir otherwise? Not every woman will react like Miss Havers.'

Nathaniel bit back a growl at the reminder of Miss Havers. He had suspected how that would end as soon as his mother had told him of the woman who had agreed to a marriage of convenience. Even the lure of his wealth and title was not enough to compensate for his scars. Miss Havers changed her mind after one meeting and Nathaniel had retreated to Shiverstone Hall, resolving to live a solitary life. She hadn't been the first woman to react to his altered appearance with horror: Lady Sarah Reece—with whom he'd had an understanding before he was injured—had lost no time in accepting another man's proposal.

He did not miss his former carefree life as one of society's most eligible bachelors: such frivolous pleasures no longer held any allure for him. Nor did he miss his erstwhile friends. He would never forget the shock on their faces, nor the speed with which they had turned their backs on him after the fire.

He was *happy* with his life, dammit. He had his animals and his hawks—*they* did not judge him by how he looked.

His mother forked a morsel of roast grouse into her mouth and then placed her knife and fork on to her plate whilst she chewed, watching Nathaniel expectantly.

'I am but thirty, Mother. There is more than enough time to produce an heir.'

'Would you pour me another glass of wine, please, Nathaniel?'

He obliged. They were dining alone in the dining room at Ravenwell Manor, the servants having been dismissed by Lady Ravenwell as soon as the dishes had been served. That had prompted Nathaniel to suspect their conversation would prove uncomfortable and his defences were already well and truly in place.

'Thank you.' His mother sipped her wine, then placed her glass on the finely embroidered tablecloth. 'Do not think I am ignorant of your plan, son,' she said. 'You arrive here after dark, at a time you know Clara will already be asleep. What is your intention? To snatch her from her bed before dawn and be away before you need to see anyone, or be seen?'

He hated the sympathy in her eyes but he also knew that behind that sympathy there existed a steely belief in duty. *His* duty: to the estate, to his family, to the memory of his father, and to the future of the marquessate. Her jibe about snatching Clara from her bed sailed too close to the truth.

'I came as soon as I could after reading your letter, Mother. My late arrival was because I did not want to wait until tomorrow to travel, but I *am* afraid I must return in the morning.'

'Must?'

'It will not do to expect a two-year-old child to travel late into the night.'

'Then stay for a few days. At least give the poor child a chance to remember you.'

He had last seen Clara four months before, when she had come up to Shiverstone with Hannah and David from their home in Gloucestershire. They had stayed with him for a week. Thinking of his sister and his friend brought that choking, aching lump into his throat once more. He bowed his head, staring unseeingly at the food in front of him, his appetite gone.

'I could invite a few neighbours for dinner. Only people you already know, not strangers.'

I can't... Bile rose, hot and bitter in his mouth.

He shoved his plate from him with a violent movement. Mother jumped, her fork clattering on to her plate and her face crumpled, the corners of her mouth jerking down as her eyes sheened. Guilt—familiar, all-encompassing—swept through him and he rounded the table to fold his mother into his arms as she sobbed.

'I'm sorry, Mother.' She had lost her precious daughter and he had been concerned only with his own selfish fears. 'Of course I will stay for a few days.' A few days would be all he could endure of his mother's efforts to reintroduce him into local society, he was certain of that. 'But no dinner parties, I beg of you. Do not forget we are in mourning.'

Mother's shoulders trembled. 'You are right,' she whispered. 'But…please…stay with me a short time.'

He dropped a kiss on her greying head. 'I will.'

Poor Mother, left with only him out of her family. He was no substitute for Hannah. Why couldn't it have been he who died? Hannah had so much to live for, whereas he… He batted that wicked thought away. No matter how black his future had seemed, he had never been tempted to take his own life. He was content enough with the life he led. The villagers avoided him and he had his dogs and his horses and his hawks: they provided all the company he needed.

Nathaniel resumed his seat, but did not draw his plate towards him again.

'What about Clara's nanny?' He remembered the woman from Hannah's last visit to Shiverstone. At least she was not a complete stranger. 'I assume she is here and will stay with Clara?'

His mother's gaze skittered past him. 'I am afraid not. She has family in Gloucester and does not want to move so far away. You will need to appoint a new nanny and then, later, she will need a governess.'

He battled to hide his dismay, but some must have shown, for she continued, 'You must put Clara's needs first. She is two years old. What do you know about taking care of such a young child? Of any child? And Mrs Sharp has enough to do with running the Hall. You cannot expect her to take on more responsibility.'

*She's right. I know she's right...*and yet every fibre of his being rebelled against the notion of not one, but two, strangers coming into his home. He eyed his mother. *Perhaps...*

'And do not think I shall yield if you try to persuade me to raise Clara on your behalf.'

His mother—one step ahead as usual. He must accept that, once again, he had no choice.

'I will advertise for a governess,' he said. One person—surely he could cope with one person. Once she was used to his appearance, all would be well. He need not see much of her. 'Then Clara will not have to adapt to another person in her life later on. She needs consistency after losing her parents.'

Poor little soul. Unwanted by her own mother—an unfortunate girl in trouble—and now losing her adoptive parents. And she was a sweet little poppet. Too young to react with horror to his scars as other children had done in the past, Clara had accepted her uncle and she, in turn, had delighted him with her gurgles and her first attempts at speech. An unaccustomed tingle warmed his chest. She would be his. She might only be two, but she would provide some human contact apart from his servants.

'You must do as you deem right for Clara.' Mother's sceptical expression, however, suggested that she was completely aware of his real reason for choosing a governess rather than a nanny. 'And for darling Hannah.'

A lone tear spilled over and tracked down her lined cheek. How had he never been aware of those wrinkles before? His mother had aged. Grief, he thought, did that to a person and poor Mother had faced more grief than most.

'I will,' he vowed.

He owed it to his sister, who had tackled her own heartbreak of trying and failing to give birth to a healthy baby with such dignity and grace. She had been besotted by Clara from the very first moment she held her in her arms and impotent anger raged through Nathaniel that she would now miss the joy of seeing her adopted daughter grow and mature. Hannah had been one of the few constants in his life since the fire that had taken his father and changed Nathaniel's life for ever. He would not let her down now. He would write to the editor of the *York Herald*, with instructions to run an advertisement for a trained governess who was willing to come and live at the Hall.

For the first time he felt a sliver of doubt—what sort of woman would agree to bury herself in such an isolated place?

Chapter One

Early November 1811

Grace Bertram breathed easier as she reached the edge of the dense woodland, with its mossy-trunked trees and its unfamiliar rustles and groans, and the barely glimpsed scurrying of invisible creatures through the undergrowth. The track she had followed from the village of Shivercombe—past the church, across a meadow and a river, and then through that spooky wood—emerged on to the edge of bleak moorland and she stopped to catch her breath, and look around.

Moorland—or, more correctly, fells according to the local villagers who had tried so hard to dissuade her from venturing to Shiverstone Hall—rose ahead of her before merging mistily with the overcast sky. She could just about make out the slate roof and tall chimneys of a house squatting in a fold of land ahead, the only sign of human habitation in that forbidding landscape.

Grace's pulse accelerated in a fusion of anticipation and fear. That must be it. Shiverstone Hall. And there, beneath those glistening black slates, was Clara. Her baby, who now lived in this isolated place with—according to those same villagers—a man who was fearful to behold and who breathed fire and brimstone on any who ventured on to his land: the Marquess of Ravenwell. Grace would not...*could* not... allow those warnings to deter her. She had survived that creepy forest and she would survive Lord Ravenwell's wrath. She would not turn back from the task she had set herself two years ago.

She owed that much to the daughter she had given away at birth.

Grace swapped her portmanteau into her left hand and glanced down at her muddied half-boots in disgust. Her left foot already squelched in her boot and the right felt suspiciously damp too. What sort of *lord* lived out here in the middle of nowhere and did not even take the trouble to build a bridge over the river between the village and his house? An uncivilised sort, that was who, in Grace's opinion. There was a ford for horses and vehicles, but the only place for a person to cross the river was by using huge, wet, *slippery* rocks set in the riverbed as stepping stones.

She was fortunate it was only her left foot that had been submerged.

Grace trudged on, muttering under her breath, still following the same track. At seventeen, and a pupil at a school for governesses, she'd had no choice but to give her baby away, but she had regretted it each and every day since then. She had promised herself that one day she would track her daughter down and make sure she was happy and loved and living the life she deserved. And now it was even more urgent that she find her daughter and make sure she was well cared for—and *wanted*—since her discovery that the couple who had adopted Clara as their own had perished in a carriage accident.

But doubts still plagued her as she walked, despite her resolve to see her mission through. She might be bold, but she was not stupid. What if this Marquess would not allow her to see Clara? What reason could she give him for seeking out the child? Not the truth. He would send her packing. No. She must find another reason.

And what if Clara is not happy and loved?

What on earth could she—a nineteen-year-old newly trained governess with no home and little money in her pocket—actually *do*? She pushed the thought aside with an impatient *tut*.

She would deal with that when and if it became necessary.

She plodded on, skirting the worst of the puddles that dotted the track. Finally, she crested the rise ahead of her and there it was. She paused. It was bigger than that first glimpse had suggested, but its appearance—grim and grey with creepers adorning the walls—and location were hardly that of a dwelling in which one might expect a wealthy lord to reside.

A shrill cry echoed through the air and she whirled around.

Nothing.

At least she wasn't still in the forest—that unearthly sound would then indeed have unnerved her. She scanned the bleak landscape, but nothing moved. Another plaintive cry brought her heart into her mouth. She looked up and caught sight of a huge bird—bigger than any she had ever seen—gliding and soaring. It then circled once, before pitching into a dive: a dark blur silhouetted against the low clouds until it disappeared behind the hill that rose behind the house.

Grace swallowed, hunched her shoulders, swapped her portmanteau over again, and soldiered on. Her upbringing at her uncle's house in Wiltshire and, since the age of nine, at Madame Dubois's School for Young Ladies in Salisbury had ill-prepared her for such nature in the raw.

Twenty minutes later the track passed through a gateway in a stone wall, at which point the surface was reinforced with gravel. A broad drive curved away to the left, only to then sweep around and across the front of Shiverstone Hall. A footpath, paved with stone setts, led from this point in a straight line to the house, bisecting a lawn. Grace followed the path until, directly opposite the front door, it rejoined the gravelled carriageway.

She paused, her heart thudding as she scanned the stone-built Hall with its blank, forbidding windows, and its massive timber door, just visible in the gloomy depths of a central, gabled porch.

There was no sound. Anywhere. Even the air was still and silent.

It is as though the house is lying in wait for me— an enchanted castle, sleeping until the fairy princess awakens it and frees the inhabitants. Or a monster's lair, awaiting the unwary traveller.

Grace bit her lip, shivering a little, castigating herself for such fanciful thoughts, worthy of one of those Gothic novels Isabel used to smuggle into school and then pass around for her awestruck friends to read. A wave of homesickness hit Grace at the thought of Isabel, Joanna, and Rachel. Her dearest friends. What were they doing now? Were they happy? Grace shook her head free of her memories: the three friends she might never see again and her heartache when the time had come for her to leave Madame Dubois's school. For a few years she had belonged and she had been loved, valued, and wanted—a rare feeling in her life thus far.

Resisting the urge to flee back the way she had come, Grace crossed the carriageway, wincing as the crunch of the gravel beneath her boots split the silence. She stepped through the arched entrance to the porch and hesitated, staring with trepidation at the door looming above her.

I have come this far... I cannot give up now.

She sucked in a deep breath and reached for the huge iron knocker. She would make her enquiries, set her mind at rest and return to the village. She had no wish to walk through that forest as the light began to fade, as it would do all too early at this time of year. She only had to knock. And state her business. Still she hesitated, her fingers curled around the cold metal. It felt stiff, as though it was rarely used. She released it, nerves fluttering.

Before she could gather her courage again, a loud bark, followed by a sudden rush of feet, had her spinning on the spot. A pack of dogs, all colours and sizes, leapt and woofed and panted around her. Heart in mouth, she backed against the door, her bag clutched up to her chest for protection. A pair of wet, muddy paws were planted in the region of her stomach, and a grinning mouth, full of teeth and lolling tongue, was thrust at her face, snuffling and sniffing. A whimper of terror escaped Grace despite her efforts to silence it. In desperation, she bent her leg at the knee and drummed her heel against the door behind her. Surely the human inhabitants of this God-forsaken place couldn't be as scary as the animals?

After what felt like an hour, she heard the welcome sound of bolts being drawn and the creak of hinges as the door was opened.

'Get down, Brack!' The voice was deep and brooked no disobedience. 'Get away, the lot of you.'

Grace turned slowly. She looked up…and up. And swallowed. Hard. A powerfully built man towered over her, his face averted, only the left side of it visible. His dark brown hair was unfashionably long, his shoulders and chest broad, and his expression—what she could see of it—grim.

She could not have run if she wanted to, her knees trembled so. Besides, there was nowhere to run to, not with those dogs lurking nearby.

'You're late,' he growled.

Time seemed to slow. The man continued to not quite look at Grace as her brain examined and rejected all the truthful responses at her disposal.

'I am sorry,' was all she said.

'You look too young to be a governess. I expected someone older.'

Governess? Are there other children here apart from Clara? The parallels with her own life sent a shiver skittering down her spine. She knew the reality of growing up with cousins who did not accept you as part of the family.

'I am fully trained,' Grace replied, lifting her chin.

Anticipation spiralled as the implications of the man's words sank in. If Lord Ravenwell was expecting a governess, why should it not be her? She was trained. If his lordship thought her suitable, she could stay. She would see Clara every day and could see for herself that her daughter was happy and loved. That she was not viewed as a burden, as Grace had been.

The man's gaze lowered, and lingered. Grace glanced down and saw the muddy streaks upon her grey cloak.

'That was your dog's fault,' she pointed out, indignantly.

The man grunted and stood aside, opening the door fully, gesturing to her to come in. Gathering her courage, Grace stepped past him, catching the whiff of fresh air and leather and the tang of shaving soap. She took two steps and froze.

The hall in which she stood was cavernous, reaching up two storeys into the arched, beamed roof. The walls were half-panelled in dark wood and, on the left-hand side, a staircase rose to a half-landing and then turned to climb across the back wall to a galleried landing that overlooked the hall on three sides. There, halfway up the second flight of stairs, a small face—eyes huge, mouth drooping—peered through the wooden balustrade. Grace's heart lurched. She moved forward as if in a dream, her attention entirely focussed on that face.

Clara.

It must be. Love flooded every cell of Grace's being as she crossed the hall, tears blurring her vision. She was real. A living little person. The memory—a tiny newborn baby, taken too quickly from her arms— could now be replaced by this little angel. A forlorn angel, she realised, recognising the sadness in that dear little face, the desolation in those huge eyes. Given away by her birth mother and now orphaned and condemned to be raised by—

Grace spun to face the man, who had followed her into the hall. His head jerked to one side, but not before she glimpsed the ravaged skin of his right cheek, half-concealed by the hair that hung around his face. Impatiently, she dismissed his appearance. The only thing that mattered was to ensure her daughter was properly cared for.

'Who are you?'

A scowl lowered the man's forehead. 'I am the master of this house. Who are *you*?'

The master. Clara's uncle. The Marquess.

Well, title or not, scarred or not, you will not frighten me.

Grace drew herself up to her full five-foot-three. 'Grace Bertram.'

'Bertram? I don't… You are not who I expected—'

'I came instead.'

'Oh.' Lord Ravenwell hesitated, then continued gruffly, 'Follow me. I'll need to know something about you if I'm to entrust my niece to your care.'

Grace's heart skipped a beat. This was the moment she should tell him the truth, but she said nothing. Could she…*dare* she…follow her heart? She needed a job and it seemed, by some miracle, there might be a position for her here.

'Clara—' Ravenwell beckoned to the child on the stairs '—come with me.'

Clara bumped down the stairs on her bottom and Grace committed every second to memory, her heart swelling until it felt like it might burst from her chest. She blinked hard to disperse the moisture that stung her eyes.

'Come, poppet.'

The Marquess held out his hand. Clara shuffled across the hall, feet dragging, her reluctance palpable. She reached her uncle and put her tiny hand into his as her other thumb crept into her mouth and she cast a shy, sideways glance at Grace. She looked so tiny and so delicate next to this huge bear of a man. Did she fear him?

'Good girl.'

The Marquess did not sound cruel or unkind, but Grace's heart ached for her sad little girl. At only two years old, she would not fully understand what had happened and why her life had changed so drastically, but she would still grieve and she must miss her mama and her papa. In that moment Grace knew that she would do everything in her power to stay at this place and to care for Clara, her daughter's happiness her only concern.

She felt Ravenwell's gaze upon her and tore her attention from Clara. She must now impress him so thoroughly he could not help but offer her the post of governess.

'You had better take those boots off, or Mrs Sharp will throw a fit.'

Grace glanced down at her filthy boots and felt her cheeks heat as she noticed the muddy footprints she had left on previously spotless flagstones.

So much for impressing him.

'Mrs Sharp?' She sat on a nearby chair and unbuttoned her boots.

'My housekeeper.'

Grace scanned the hall. Every wooden surface had been polished until it gleamed. She breathed in, smelling the unmistakable sweet scent of beeswax. Appearances could be deceptive, she mused, recalling her first view of the Hall and its unwelcoming exterior. Although…looking around again, she realised the impeccably clean hall still felt as bleak as the fells that rose behind the house. There was no fire in the massive stone fireplace and there were no homely touches: no paintings, vases, or ornaments to brighten the place. No rug to break up the cold expanse of stone floor. No furniture apart from one console table—incongruously small in that huge space—and the simple wooden chair upon which she now sat. It lacked a woman's touch, giving it the atmosphere of an institution rather than a home. Grace darted a look at the Marquess. Was he married? She had not thought to ask that question before she had travelled the length of the country to find her daughter.

She placed her boots neatly side by side next to the chair and stood up, shivers spreading up her legs and across her back as the chill of the flagstones penetrated her woollen stockings.

Ravenwell gestured to a door that led off the hall. 'Wait in there.'

Chapter Two

Grace entered a large sitting room. Like the entrance hall, it was sparsely furnished. There were matching fireplaces at each end of the room—one lit, one not—and the walls were papered in dark green and ivory stripes above the same dark wood panelling as lined the hall. On either side of the lit fireplace stood a wing-back chair and next to each chair stood a highly polished side table. A larger table, with two ladder-back wooden chairs, was set in front of the middle of three tall windows. At the far end of the room, near the unlit fireplace, were two large shapes draped in holland covers. Her overall impression of the room was of darkness and disuse, despite the fire burning in the grate.

This was a house. A dwelling. Well cared for, but not loved. It was not cold in the room and she stood upon polished floorboards rather than flagstones, but she nevertheless suppressed another shiver.

Lord Ravenwell soon returned, alone and carrying a letter.

'Sit down.'

He gestured at the chair to the right of the hearth and Grace crossed in front of the fire to sit in it. Ravenwell sat in the opposite chair, angling it away from the fire, thus ensuring, Grace realised, that the damaged side of his face would be neither highlighted by firelight nor facing her. His actions prompted a desire in her to see his scarred skin properly. Was it really as horrific as he seemed to believe?

'Why did the other woman—' Ravenwell consulted the letter '—Miss Browne, not come? I expected her three days ago.'

His comment sparked a memory. 'I believe she found the area too isolated.'

The villagers had regaled her with gleeful tales of the other young lady who had listened to their stories, headed out from the village, taken one look at the dark, ancient woodland through which she must walk to reach Shiverstone Hall and fled.

'And did our isolation not deter you?'

'I would not be here if it did.'

His head turned and he looked directly at her. His eyes were dark, deep-set, brooding. His mouth a firm line. On the right side of his face, in a broad slash from jaw to temple, his skin was white and puckered, in stark contrast to the tan that coloured the rest of his face. Grace tried not to stare. Instead, she allowed her gaze to drift over his wide shoulders and chest and down to his muscular thighs, encased in buckskin breeches and boots. His sheer size intimidated her. How furious would he be if he discovered her deception? Her heartbeat accelerated, thumping in her chest, and she sought to distract herself.

'Will Mrs Sharp not scold *you* for wearing boots indoors?' she said, before she could curb her tongue.

His shoulders flexed and a muffled snort escaped him. 'As I said, I am the master. And *my* boots,' he added pointedly, 'are clean.'

Chastised, Grace tucked her stockinged feet out of sight under her chair. She was in an unknown place with a strange man she hoped would employ her. This was not school. Or even her uncle's house, where she had grown up. She was no longer a child and she ought to pick her words with more care. She was a responsible adult now, with her own way to make in the world. Ravenwell had already commented on her youthfulness. She must not give him a reason to think her unsuitable to take care of Clara.

She peeped at him again and saw that the back of his right hand, in which he held the letter, was also scarred.

Like Caroline's. One of her fellow pupils had similar ravaged skin on her legs, caused when her dress had gone up in flames when she had wandered too close to an open fire as a young child. She was lucky she had survived.

Is that what happened to Ravenwell? Was he burned in a fire?

As if he felt her interest, the Marquess placed the letter on a side table and folded his arms, his right hand tucked out of sight, before bombarding Grace with questions.

'How old are you?'

'Nineteen, my lord.'

'Where did you train?'

'At Madame Dubois's School for Young Ladies in Salisbury.'

'Where are you from?'

'I grew up in my uncle's house in Wiltshire.'

'What about your parents?'

'They died when I was a baby. My uncle and aunt took me in.'

Ravenwell unfolded his arms and leaned forward, his forearms resting on his thighs, focussing even more intently on her. Grace battled to meet his eyes and not to allow her gaze to drift to his scars. It was just damaged skin. She must not stare and make him uncomfortable.

His voice gentled. 'So you know what it is like to be orphaned?'

'Yes.'

It is lonely. It is being second-best, unimportant,

overlooked. It is knowing you are different and never feeling as though you belong.

'I do not remember my parents. I was still a babe in arms when they died.'

Like Clara, when I gave her away.

He sat back. 'I hope Clara will remember her parents, but I am not sure she will. She is only two.'

'She will if you talk to her about them and keep their memory alive,' Grace said. 'My uncle and aunt never spoke to me of my parents. They had quarrelled over something years before and they only took me in out of what they considered to be their Christian duty.'

Silence reigned as Ravenwell stared, frowning, into the fire. Grace knitted the strands of her thoughts together until she realised there were gaps in her understanding.

'You speak only of Clara,' she said. 'You said you will need to know about me if you are to entrust her to my care. Is she not rather young, or do you and Lady Ravenwell have need of a governess for your other children, perhaps?'

Her question jerked Ravenwell from his contemplation of the flames. 'There is no Lady Ravenwell. Clara would be your sole charge.'

'Would a nanny, or a nursery maid, not be more suitable?' The words were out before Grace could stop them. *What are you trying to do? Talk him out of employing you?*

Ravenwell scowled. 'Are you not capable of looking after such a young child? Or perhaps you think it beneath you, as a trained governess?'

'Yes, I am capable and, no, it is not beneath me. I simply wondered—'

'I do not want Clara to grow fond of someone and then have to adjust to a new face in a few years' time. She has faced enough disruption. Do you want the position or not?'

'Yes…yes, of course.' Grace's heart soared. How could life be any sweeter?

Ravenwell was eyeing her, frowning. 'It will be lonely out here, for such a young woman. Are you sure?'

'I am sure.'

Joy bubbled through her. *Real* joy. Not the forced smiles and manufactured jests behind which she had concealed her aching heart and her grief from her friends. Now, her jaw clenched in her effort to contain her beaming smile, but she knew, even without the aid of a mirror, her delight must shine from her eyes. She could not fake nonchalance, despite Madame Dubois's constant reminders that unseemly displays of emotion by governesses were not appreciated by their employers.

'I will fetch Clara and introduce you.'

Grace's heart swelled. She could not wait to speak to Clara. To touch her.

Lord Ravenwell stood, then hesitated and held out his hand. 'Give me your cloak. I will ask Mrs Sharp to brush it for you.'

Startled by this unexpected courtesy, Grace removed her grey cloak—warm and practical, and suitable garb for a governess—and handed it to him. Doubts swirled. Until this moment she had not fully considered that accepting the role of governess to Clara actually meant becoming part of this household and living here with Ravenwell. She thought she had learned her lesson of acting first and thinking about the consequences second, but perhaps, deep down, she was still the impulsive girl she had always been. Her entire focus had been on the lure of staying with Clara. She swallowed. Ravenwell—who had not smiled once since her arrival and who appeared to live as a recluse in this cold, isolated house—was now her employer. This terse, scowling man was now part of her future.

It will be worth it, just to be with Clara. And what kind of life will my poor little angel have if I do not stay?

There was no question that she would accept the post, even if she had not considered all the implications. She would bring sunshine and laughter and love to her daughter's life. Clara would never doubt she was loved and wanted. Grace would make sure of it.

'How many servants are there here?' she asked.

'Three indoors and two men outdoors. We live quietly.'

And with that, he strode from the room, leaving Grace to ponder this unexpected path her life had taken. What would Miss Fanworth say if she could see Grace now? Doubt assailed her at the thought of her favourite teacher. It had been Miss Fanworth who had come to her aid on that terrifying night when she had given birth, Miss Fanworth who had advised Grace to give her baby up for adoption and Miss Fanworth who had taken Grace aside on the day she left the school for the final time and revealed the name of the couple her baby daughter had been given to.

'It is up to you what you choose to do with this information, Grace, but I thought you deserved to know.'

Grace had left school that day, full of determination to find the people who had adopted her daughter, knowing nothing more than their name and that they lived in Gloucestershire. When she eventually tracked them down, it had been too late. They were dead and Grace's daughter had been taken to live with her uncle and guardian, the Marquess of Ravenwell.

Undeterred, Grace had travelled to Ravenwell's

country seat, south of Harrogate, where—after some persistent questioning of the locals—she had discovered that the Marquess lived here, at Shiverstone Hall. And, finally, here she was. She had succeeded. She had found her baby.

She could almost hear Miss Fanworth's measured tones in her head: *'Do take care, Grace, dear. You are treading on very dangerous ice.'*

Those imagined words of caution were wise. She must indeed take care: her heart quailed again at the thought of the forbidding Marquess discovering her secret.

I am not really doing wrong. I am a governess and he needs a governess. And I will protect Clara with the last breath of my body. How can that be wrong?

The door opened, jolting her from her thoughts. Ravenwell entered, walking slowly, holding Clara by the hand as she toddled beside him, a rag doll clutched in the crook of her arm.

'Clara,' he said, as they halted before Grace. 'This is Miss Bertram. She has come to take care of you.'

A tide of emotion swept through Grace, starting deep down inside and rising…swelling…washing over her, gathering into a tight, aching knot in her chest. Her throat constricted painfully. She dropped to her knees before her little girl, drinking her in… her light brown curly hair, her gold-green eyes—*the image of mine*—her plump cheeks and sweet rose-bud lips.

Oh, God! Oh, God! Thank you! Thank you!

She reached out and touched Clara's hand, marvelling at the softness of her skin. How big that hand had grown since the moment she had taken her baby's tiny fist in hers and pressed her lips to it for the last time. She had tucked away those few precious memories, knowing they must last a lifetime. And now, she had a second chance.

She sucked in a deep breath, desperately trying to suppress her emotion. Ravenwell had released Clara's hand and moved aside. Grace could sense his eyes on her. Watching. Judging.

'What a pretty dolly.' Her voice hitched; she willed the tears not to come. 'Does she have a name?'

Clara's thumb crept into her mouth as she stared up at Grace with huge eyes—too solemn, surely, for such a young child?

'She has barely spoken since she lost her parents.'

Powerless to resist the urge, Grace opened her arms and drew Clara close, hugging her, breathing in her sweet little-girl scent as wispy curls tickled her neck and cheek.

She glanced up at Ravenwell, watching her with a puzzled frown. She dragged in a steadying breath. She must not excite his suspicions.

'I know what it is l-like to be orphaned,' she reminded him. 'But she has us. W-we will help her to be happy again.'

She rubbed Clara's back gently, rocking her and revelling in the solid little body pressed against hers. She was rewarded with a slight sigh from the child as she relaxed and wriggled closer. The tears welled. She was powerless to stop them. A sob shook her. Then another.

'Are you crying?'

The deep rumble penetrated Grace's fascination with this perfect being in her arms. Reluctantly she looked up, seeing Ravenwell mistily through drowning eyes. He was offering her his hand. Grace blinked and, as the tears dispersed, she saw the handkerchief he proffered. She reached for it and dabbed her eyes, gulping, feeling a fool.

She prised her arms loose, releasing Clara. There would be plenty of time to hold her, as long as Ravenwell did not now change his mind about employing her. Grace's head rang with Madame Dubois's warnings on the necessity of staying in control of one's emotions at all times.

It's all very well for Madame. She hasn't a sensitive bone in her body.

The words surfaced, unbidden, in Grace's mind but, deep down, she knew she was being unfair to the principal of her old school. If rumour was true— and Miss Fanworth's words on the day Joanna had left the school, as well as Rachel's discovery of Madame weeping over a pile of old letters suggested it was—Madame had suffered her own tragedies in the past. Thinking of the stern Madame Dubois steadied Grace. The knowledge she had let herself down set her insides churning.

Would Ravenwell be thoroughly disgusted by her display of emotion? Would he send her away? She pushed herself—somewhat inelegantly—to her feet, hoping she had not disgraced herself too much. She must say something. Offer some sort of explanation. Not the truth, though. She could not possibly tell him the truth. She mopped her eyes again, and handed him back his handkerchief. His expression did not bode well.

'Th-thank you,' she said. 'I apologise for giving way to my emotions. I—'

Her heart almost seized as she felt a small hand creep into hers. Clara was by her side and, with her other hand, she was offering her dolly to Grace. Tears threatened again and Grace blinked furiously, took the doll, and crouched down by the child, smiling at her.

'Thank you, Clara. N-now I can see your dolly properly, I can see she is even prettier than I first thought—almost as p-pretty as you.'

She stroked Clara's satiny cheek and tickled her under the chin. She was rewarded with a shy smile.

Heart soaring, Grace regained her feet and faced the Marquess, holding his gaze, strength and determination stiffening every fibre of her being. She would give him no opportunity to change his mind. She was staying, and that was that.

'As I was about to explain, I was overcome by the similarities between Clara's situation and my own as a child and also by relief at having secured such an excellent position.' She raised her chin. 'It was an unforgivable lapse. It will not happen again, I promise.'

Chapter Three

Nathaniel felt his brows lower in yet another frown and hastily smoothed his expression, thrusting his doubts about Grace Bertram aside. Would he not harbour doubts about anyone who applied for the role of governess simply because, deep down, he still rebelled at the idea of a stranger living under his roof?

He loathed this sense of being swept along by an unstoppable tide of events, but, from the very moment he had read his mother's letter, he had known his fate was sealed. He was Clara's legal guardian and he must...no, he *wanted* to do what was right for her, both for her own sake and for Hannah's. The familiar ache of loss filled his chest and squeezed his throat, reminding him it was not mere obligation that drove him, but his love for Hannah and David, and for their child. He had vowed to make Clara's childhood as happy and carefree as possible, but the three weeks since his return from Ravenwell had confirmed he needed help.

But is she the right woman for the job?

Those doubts pervaded his thoughts once more.

There were all kinds of very good reasons why he should not employ Grace Bertram as Clara's governess. She was too young and, he had silently admitted as he had watched her with Clara, too pretty. Mrs Sharp would disapprove on those grounds alone—his housekeeper had made no secret of her opinion he should seek a mature woman for Clara's governess. Nathaniel knew her concern was more for his sake than for Clara's and it irritated him to be thought so weak-willed he could not withstand a pretty face in his household. He had learned the hard way to protect his heart and his pride from ridicule and revulsion.

Miss Bertram also wore her heart on her sleeve in a manner most unsuited to a woman to whom he must entrust not only his niece's well-being but also her moral character. And, in the short time she had been here, she had demonstrated an impulsiveness in her speech that gave him pause. Did she lack the sense to know some thoughts were best left unsaid, particularly to a prospective employer? Take his boots off indeed! But, in fairness, this *would* be her first post since completing her training and she was bound to be nervous.

There were also very compelling reasons why he would not send Grace Bertram packing. She was pleasant and she was warm-hearted. With a young child, that must be a bonus. He refused to relinquish the care and upbringing of his two-year-old niece to a strict governess who could not—or would not—show her affection. More importantly, Clara appeared to like Miss Bertram. Besides, if he was honest, there *was* no one else. He had no other option. He had interviewed two women whilst he was still at Ravenwell Manor, hoping to find someone immediately. Neither wanted the job. And that other woman, Miss Browne, had not even arrived for her interview.

He eyed Grace Bertram as she faced him, head high. Despite her youth, he recognised her unexpected core of steel as she threw her metaphorical gauntlet upon the ground. She wanted to stay. Her eyes shone with determination as she held his gaze.

She does not recoil at my appearance.

She had not flinched once, nor stared, nor even averted her gaze. It was as though his scars did not matter to her.

Of course they do not, you fool. You are interviewing her for the post of a governess, not a wife or a mistress.

That thought decided him. They would spend little time together, but her acceptance of his appearance was a definite point in her favour.

'Come,' he said. 'I will introduce you to Mrs Sharp and she will show you around the house.'

He swung Clara up on to his shoulders, revelling in

her squeal of delight, and led the way to the kitchen, awareness of the young woman following silently at his heels prickling under his skin. He needed to be alone; he needed time to adjust. By the time they reached the door into the kitchen, his nerves were strained so tight he feared one wrong word from his housekeeper or from Miss Bertram might snap them with disastrous consequences. He pushed the door wide, ducking his knees as he walked through the opening, to protect Clara's head. Mrs Sharp paused in the act of slicing apples.

'Was she suitable, milord?'

Miss Bertram was still behind Nathaniel; he stepped aside to allow her to enter the kitchen.

'Yes. Mrs Sharp—Miss Bertram.'

Mrs Sharp's lips thinned as she looked the new governess up and down. 'Where are your shoes?'

Nathaniel felt rather than saw Miss Bertram's sideways glance at him. He should ease her way with Mrs Sharp, but he felt the urge to be gone. Miss Bertram must learn to have no expectations of him: he had his own life to live and she would get used to hers. He lifted Clara from his shoulders, silently excusing himself for his lack of manners. She was only a governess, after all. He would be paying her wages and providing her with food and board. He need not consider her feelings.

'I'll leave you to show Miss Bertram the house:

where she is to sleep, the child's new quarters and so forth.'

He turned abruptly and strode from the kitchen, quashing the regret that snaked through him at the realisation of how much less he would now see of Clara. The past few weeks, although worrying and time-consuming, had also revived the simple plea-sure of human company, even though Clara was only two. She'd been restless at night and he'd put her to sleep in the room next to his, needing to know some-one would hear her and go to her if she cried. Al-though the Sharps and Alice, the young housemaid who had travelled back with him from Ravenwell, had helped, he could not expect them to care for Clara's welfare as he did. Now, that would no longer be necessary. A suite of rooms had already been pre-pared for when a governess was appointed and Clara would sleep in her new room—at the far side of the house from his—tonight.

He snagged his greatcoat from a hook by the back door and shrugged into it as he strode along the path to the barns. The dogs heard him coming and milled around him, leaping, tails wagging frantically, pant-ing in excitement.

'Steady on, lads,' he muttered, his agitation settling as he smoothed the head of first one, then another. His favourite, Brack—a black-and-tan hound of in-determinate breeding—shouldered his way through the pack to butt at Nathaniel's hand, demanding attention. He paused, taking Brack's head between his hands and kneading his mismatched ears—one pendulous and shaggy, the other a mere stump following a bite when he was a pup—watching as the dog half-closed his eyes in ecstasy. Dogs were so simple. They offered unconditional love. He carried on walking, entering the barn. Ned, his groom, emerged from the feed store at the far end.

'Be riding, milord?' Ned was a simple man of few words who lived alone in a loft above the carriage house.

'Not now, Ned. How's the mare?'

'She'll do.' One of the native ponies they kept for working the sheep that grazed on the fells had a swollen fetlock.

Nathaniel entered the stall where she was tethered, smoothing a hand down her sleek shoulder and on down her foreleg.

'Steady, lass. Steady, Peg,' he murmured. There was still a hint of heat in the fetlock, but it was nowhere near as fiery as it had been the previous day. He straightened. 'That feels better,' he said. 'Keep on with the good work. I'm off up to the mews.'

'Right you are, milord.'

The dogs, calmer now, trotted by his side as he walked past the barn and turned on to the track that led up to the mews where he kept his birds, cared for by Tam. There was no sign of Tam, who lived in a cottage a few hundred yards further along the track with his wife, Annie. The enclosures that housed his falcons—three peregrine falcons, a buzzard, and a kestrel—came into view and Nathaniel cast a critical eye over the occupants as he approached. They looked, without exception, bright-eyed, their feathers glossy, as they sat on their perches. He had flown two of them earlier and now they were fed up and settled.

Loath to disturb the birds, he did not linger, but rounded the enclosures to enter the old barn against which they were built, shutting the door behind him to keep the dogs out. Light filtered in through gaps in the walls and the two small, unglazed windows, penetrating the gloomy interior. A flap and a shuffle sounded from the large enclosure built in one corner, where a golden eagle—a young female, they thought, owing to her size—perched on a thick branch.

The eagle had been found with a broken wing by Tam's cousin, who had sent her down from Scotland, knowing of Nathaniel's expertise with birds of prey. Between them, he and Tam had nursed the bird back to health and were now teaching her to fly again. Nathaniel had named her Amber, even though he knew he must eventually release her back into the wild. His other birds had been raised in captivity and would have no chance of survival on their own. Amber, however, was different and, much as Nathaniel longed to keep her, he knew it would be unfair to cage her when she should be soaring free over the mountains and glens of her homeland.

Nathaniel selected a chunk of meat from a plate of fresh rabbit on Tam's bench, then crossed to the cage, unbolted the door, and reached inside. His soft call alerted the bird, who swivelled her head and fixed her piercing, golden eyes on Nathaniel's hand. With a deft flick of his wrist, Nathaniel lobbed the meat to the eagle, who snatched it out of the air and gulped it down.

Nathaniel withdrew his arm and bolted the door, but did not move away. He should return to the house. He had business to deal with: correspondence to read and to write, bills to pay, decisions to make over the countless issues that arose concerning his estates. He rested his forehead against the upright wooden slats of Amber's cage. The bird contemplated him, unblinking. At least she wasn't as petrified as she had been in the first few days following her journey from Scotland.

'I know how you feel,' he whispered to the eagle. 'Life changes in an instant and we must adjust as best we can.'

The turning point in his life had been the fire that destroyed the original Ravenwell Manor. It had been rebuilt, of course. It was easy to restore a building— not so easy to repair a life changed beyond measure.

He touched his damaged cheek, the scarred skin tight and bumpy beneath his fingertips. And it was impossible to restore a lost life. The familiar mix of guilt and desolation washed over him at the memory of his father.

And now another turning point in his life had been reached with Hannah's death.

As hard as he strove to keep the world at bay, it seemed the Fates deemed otherwise. His hands clenched, but he controlled his urge to slam his fists against the bars of the cage—being around animals and birds had instilled in him the need to control his emotions. He pushed away from the bars and headed for the door, turning his anger upon himself. Why was he skulking out here, when there was work to be done? He would shut himself in his book room and try to ignore this latest intrusion into his life.

Grace winced as the door banged shut behind the Marquess. She tried not to resent that he had left her here alone to deal with Mrs Sharp, who looked as disapproving as Madame Dubois at her most severe, with the same silver-streaked dark hair, scraped back into a bun. Grace tried to mask her nervousness as the housekeeper's piercing grey eyes continued to rake her. Clara, meanwhile, had toddled forward and was attempting to clamber up on a chair by the table. Grace moved without conscious thought to help her.

Clara didn't appear to be intimidated by the house-keeper, so neither would she.

'Well? Your shoes, Miss Bertram?'

'His lordship requested that I remove them when I came inside,' Grace said. 'They were muddy.' She looked at the bowl of apples. They would discolour if not used shortly. 'May I help you finish peeling those before you show me where my room is? I should not like them to spoil.'

Wordlessly, Mrs Sharp passed her a knife and an unpeeled apple. They worked in silence for several minutes, then Mrs Sharp disappeared through a door off the kitchen and re-emerged, carrying a ball of uncooked pastry in one hand and a pie dish in the other. As she set these on the table, she reached into a pocket of her apron and withdrew a biscuit, which she handed to Clara, who had been sitting quietly— too quietly, in Grace's opinion—on her chair. Clara took the biscuit and raised it to her mouth. Grace reached across and stayed her hand.

'What do you say to Mrs Sharp, Clara?'

Huge green eyes contemplated her. Grace crouched down beside Clara's chair. 'You must say thank you when someone gives you something, Clara. Come, now, let me hear you say *Thank you.*'

Clara's gaze travelled slowly to Mrs Sharp, who had paused in the act of sprinkling flour on to the table and her rolling pin.

'Did his lordship not say? She has barely said a word since she came here.'

'Yes. He told me, but I shall start as I mean to go on. Clara must be encouraged to find her voice again,' Grace said. 'Come on, sweetie, can you say, *Thank you?*'

Clara shook her head, her curls bouncing around her ears. Then, as Grace still prevented her eating the biscuit, her mouth opened. The sound that emerged was nowhere near a word, it was more of a sigh, but Grace immediately released Clara's hand, saying, 'Clever girl, Clara. That was nice of you to thank Mrs Sharp. You may now eat your biscuit.'

She glanced at Mrs Sharp, but the housekeeper's head was bent as she concentrated on rolling out the pastry and she did not respond. Grace bit back her irritation. It wouldn't have hurt the woman to praise Clara or to respond to her. But she held her tongue, wary of further stirring the housekeeper's hostility.

Once the apple pie was in the oven, Mrs Sharp led the way from the kitchen. They went upstairs first— Grace carrying Clara—then crossed the galleried landing and turned into a dark corridor, lit only by a window at the far end.

'This is your bedchamber.'

Grace walked through the door Mrs Sharp indicated into a plain room containing a bed, a massive wardrobe and a sturdy washstand. The curtains were half-drawn across the windows, rendering the room as gloomy and unwelcoming as the rest of the house. Grace's portmanteau was already in the room, by the foot of the bed.

'Who brought this up?' she asked, bending to put Clara down. The thought of the burly Lord Ravenwell bringing her bag upstairs and into her bedchamber set strange feelings stirring deep inside her.

'Sharp. My husband.'

'So he works in the house, too?'

'Yes.'

Thoroughly annoyed by now, Grace refused to be intimidated by the older woman's clipped replies.

'His lordship mentioned three inside servants and two outside,' she said. 'Who else is there apart from you and your husband?'

A breath of exasperation hissed through Mrs Sharp's teeth. 'Indoors, there's me and Sharp, and Alice, the housemaid. She's only been here three weeks. His lordship brought her back with him and Miss Clara from Ravenwell, to help me with the chores.

'Outside, there's the men who care for his lordship's animals. Ned is unmarried and lives in quarters above the carriage house. Tam lives in a cottage on the estate. His wife, Annie, spins wool from the estate sheep and helps me on laundry days.

'Now, I have dinner to prepare. I don't have time for

all these questions.' She headed for the door. 'Hurry along. There's more to show you before we're finished.'

'I shall just find my shoes.'

Her stockinged feet were thoroughly chilled again, after standing in the stone-flagged kitchen. Ignoring another hiss from the housekeeper, Grace unclasped her bag and pulled out her sturdy shoes, part of the uniform deemed by Madame Dubois to be suitable for a governess, along with high-necked, long-sleeved, unadorned gowns, of which she had two, one in grey and one in brown.

She hurried to put on her shoes whilst Mrs Sharp tapped her foot by the door. As soon as Grace was done, Mrs Sharp disappeared, her shoes clacking out her annoyance as she marched along the wooden-floored corridor. Grace scooped Clara up and followed.

'This is the eastern end of the house,' the housekeeper said, opening the next door, 'which will be your domain upstairs. Your bedchamber you've seen, this is the child's room—there's a door between the two, as you can see. Then there's a small sitting room, through that door opposite, for your own use, and the room at the far end will eventually be the schoolroom but, for now, it will be somewhere Miss Clara can play without disturbing his lordship.'

All the rooms were furnished in a similar style to

Grace's bedchamber and they felt chilly and unwelcoming as a result. Clara deserved better and Grace
vowed to make the changes necessary to provide a
much cosier home for her.

'Is his lordship wealthy?'

Mrs Sharp glared. 'And why is that any business
of yours, young lady?'

Chapter Four

Too late, Grace realised how her question might be misconstrued by the clearly disapproving housekeeper.

'No…no…I did not mean…' She paused, her cheeks burning with mortification. 'I merely meant… I should like to make these rooms a little more cheery. For Clara's sake.'

Mrs Sharp stiffened. 'I will have you know this house is spotless!'

'I can see that, Mrs Sharp. I meant no offence. You do an excellent job.' She would ask the Marquess. Surely he could not be as difficult to deal with as his housekeeper? 'Perhaps you would show me the rest of the house now?'

They retraced their steps to the head of the staircase. 'His lordship's rooms are along there, plus two guest bedchambers.' Mrs Sharp pointed to the far side of the landing, her tone discouraging. 'You will have no need to turn in that direction. Alice, Sharp, and I have our quarters in the attic rooms. I will show you the rooms on the ground floor you have not yet seen and then I must get back to my kitchen. The dinner needs my attention and Miss Clara will want supper before she goes to bed.'

Grace followed Mrs Sharp to the hall below, helping Clara to descend the stairs. She bit her lip as she saw the trail of mud from the front door to where she had left her half-boots by the only chair in the hall and was thankful the housekeeper did not mention the mess. The longcase clock in the hall struck half past four as Mrs Sharp hurried Grace around the rest of the ground floor: the drawing room—as she called it—where Ravenwell had interviewed her, a large dining room crammed with furniture shrouded in more holland covers, a small, empty sitting room and a morning parlour furnished with a dining table and six chairs where, she was told, Lord Ravenwell ate his meals.

Grace wondered, but did not like to ask, where she would dine. With Clara in the nursery suite? In the kitchen with the other servants? Clara was flagging and Grace picked her up. The house was, as her first impression had suggested, sparse and cold but clean. She itched to inject some light and warmth into the place, but realised she must tread very carefully where the prickly housekeeper was concerned.

They reached the final door off the hall, to the right

of the front door. Clara had grown sleepy and heavy in Grace's arms.

'This,' Mrs Sharp said, as she opened the door and ushered Grace into the room, 'is the book room.'

Grace's gaze swept the room, lined with glass-fronted bookcases, and arrested at the sight of Lord Ravenwell, glowering at her from behind a desk set at the far end, between the fireplace and a window.

From behind her, Mrs Sharp continued, 'It is where—oh!' She grabbed Grace's arm and pulled her back. 'Beg pardon, milord. We'll leave you in peace.'

'Wait!'

Grace jumped at Ravenwell's barked command and Clara roused with a whimpered protest. Grace hugged her closer, rubbing her back to soothe her, and she glared at the Marquess.

'Clara is tired and hungry, my lord,' she said. 'Allow me to—'

'Mrs Sharp. Take Clara and feed her. I need to speak to Miss Bertram.'

'Yes, my lord.'

Grace gave her child up with reluctance, her arms already missing the warmth of that solid little body. She eyed Ravenwell anxiously as the door closed behind Mrs Sharp and Clara. His head was bowed, his attention on a sheet of paper before him.

Has he found me out? Will he send me away?

Her knees trembled with the realisation of just how much she wanted...*needed*...to stay.

'Sit!'

Grace gasped. She might be only a governess, but surely there was no need to speak to her quite so brusquely. He had not even the courtesy to look at her when he snapped his order, but was directing his attention down and away, to his right. Was he still attempting to hide his disfigurement? Grace stalked over to the desk and perched on the chair opposite his.

He lifted a brow. She tilted her chin, fighting not to relinquish eye contact, determined not to reveal her apprehension. After what seemed like an hour, one corner of his mouth quirked up.

'Did you think I meant you?'

'I...I beg your pardon?'

'I was talking to the dog.' He jerked his head to his right.

Grace followed the movement, half-standing to see over the side of his desk. There, sitting by his side, was the rough-coated dog that had jumped up at her when she first arrived at Shiverstone Hall.

'Oh.' She swallowed, feeling decidedly foolish and even more nervous; the dog was very big and she had little experience of animals.

'Now, to business.' Any vestige of humour melted from Ravenwell's expression as if it had never been and Grace recalled, with a thump of her heart, that she might have a great deal more to worry about than a dog. 'I cannot understand how your letter applying for the post can have gone astray but, now you are here, we must make the most of it. You said this is your first post since finishing school, is that correct?'

Grace swallowed her instinctive urge to blurt out that she had written no letter of application. 'Yes, my lord.'

'Do you carry a reference or—?'

'I have a letter of recommendation from my teacher, Miss Fanworth,' Grace said, eagerly. Mayhap she was worrying about nothing. He did not sound as though he planned to send her away. 'It is in my bag upstairs.'

'Go and get it now, please. I shall also require the name of the principal of the school and the address.'

'The…the principal?' Grace's heart sank. 'Wh-why do you want that when I already have a letter from Miss Fanworth?'

Out of the four friends, she had been Madame Dubois's least favourite pupil, always the centre of any devilment. *You are the bane of my life*, the Frenchwoman had once told Grace after a particularly naughty prank. Of course, that was before Grace had Clara—thank goodness Madame Dubois had never found out about *that* escapade—and Grace's behaviour had improved considerably since then. Perhaps Madame would not write too damning a report about Grace's conduct at school.

The Marquess continued to regard her steadily. 'I should have thought that was obvious,' he said, 'and it is not for you to question my decision.'

'No, my lord.'

Grace rose to her feet, keeping a wary eye on the dog as she did so. His feathery tail swished from side to side in response and she quickly averted her eyes.

'Are you scared of him? Brack, come here, sir.'

Ravenwell walked around the desk to stand next to Grace and she quelled her impulse to shrink away. She had forgotten quite how tall and intimidating he was, with his wide shoulders and broad chest. He carried with him the smells she had previously noted: leather, the outdoors, and soap. Now, though, he was so close, she caught the underlying scent of warm male and she felt some long-neglected hunger within her stretch and stir. His long hair had swung forward to partially obscure the ravaged skin of his right cheek and jaw, but he did not appear to be deliberately concealing his scars now and Grace darted a glance, taking in the rough surface, before turning her wary attention once again to Brack. The dog had moved closer to her than she anticipated and now she could not prevent her involuntary retreat.

'It is quite all right. You must not be scared of him.'

There was a hint of impatience in Ravenwell's tone.

Grace peeped up at him again, meeting his gaze. He might be intimidating in size, and brusque, but she fancied there was again a hint of humour in his dark brown eyes.

'Try to relax. Hold out your hand. Here.'

He engulfed her hand in his, eliciting a strange little jolt deep in her core. Her pulse quickened. Ravenwell called to Brack, who came up eagerly, sniffed and then pushed the top of his head under their joined hands, his black-and-tan coat wiry under Grace's fingers. The dog had a disreputable look about him, one ear flopping almost over his eye whilst the other was a ragged stump. Grace swallowed. Ravenwell wouldn't keep a dangerous animal indoors. Would he?

'All he wants is some attention,' Ravenwell said, his warm voice rumbling through her.

Grace's chest grew tight, her lungs labouring to draw air.

'Where are the other dogs?'

'Brack's the only one who is allowed inside.' Ravenwell released Grace's hand and moved away, and Grace found she could breathe easily again. 'I reared him from a pup after his mother died.'

Grace stroked along Brack's back, feeling very daring. 'I am sure I will get used to him.'

She imagined telling the other girls about this: how they would laugh at her fear of a simple dog. Then, with a swell of regret and sorrow, she remembered she would never again share confidences with her friends. They could write, of course, but letters were not the same as talking face to face—sharing their hopes and fears and whispering their secrets as they lay in bed at night—or as supporting and comforting each other through the youthful ups and downs of their lives. And those friends, her closest friends— her dearest Joanna, Rachel, and Isabel—had supported and comforted Grace through the worst time of her life. Theirs had been the only love she had ever known.

She longed to hear how they all fared in their new roles as governesses and she knew they would be waiting to hear from her—wondering if she had found the baby she had vowed to trace. But they would not know how to contact her—none of them, no one from her former world, knew where she had been since she left the school or where she was at this moment in time.

She must let them know.

'My lord…if you are to write to Madame Dubois, do you think…might I write to Miss Fanworth too? I should like her to know I arrived safely.'

'What about your aunt and uncle? Will they not also wish to know you are here?'

'Yes, of course.'

She uttered the words, but she doubted they would

concern themselves one way or the other as to her welfare, as long as she did not end up back on their doorstep, costing them money. She had visited them before starting her quest to find Clara. They had made it clear their home was no longer hers, now she was an adult.

'I shall write to them as well.'

'You may write your letters in here. Ned rides into the village most mornings with the post.'

'Thank you.'

Grace ran upstairs to fetch her letter of recommendation, deliberating over her strange reaction to the Marquess. There had been a moment…when he had been standing so close…when he had taken her hand… She shook her head, dismissing her reaction as nonsense. It was fear of the dog, that was all. Nevertheless, she would avoid using the book room to write her letters whilst he was present. She would wait until her disturbing employer was elsewhere in the house.

Nerves knotted her stomach when she returned downstairs and handed him Miss Fanworth's letter.

'I must go now and see to Clara.' The words tumbled from her, and his brow rose. 'I shall write my letters later, so they will be ready for the morning. Thank you.'

She did not wait for his response, but hurried from the room, feeling her tension dissipate as she closed the door behind her. She went to the kitchen, where Clara was eating some bread and butter with a bowl of broth. The room was warm, and steamy with a mouthwatering aroma that made Grace's stomach growl in protest, reminding her she had not eaten since her breakfast that morning.

A man with ruddy cheeks, small blue eyes and sleeked-down mousy hair sat beside Clara. He was helping her to spoon the broth into her mouth, in between supping from a tankard of ale. He grinned at Grace, but Mrs Sharp—sitting on the opposite side of the scrubbed table—scowled as she entered.

'What did his lordship want with you?'

Grace tilted her chin. 'I suggest you ask him, Mrs Sharp,' she said. 'If he wishes you to be privy to our conversation, I am sure he will enlighten you.'

Mrs Sharp's eyes narrowed, but she said nothing more. Grace switched her attention to the man, whose grin had widened, his eyes almost disappearing as his face creased.

'Good afternoon,' she said. 'My name is Grace Bertram and I expect you already know I have come to take care of Clara.'

The man bobbed to his feet and nodded. 'Pleased to meet you, miss. I'm Sharp—husband of this one.' He winked at Mrs Sharp, whose lips thinned so much they almost disappeared. 'I look after his lordship, such as he'll allow, bring in the wood and coal and tend the fires, and do a bit of gardening.

'I'll wager this little one—' he ruffled Clara's curls '—will be happy to have you here. As am I,' he added, with a defiant look at his wife, who huffed audibly and got up to stir a pot suspended over the range.

Sharp's eyes twinkled as he raised his tankard in a silent toast to his wife's back. He tilted his head back, drinking with evident enjoyment.

'Sit yourself down, missy...' he put the tankard down with a clatter, earning him another irritable look from his wife '...and tell us a bit about yourself while Miss Clara finishes her meal.'

Grace took care to tell the Sharps no more than she'd already told his lordship. It was not lying. Not precisely. She merely omitted certain facts. Sharp—as garrulous and inquisitive as his spouse was taciturn—continued to interrogate Grace until, the minute Clara finished eating, Grace shot to her feet.

'I must take Clara upstairs now, so she can become accustomed to her new room before it is time for her to sleep.'

She smiled at Sharp to soften her abruptness and picked Clara up, hefting her on to one hip. She couldn't wait to have her little girl all to herself, nor to get away from Sharp's questions and Mrs Sharp's suspicious looks. Quite why the housekeeper disliked her she could not begin to guess, unless…

'Will Mrs Sharp miss looking after Clara?' she asked Sharp. His wife was rattling around in the pantry and Grace kept her voice low so she would not hear. 'Is that why she does not care for me being here?'

'Bless 'ee, no.' Sharp's words, too, were quiet and he darted a glance at the pantry door before continuing, 'It's his lordship she's protecting. She's worried he'll—' He clamped his lips and shook his head. 'Nay, I'll not tell tales. You'll soon find out, if'n you don't already know.'

'What?' Grace hissed. Why would a housekeeper worry about a marquess? And protect him against whom? Her? That made no sense. 'What were you going to say?'

Mrs Sharp chose that moment to emerge from the pantry and Sharp smirked at Grace. She couldn't question him further now.

'His lordship dines at six,' Mrs Sharp said. 'And we have our meal after he's been served. Do not be late.'

Nasty old crow. Grace left the kitchen and carried Clara upstairs.

'Alone at last, sweetie,' she said, as she shut the nursery door firmly behind them.

She shivered. There was no fire lit and the only illumination was from the single candlestick she had carried up to light their way. The room had bare, polished floorboards, a large cabinet, two wooden chairs and a small, low table.

Grace lowered Clara to the floor. 'We shall have to do something about this, Clara. This is simply not good enough.'

She glanced down at her daughter, who was gazing up at her with worry creasing her forehead and her mouth drooping. Grace's heart faltered and she crouched down.

'Don't look so sad, little one,' she whispered. 'I am not cross with you.'

The enormity of the task she had undertaken dawned on her. What did she know about caring for such a young child? Had she thought, because she was Clara's mother, she would magically know what to do and how to raise her properly? All her training had been about older children. She cupped Clara's face between her palms and pressed a kiss to her forehead.

'We shall learn how to go on together,' she said. 'But first, I shall talk to your uncle and I will make sure you want for nothing. And the first step will be a lovely cosy room where you can play and have fun.'

'Unc' Nannal.'

Grace froze. 'What did you say, Clara?'

Clara—eyes wide, thumb now firmly jammed in

her mouth—remained silent. Grace gently pulled Clara's hand from her face. 'Say it again, sweetie.'

'She said *"Uncle Nathaniel"*.'

Chapter Five

Grace's heart almost seized in her chest. She twisted to look over her shoulder, then scrambled to her feet to face the Marquess, who filled the open doorway. How long had he been there? What had he heard? Her thrill at hearing Clara speak faded, to be replaced by anxiety. She could barely remember what she had said out loud and what she had thought.

'I did not see you there,' she said.

'Evidently.'

Her heart began to pound as he continued to stare at her, frowning.

'You shall have a fire up here tomorrow and Mrs Sharp will show you where there is furniture and so forth in storage. You may make use of anything you need to make these rooms comfortable for you and for Clara.'

He does not seem to think of Clara as an unwanted burden. He accepts her as though she is truly his niece.

'Thank you, my lord.'

He looked at Clara and his expression softened. 'You are a clever girl, saying my name. Will you say it again? For me?'

'Unc' Nannal,' Clara whispered.

Ravenwell beamed. 'Well done, poppet. Now, where's my goodnight kiss?

Clara toddled over to the Marquess, her arms stretched high, and he swung her aloft, kissing her soundly on her cheek. Her arms wrapped around his neck and she kissed him twice, firstly on his left cheek and then—crooning softly and chubby fingers stroking—she kissed him on his scarred cheek. Ravenwell's gaze flicked to Grace and then away. He turned from her, Clara still in his arms.

'Come.' His voice was gruff. 'Let Uncle Nathaniel see your new bedchamber.'

He strode from the room, leaving Grace to ponder that scene. She had thought Clara was scared of her uncle but—picturing again her first meeting with Clara, she now wondered if her daughter's reluctance as she bumped down the stairs and dragged her feet across the hall was not wariness of the Marquess, but of Grace. The stranger.

That will teach me not to make assumptions.

A chastened Grace hurried from the room to join Ravenwell and Clara in the child's bedchamber, which adjoined Grace's.

Grace froze by the door. Here, a fire had been lit—presumably by the elusive Alice—and the room had taken on a warm glow. A rug lay before the fire and there, stretched full length, was Brack. He lifted his head to contemplate Grace and his tail thumped gently on the floor. Twice.

'I do not think...'

Grace's objection drifted into silence as Clara squirmed in her uncle's arms.

'Brack! Brack!'

The Marquess placed her on the floor and, squealing, she rushed over to the dog and launched herself on top of him, wrapping her arms around his neck as his tail continued to wag.

Grace watched, open-mouthed.

'You do not think...?' Ravenwell's voice had a teasing note she had not heard before.

'It does not matter. Clara is clearly fond of Brack.'

'And *she* is not scared of him, despite his size.'

Grace bristled at his emphasis on *she*. 'No, but I did not know he was friendly when I first saw him.'

'That is true. And as you said earlier, you will soon become accustomed to the dogs.'

'I will try.'

Watching Clara with Brack warmed Grace's heart and she could not help smiling at the sight. She turned to the Marquess to comment on Clara's delight but, before she could speak, the good humour leached from Ravenwell's expression and he averted his face. It was only a fractional movement, but she did not miss it.

'Come, Brack.'

He stalked from the room.

Nathaniel sought the sanctuary of his book room. He stood by his desk, staring unseeingly at the surface, tracing with his forefinger the pits and scratches that had accumulated over the years, pondering his gut reaction to Miss Bertram.

Specifically, to Miss Bertram's smile.

Clara needed a governess. That was an irrefutable fact.

Grace Bertram had appeared on his doorstep at a time he was beginning to fear he would never find anyone willing to move to Shiverstone Hall and care for his niece. The alternative—moving back to Ravenwell Manor—had begun to haunt him. So, despite his reservations, he had offered Miss Bertram the post, secured her behind a door marked *Employee* in his mind and banished any thoughts of her as a female. She was as welcome or as unwelcome as any woman taking that post. Her looks were...*must be...* immaterial.

And then she had smiled. And the memories had swarmed up from the depths of his mind, overwhelming him with images from his past: the flirtations, the fun, the laughter.

Memories of how life had used to be.

Unwanted memories of pretty girls who would smile spontaneously at him.

An aggravating reminder of his world before he chose this reclusive life.

With a muttered curse, Nathaniel hauled his chair from under his desk, sat down and pulled a ledger towards him. He flipped it open and forcibly applied his mind to business until it was time to dress for dinner.

He always dined at six and he always—despite dining alone—dressed for dinner. It was the one custom he continued from his former life, allowing him the illusion he was still a gentleman. He contemplated his appearance in the mirror as he wound his neckcloth around his neck and tied it in a neat knot. Would Miss Bertram think he made this effort on her behalf?

And if she does, why should it matter? You are not answerable to her. You are answerable to no one.

The pit of his stomach tangled into knots as the evening ahead stretched before him. Something about the thought of sitting at the table with her, eating and talking, fuelled his vulnerability. But he was sure, once the meal was underway, those knots would untangle. Miss Bertram had already demonstrated a welcome lack of disgust at his scars and that would help him become less self-conscious.

And those memories that glorious smile of hers had awoken? They were just that. Memories. They could wield no power over him as long as he banished them from his mind.

He tugged a comb through the knots in his hair—the winds out on the fells had, as usual, played havoc with it. Should he ask Sharp to cut it? He ran his hand over the side of his face, feeling the now-familiar roughness, as though twists of rope lay beneath the surface. His hair helped to hide the worst of the ravages the fire had wrought, particularly into the hairline where some of his hair had not grown back, but it could not completely conceal it, so it served little purpose.

The sound of his bedchamber door opening jolted him from his musings.

'Sorry, milord,' Sharp said. 'I thought, with the time…'

'No, do not apologise,' Nathaniel said. 'I am late, but I am going down now, so you may continue.'

It was Sharp's custom to tidy Nathaniel's bedchamber and bank up the fire when Nathaniel went downstairs to eat his dinner.

Nathaniel ran down the stairs. The parlour door was ajar and he entered, stopping short on seeing the table was only set for one. He spun on his heel and made for the kitchen. Mrs Sharp was there, ladling food into a serving dish, whilst Ned—who ate all his meals at the Hall—and Alice both sat ready at the table, awaiting their supper, which would be served when Sharp finished upstairs.

'I heard you come down the stairs, milord. Your dinner is ready. I—'

'Why is there only one place set in the parlour, Mrs Sharp?'

The housekeeper frowned. 'I did not think you would want to dine with her, milord.'

Nathaniel bit back a terse retort. This was his fault. He had not specified where Miss Bertram would dine. He had made an assumption.

'A governess would not expect to dine in the kitchen,' he said, 'and it would be too much work for her to dine upstairs in her room. Be so good as to lay another place in the parlour, Mrs Sharp.'

'But...milord...'

'*Now*, please.'

The sound of a throat being cleared delicately behind him had him whirling to face the door. Miss Bertram stood there, hands clasped in front of her, fingers twisting together. She had changed into a dowdy grey dress and the slight blush that tinted her cheeks was the only hint of colour on her person.

'I do not mind where I eat, my lord,' she said.

He did not want a debate. 'I do,' he said. 'You will

dine with me in the parlour. Set another place, Mrs Sharp.'

He gestured for Miss Bertram to precede him out of the kitchen. In the morning parlour, he pulled a chair out for her—choosing the place to his left— and then sat in his customary place at the head of the table.

Silence reigned.

Mrs Sharp came in, set a plate and cutlery in front of Miss Bertram and left again, spine rigid.

'Clara went to sleep without any problems.'

He grunted discouragingly.

'I thought you might like to know that.'

Mrs Sharp returned with a tray of serving dishes, saving him from further response.

'It is venison stew, milord.' She placed the first dish in the centre of the table. 'And there are potatoes and some of the pie from yesterday, warmed up.'

Miss Bertram smiled at Mrs Sharp. 'Thank you,' she said. 'It smells delicious.'

'Thank you.'

It was said grudgingly at the same time as the housekeeper darted a worried glance at Nathaniel. The Sharps had been with him since before the fire—had cared for him when the emotional pain had outstripped any physical pain resulting from his injuries, had remained loyal, burying themselves here at Shiverstone without complaint. They clearly worried over the choices he had made for his life.

'Yes, it does,' he said. 'Thank you, Mrs Sharp.'

And he meant for more than just the food. He understood her concern and the reason why she had not set a place for Miss Bertram in the parlour. She was afraid for him.

Thank you for caring.

She treated him to a fleeting smile before she left the room to fetch the rest of the food.

Nathaniel glanced at Miss Bertram, who was watching him, a glint of speculation in her eyes. He quashed his instinct to avert his face. He could hardly fault her for being curious and he knew he must overcome his natural urge to hide his scars, as he had with his servants. They were impossible to hide; she would see them often enough and, to her credit, her reaction so far had been encouraging. The sooner she accepted his appearance, the sooner he could also forget about it and then his awkwardness would fade.

He reached for her plate to serve her some stew.

As they ate their meal, Nathaniel watched Miss Bertram surreptitiously. Why would such a young, beautiful girl choose to travel all this way north for a post in a bleak place like Shiverstone? She struck him as a sociable sort. It made little sense, but she was here now and he did not doubt she would care for Clara. Whatever the reason, he must count it as a blessing for his niece. He was certain Hannah and David would approve of Miss Bertram.

The thought of his sister and brother-in-law brought the usual swell of anguish, followed by another thought. Miss Bertram had shown no curiosity whatsoever about how Clara had come to be orphaned. She had not enquired once about Clara's parents. Would it not be natural to have some curiosity over how they had died?

Then his conscience pricked him. He had actively discouraged her from conversation, never stopping to consider that if Miss Bertram failed to settle at Shiverstone, she might leave. And then what would he do about Clara? Besides, no matter how he had chosen to live these past nine years, he was still a gentleman and this prolonged silence at the dinner table went against every tenet of his upbringing.

'What made you choose to come to Shiverstone?'

There was a slight choking noise from the woman to his right. His fault, surprising her with a sudden question whilst she was eating.

'Were there no positions closer to where you grew up? Wiltshire, was it not?'

Miss Bertram cleared her throat, then sipped her wine. 'My uncle encouraged me to look for a post outside the county.' She directed a wry smile at her plate, avoiding eye contact. 'He did not want the embarrassment of his niece working for someone he is acquainted with.' There was a hint of disgust in her tone. 'I was the last of my friends to leave the school after our training finished, but when I went back to my uncle's house it was clear I was not welcome. My father had bequeathed me a little money, so I took a room in a lodging house in Cheltenham…and…and I heard about this post and I thought it would be interesting to see the North Country.'

'It is certainly a long way from Salisbury. And Cheltenham. Does it meet your expectations?'

'I…I…no, if I am to be honest. It is wilder than I imagined, but it is very…impressive, also.'

'And do you think you will grow to like it?'

'Oh, yes.' Her vehemence surprised him. 'I am certain of it.'

Nathaniel chewed another mouthful of venison. Was she running from something? Is that why she was content to bury herself out here? He had not yet penned his letter to this Madame Dubois. He would ask her, couching his question in discreet terms.

'If I might ask…' Miss Bertram hesitated. Her head was bent, her concentration still on her plate of food. 'I have no wish to revive painful memories, but I should like to know a little of Clara's parents. So I may speak to her of them.'

Almost as though she senses my suspicions.

'The memories are not all painful.' He closed his eyes, allowing his thoughts to travel back. 'Hannah was a year younger than me and we were very close growing up. There is a portrait of her in the dining room, painted by David, my brother-in-law, if you would care to see it. It is under a dust cover.'

He told himself he covered the picture to protect Clara, but he knew, deep down, it was because he could not bear seeing Hannah's likeness after her death, so he had removed it from the drawing-room wall.

Out of sight, out of mind. Except that did not really work.

'David was a fine artist and painted landscapes for the most part, but he painted Hannah and they presented the result to me when they were last here in June.'

Under the pretence of sipping his wine, Nathaniel swallowed his burgeoning pain. *Concentrate on the happy times.* 'Hannah loved to sing and to play the pianoforte.'

'She sounds a lovely lady. Let us hope Clara will remember something of her and her father.'

'I hope so. She had a fine character and she always remained positive, even in the face of heartache.'

'Heartache?'

The question dropped into the silence. He had said more than he meant to. They had both finished eating and Miss Bertram leant forward, her gaze intense.

'She was unable to bear children. Clara was adopted.'

There was another silence. Miss Bertram pressed her lips together and her lashes swept down, casting a lacy shadow on her cheeks as she fidgeted with the knife and fork she had placed neatly on her empty plate. Her hands were small and delicate, with slender fingers and beautifully shaped oval nails.

She cleared her throat. 'I…I did not know that.'

'As far as Hannah and David were concerned, Clara was theirs. They doted on her. She was such a happy little girl. So very much wanted and loved.'

She raised her head, her large gold-green eyes shimmering as they reflected the candlelight. 'She will be again. I promise you that.'

Chapter Six

Nathaniel's heart lightened at the sincerity that shone through Miss Bertram's words. Here was someone who would help him. The responsibility—he would never call it a burden—of raising Clara and making her happy was no longer his alone. Only now did he recognise the deep-seated worries that had plagued him ever since he read his mother's letter. Only now could he contemplate the coming months and years with a sense of peace and control.

'Thank you.'

Her fine brows drew together. 'Why do you thank me, my lord?' Her eyes searched his.

Nathaniel spoke from his heart. 'I am grateful you are prepared to live out here in order to help me raise Clara. I pray you will remain for a very long time. I do not wish my niece to suffer any more abandonment in her life.'

She stared at him, wordlessly, then dropped her

gaze to her plate again. He had to strain to make out her next words.

'I will never abandon her a—'

Her jaw snapped shut and Nathaniel wondered what she had been about to say. Then she hauled in a deep breath, looked up and smiled, driving further conjecture from his mind. The glory of that smile, once again, hit him with the force of a punch to his gut. How long had it been since a woman had smiled at him…genuinely, and not forced or with disgust in her eyes? For the second time that evening, he battened down his visceral reaction. Miss Bertram was his employee. It behoved him, as a gentleman, to protect her, not to lust after her. He made himself imagine her likely reaction to any hint of an approach from him and the thought of her disgust had the same effect on his desire that a sudden squall might have on a summer's day. The resulting chill chased over his skin and his insides shrivelled, as though by shrinking away from his surface they might protect him from the result of his momentary lapse.

The door opened and Sharp ambled in, bringing with him the smell of a brewery. Nathaniel did not grudge him his weakness. At least the man did not overindulge through the day and he deserved some compensation for moving to Shiverstone and leaving his friends and his favourite alehouse in Harrogate behind. Normally garrulous in the evening, Sharp cleared the dishes in silence and, shortly after he left the room, Mrs Sharp came, carrying a warm pie—apple, by the smell of it—and a jug of cream.

Nathaniel took advantage of the distraction to study the newest member of his household even further. So very delicate and pretty, with fine cheekbones and clear skin and silky, blonde hair…no wonder he had been momentarily attracted to her. Familiarity would help. He would cease to notice her appearance, much as she would cease to notice his scars. At least Clara would be cared for and happy.

'I am pleased to hear you say that,' he said, resulting in a swift sideways glance from Mrs Sharp, whose long nose appeared to twitch, as if to say, *What are you talking about?*

Miss Bertram pursed her lips, her eyes dancing, as she watched the housekeeper.

'Mrs Sharp—' amusement bubbled through her voice '—the stew was delicious and the pie smells wonderful. I can see I shall have to restrain my appetite if I am not to increase to the size of a house.'

'Hmmph. I am sure it matters not to anyone here if you should gain weight, miss.'

Miss Bertram's gaze flicked to meet Nathaniel's and this time he was certain she was biting back a smile. A conspirator's smile. He had talked overmuch. Given her the impression they were allies.

Even that they might become friends. Every instinct he possessed told him to beware.

'When you have finished your dessert, you may use the book room to write those letters we discussed,' he said.

He steeled his heart against the hurt that flashed across her face. Better she did not get the wrong impression. He was not here to be her friend.

'Mrs Sharp, please be so good as to serve tea to Miss Bertram in the book room. Shall we say in fifteen minutes? And tell Sharp to bring my brandy here.'

'Yes, milord.' Such satisfaction communicated in just two words.

They finished their meal in silence.

What to write?

Grace brushed the untrimmed end of the quill pen against her cheek as she pondered how much she should reveal to Miss Fanworth.

The letter to her uncle had been easy: an enquiry after his health and that of the rest of the family, the news that she had obtained a position as governess to the niece of the Marquess of Ravenwell and her address, should they wish to contact her. She decided, with an inner *hmmph*, that it would be unwise for her to hold her breath waiting for that last to occur.

But... Miss Fanworth... She bent her head and began to write.

My dear Miss Fanworth,
I hope you will be happy to know that I found my child. She is happy and loved, and I am re-assured that she is well cared for, so I am con-tent. Thank you so much for trusting me with the names of her new parents. I shall be in your debt for ever.

I must also acquaint you with my good for-tune in securing a position as governess for the Marquess of Ravenwell. He has the intention of writing to Madame for a reference—despite your letter of recommendation—and I am hopeful that she will find it in her heart to dwell less upon my early escapades and more upon my later years at the school when she pens that reference!

My new address is at the top of this letter and I would count myself fortunate if you might write to me once in a while to tell me how everyone at school fares. Please, also, should you write to them, communicate my address to my dear friends Rachel, Joanna, and Isabel. Might I also request that you send on any letters addressed to me that may have arrived at the school?

Please convey my most sincere regards to Madame and to the other teachers and staff.
Your very grateful former pupil,
Grace Bertram

Grace read and reread her effort anxiously. No, she had not lied, but she had successfully masked the truth. If Madame was to discover the actuality of her new position, she would surely inform his lordship and he would banish her immediately.

She could not fathom the brusque Marquess. His initial reluctance to converse over their meal had disappointed, but not surprised her—no one would choose to live such a reclusive life if they craved company. But the man was not shy and, in Grace's opinion, it was plain bad manners not to make the smallest effort at civilised conversation. Although—she had told herself as she concentrated on her meal—she must remember she was only the governess and not a guest to be treated with due deference.

But then he began to talk and she had relaxed, thinking he was merely unused to company. And her thoughts had raced ahead and, in her imagination, she helped him to overcome his awkwardness and taught him to enjoy socialising, for Clara's sake, and the house would be filled with light and laughter…but then Mrs Sharp—that wicked old crow—had come in and jerked her back to reality and Ravenwell had pokered up all over again.

The prospect of the evenings to come filled her with dismay, but at least she would not lack company entirely at Shiverstone Hall. Sharp was as affable as his wife was hostile, Alice, the newly arrived fourteen-year-old housemaid, was a plump chatterbox and Ned, although he had little to say, did not appear unfriendly.

And there was always Clara. A warm, comforting glow spread through Grace. Her child. The days ahead would be filled with Clara, and the Marquess and his moodiness, and Mrs Sharp and her meanness could go to… Grace squashed that thought before it could form into the word in her brain. She was a mother now, with responsibilities. She was no longer a rebellious girl with a penchant for trouble.

Her letter would suffice. She would leave her letters with his lordship's, on the console table in the hall, for Ned to take to Shivercombe village in the morning.

She leaned back in Ravenwell's chair, her lids heavy. It had been an exhausting day, both physically and emotionally. The homesickness for her school days and for the companionship, laughter and love of her friends welled up, and hot tears prickled. She blinked furiously. Life had taught her that self-pity was not an option. It achieved nothing. She and her friends were grown women now. She'd wager *they* were not wallowing in nostalgia, but embracing their new lives with hope and confidence.

Well, she was sure Isabel and Rachel would be doing just that, but what of gentle, reserved Joanna, abandoned on the doorstep of Madame's school as a baby? She had been taken in and brought up by Madame and the other teachers and it had been a lonely existence until the age of nine, when other girls her age were taken in as boarders. Grace, Isabel, and Rachel were the closest to family Joanna had ever known and she prayed the family who had employed her would be kind.

As for Rachel, there was no doubt in Grace's mind her independent, self-sufficient friend would be in her element with the opportunity to travel to exotic places after she had been employed by a sheikh, in the kingdom of Huria. The girls had found the country on the map—beyond the furthest reaches of the Mediterranean Sea—and Grace had marvelled at the distance Rachel must travel. Journeying as far as Shiverstone Hall had been quite far enough!

And Isabel—a momentary disquiet sneaked through Grace. There had been something about Isabel and her insouciance when she left the school. Her meek acceptance of her future as a governess had seemed out of character, when they all knew her great ambition was to become a famous singer.

Would she settle in her new life? Or would she risk everything in her bid for excitement?

She longed to hear all their news and hoped that, as promised, they had written to her care of the school as she had not known where she might eventually find employment. Selfishly, she was relieved she had mislaid her friends' addresses during her travels for, even if she *could* write to them today, how much of the truth would she dare reveal? Could she admit the reality of her new situation? She had never kept secrets from them before, not even the greatest secret of her life, when she discovered she was with child, but…would they understand what she had done, or would they condemn? They would worry about her, of that she was certain.

That brief interlude, when Lord Ravenwell had reminisced so movingly about his sister, might never have happened. Over her first few days at Shiverstone Hall, Grace barely saw her employer. He only appeared at dinner, dressed in his black tail coat and meticulously knotted neckcloth, adorned with a ruby pin. He remained distant and, after another few abortive attempts at conversation, Grace gave up. Her days were long and full, and by the evening she was exhausted, so she followed her employer's lead and ate in silence.

The quietness and calm of their meals gave her

time to think. Time to wonder why he lived as a recluse, what had caused his scars, why he had talked that one time on her first night and then clammed up. He was a puzzling man.

The silence also gave her time to observe. He had been a handsome man. Still was, if one ignored the scarring. The skin of his jaw and up the side of his face on the right-hand side was uneven and pale in contrast to the rest of his face, which was lightly tanned, no doubt from exposure to the sun and the wind out on the fells.

Then, one evening when he was in his cups and his wife was out of earshot, Sharp had told her how his lordship had been burned nine years ago in a fire at Ravenwell Manor. A fire that had killed his father. Before that Ravenwell had been one of society's most eligible bachelors and had led a carefree life filled with fun and pleasure. The fire had scarred more than his skin, Sharp had slurred. It had scarred the very essence of the man. Grace's natural sympathy had been stirred, but she knew the Marquess would not wish for pity and so she said nothing. But still she wondered at the reclusive life he led. He must be lonely.

His size no longer intimidated her, but his silence did. And his dogs—other than Brack, to whom she was slowly becoming accustomed. Ravenwell spent much of his time outside and, although Grace and

Clara ventured into the fresh air almost every day, they remained close by the house and they saw nothing of Clara's uncle. Grace's heart bled for Clara. For all his lordship's fine talk about not wanting his niece's life disrupted, what did he think he was doing now by avoiding all contact with her every day? He might just as well not live here, for all Clara saw of him.

Grace kept her counsel. For the time being. For now, she was content to expend her energy in making their upstairs rooms more homely and in coaxing smiles and more words from her daughter.

Chapter Seven

'Good afternoon.'

It was the fourth day of her new life at Shiverstone Hall. Grace and Clara had been playing on the lawn in front of the house and now Clara was chirruping away to herself as she gathered pretty stones from the carriageway, piling them into a heap. Grace tore her attention from Clara, shielding her eyes against the low-lying sun. A young man, clad in a black coat and black, low-crowned hat, stood a few yards away, smiling at her.

'Good afternoon. Mr…?'

'Rendell. Ralph Rendell.' He raised his hat, revealing a mop of curly light brown hair. 'I am the curate at St Mary's.'

Grace's ignorance of the existence of St Mary's must have shown in her expression for Mr Rendell laughed, and said, 'The church in Shivercombe village.'

'I am pleased to meet you, Mr Rendell. Are you a frequent visitor to the Hall?'

The curate's smile broadened. 'And that, I surmise, is a delicate way of enquiring the purpose of my visit.'

Grace bit her lip against her answering smile.

'My visit,' he continued, 'appears to have already achieved its purpose.'

'Which was?'

'To satisfy myself as to your safety, Miss…?'

'Oh, I am sorry. I am Miss Bertram. Miss Grace Bertram.'

Mr Rendell bowed. 'I am delighted to make your acquaintance, Miss Bertram. Am I correct in assuming you are the young lady who enquired for directions to the Hall in Shivercombe last Tuesday and has not been seen since?'

'Yes, indeed,' Grace replied. 'I came in response to an advertisement for the post of governess.' She felt her face heat and, unable to meet his eyes after such a blatant lie to a man of God, she lowered her gaze to Clara, who now stood watching them, her thumb jammed in her mouth. Grace bent and gently tugged at Clara's hand. 'No, sweetie. Your hands are dirty.'

'To this little one? So the rumours *were* true. I did not know the Marquess had a child.'

'Clara is his lordship's niece. She is an orphan.'

Except she still has me, even though she will never know it. Poor Clara: her adoptive parents dead, her father killed at the Battle of Bussaco and me, her real mother, never able to tell her the truth.

Grace buried the sorrows of the past as Clara crouched down again to continue piling up stones. She was here now. That was all that mattered.

'Why should you have a concern for my safety, sir?'

'There was a certain amount of disquiet in the village after you failed to return. Lord Ravenwell is something of an enigma to the good folk of Shivercombe and—in the nature of filling the vacuum resulting from his servants' most unsatisfactory refusal to gossip about him—the villagers have developed their own theories and stories about this place and its master.'

Grace laughed. 'Yes. I recall. When I asked for directions, I was earnestly advised not to risk coming here. But I am pleased I did.'

Those tales had strengthened her resolve to find her daughter.

'And I am pleased to discover you safe and well, Miss Bertram.' Mr Rendell smiled, his hazel eyes creasing at the outer corners. He squatted next to Clara and handed her an attractively veined stone to add to her pile. 'And to make the acquaintance of this little treasure.'

Clara smiled at the curate. 'Fank 'oo.'

'She has beautiful eyes,' Mr Rendell said. 'A most unusual colour.'

Grace strived to sound nonchalant. 'They are lovely indeed.' She bent to take Clara's hand. 'Come, sweetie. It is time we went indoors.'

Mr Rendell stood up and brushed at the hem of his coat, before smiling at Grace. 'And it is time I took my leave of you. I have achieved what I set out to accomplish.'

Guilt over her abruptness prompted Grace to say, 'Would you care for a cup of tea, Mr Rendell? Did you walk all the way here?'

'No, I drove. I left my gig at the stable yard with Tam.' He stared up at the Hall, scanning the frontage, then returned his gaze to Grace. 'Yes, I should welcome a cup of tea, Miss Bertram. Thank you.' His reply was laced with determination.

Grace puzzled over the curate's tone as she led the way to the front door. He had given the impression of a man waging an internal battle…no doubt he was fully aware her enigmatic employer discouraged visitors. But good manners dictated she should offer her visitor some hospitality. After all, he had come all this way, merely to assure himself of her well-being.

Conscious she might be violating an unwritten rule that strangers were not to be invited inside the Hall, Grace lifted the latch and, straightening her spine, marched into the entrance hall. Mrs Sharp was descending the stairs and Grace's courage almost failed at the sight of the hostile housekeeper. Almost, but not quite, for Clara must meet and socialise with others if she was not to grow up shy and awkward in company. And did not she… Grace…deserve to have some friends outside the Hall?

'Mrs Sharp,' she said, 'this is…' Her words faded into silence as Mrs Sharp smoothed her hair back with both hands before hurrying down the remaining stairs, a welcoming smile on her face.

Well!

'Mr Rendell, how very good of you to call. Miss Bertram, please show our visitor into the drawing room and I will bring you refreshments.'

'You have been here before?' Grace asked the curate as she sat down.

'No, never. Mrs Sharp is a regular at church, however, so we are acquainted, although it must be a month since her last attendance. I confess I am a little bemused by her welcome—such visits have been positively discouraged in the past.'

'Does Lord Ravenwell attend church as well?'

'No. We have never seen him in the village. All the servants come to church, when the weather permits, for the track between here and the village can become treacherous in inclement weather. They do not mix with the villagers, however. That fact, in itself, spawns even more speculation about his lordship.' He leaned forward, suddenly intense. 'You are happy here, Miss Bertram? You must know you can rely upon me to help if ever you need it.'

'I am…content enough, sir.'

Was she happy? She was thrilled to be with Clara and nothing would tear her away. But happy with the rest of her situation? With her brusque employer and the taciturn housekeeper—although Mrs Sharp had been surprisingly helpful with Grace's efforts to refurbish the nursery wing upstairs once she accepted there was no criticism of her housekeeping skills. Or with the regularly tipsy Sharp and friendly but unsophisticated Alice? It was too soon to say. And yet, what choice did she have? She had nowhere else to go. And Clara needed her.

'But I thank you for your concern and you may rest assured you will be the first person to whom I shall apply should I ever need help.'

'Then I am satisfied. And I shall look forward to seeing you on the morrow in church, together with this little one.' He reached out and ruffled Clara's curls and she tilted her head to stare at him from her seat on the rug. 'It is never too early to educate a child in the ways of the Lord.'

'I shall be there.'

Grace's heart lifted. It might only be a church service, but it would break the monotony of life at the Hall. So far, she had ventured no further than the kitchen garden to watch Sharp digging the soil in preparation for planting in the spring.

'If not this week, then next,' she continued, 'for I have no idea how we might get to the village. Clara cannot walk that far.'

'You may ride in the carriage with Annie and me.' Mrs Sharp had returned and was pouring the tea. She passed a cup to Mr Rendell and then one to Grace. 'Ned usually drives us and Sharp sits with him up on the box whilst Tam rides.'

Grace stared at the change in the housekeeper— was this all to impress the curate with her good Christian values?

Before she could respond, the sound of boots on the flags of the hall floor rang out.

Clara scrambled to her feet. 'Unc' Nanniel,' she said.

Nathaniel strode through the hall, Brack at his heels. A morning out on the fells, flying Amber, had given him a raging appetite. He was delighted with the eagle's progress. Her wing was growing stronger and she was becoming accustomed to hunting again, in preparation for her release back into the wild.

A scuffle from the direction of the drawing room distracted him. He stopped, then forgot his hunger as a beaming Clara erupted from the room, arms aloft.

'Unc' Nanniel!'

'Clara!'

He bent to catch her up in his arms, then swung her in a wide circle, revelling in her giggles. He hugged her close and kissed her cheek. How he had missed her.

Your fault, came the silent riposte.

It was true. He had deliberately avoided Miss Bertram—and thus, by association, Clara—since her arrival. That first evening, he had found himself relaxing…talking too much…*revealing* too much. He did not want a friend. The danger of becoming dependent upon her company, upon *anyone's* company, disturbed his sleep. What if she did not stay after all? He could not bear to become accustomed to her company and then lose it, leaving him to endure the agony of readjusting to his self-imposed exile.

It was bad enough having to dine together every evening. The silence—yet again, his choice—gave him too much time to think. And to remember. Miss Bertram, with her delicate lily-of-the-valley scent, her prettiness and her femininity was a constant reminder of what he had given up and an ever-growing challenge to his male instincts, kept suppressed for so very long. Not that he would ever risk an overture towards her. A beauty like Miss Bertram would be disgusted by the mere thought of intimacy with a man like him. Besides, the standards he expected of himself would not allow him to take advantage of an innocent woman in his employ.

But…he was increasingly irked by his own behaviour. It smacked of cowardice. If Miss Bertram should decide to leave, then he would simply have to deal with it. He had dealt with worse things. Hannah's face floated into his mind, and his heart clenched. *Far worse*. He would put his caution aside and accept Miss Bertram's presence in his household. He could not run away for ever. He strode towards the drawing room. Clara had come from there. Ergo, Miss Bertram must be in there.

It was time he changed.

He walked in through the door and slammed to a halt as he took in the three faces turned towards him. Of the three, both Mrs Sharp and Miss Bertram wore identical expressions of consternation. The third— a young man—smiled as he rose to his feet and extended his right hand.

'I beg you will forgive my intrusion, sir. Ralph Rendell, curate of St Mary's, at your service.' The young man did not approach Nathaniel, but remained standing with his hand thrust out, a confident smile on his face. His clear-skinned, handsome face.

Nathaniel put Clara down and walked towards the young curate, fighting the urge to twist his neck to shield his scars from Rendell. He shook the proffered hand, steeling himself not to flinch as the other man's fingers closed around his hand, touching the scarring on the back of his hand, even though it gave him no physical pain. The curate showed no flicker of reaction and some of Nathaniel's tension dissipated.

'Ravenwell.'

He gestured to the other man to sit, aware he now had two choices. He could stalk out. It was common knowledge visitors were not welcome at the Hall and no one would be surprised. Or he could be a gentleman. Only moments ago he had accepted it was time to change. Out of the corner of his eye he saw Miss Bertram chew at her bottom lip, worry creasing her brow. Her clear unease settled the matter.

'Mrs Sharp, be so good as to bring another cup, will you?' And he sat down.

Clara immediately clambered on to his lap and settled into the crook of his arm, sighing contentedly.

'Clara is happy to see you, my lord.'

He caught the hint of reproach. 'I have been busy these past days,' he said. It was true. Gradually accustoming Amber to flying and to her new freedom had taken much of his time. He bent his head, rubbing his cheek against Clara's. 'I am happy to see you too, poppet.'

Clara pulled her thumb from her mouth with a pop. 'Unc' Nanniel,' she whispered.

Nathaniel turned his attention to Mr Rendell. 'It is seldom we get visitors to the Hall, Rendell.'

'Indeed.' Light brown eyes regarded him steadily. 'I came to ensure myself of Miss Bertram's well-being.'

Nathaniel heard Miss Bertram's stifled gasp and felt his brows snap together in a frown.

'Well-being?'

Rendell continued to hold his gaze. 'Yes. She was known to have come out to Shiverstone on Tuesday last. I came to make certain of her safe arrival.'

Tactful wording. Nathaniel could not but be impressed by the young man's courage in braving Nathaniel's carefully nurtured reputation to ensure the safety of a stranger.

'Most commendable.'

Mrs Sharp bustled in with another cup and a plate piled with slabs of fruit cake. Nathaniel's stomach growled at the sight, his hunger pangs resurfacing with a vengeance. He accepted a slice of cake and bit into it as Mrs Sharp poured him a cup of tea.

'I have promised Mr Rendell that Clara and I will attend the church service tomorrow,' Miss Bertram said. 'That is, if you are happy to give your permission, my lord?'

With his mouth full of cake, Nathaniel could not immediately reply.

'I am sure his lordship will not stand in the way of your moral enlightenment, Miss Bertram,' Rendell said.

Nathaniel swallowed his food. 'I would not dream

of objecting to your attendance at church, Miss Bertram.'

'And,' Rendell continued, 'I would deem it an honour if you would call upon us at the rectory if you can spare the time to visit Shivercombe, Miss Bertram. The rector's daughter is a similar age to yourself, and...' he leant over to tickle under Clara's chin, causing her to squirm with delight '...we have a litter of kittens this young lady might enjoy meeting.'

'Kittens, Clara! How exciting.' Miss Bertram switched her attention from Clara to the curate. 'I am sure she would love to see them, sir. She already takes great delight in his lordship's dogs. But will you not be too busy, with tomorrow being Sunday?'

'Oh, I did not mean tomorrow. You will surely welcome an excuse to visit your neighbours on occasion. After all, living in seclusion is not everybody's choice.'

Nathaniel bit back an angry retort. How dare Rendell chastise him in his own house, and back him into a corner like this?

Outmanoeuvred, by God...and by a man of God, at that.

Then his exasperation subsided, to be replaced by an impulse to laugh. What was he thinking? Was it his intention to keep Miss Bertram a prisoner at the Hall? He had chosen not to mix with his neighbours, but had no justification for forcing her to do likewise. And it would be good for Clara.

'You are right,' he said. 'Can you drive?' he added, to Miss Bertram.

'No.' It was said with regret. 'My uncle did not think it worth having me taught. I thank you for your offer, Mr Rendell, but I am afraid I am unable to accept your invitation.'

'Your man rides or drives in most days, does he not, my lord? Surely Miss Bertram and Clara could come in with him?'

'They could, but he normally leaves here very early and returns immediately. It would not be long enough for a social visit.'

The stubborn tilt of the curate's chin suggested he would not easily give in, prompting Nathaniel to add, 'You may drive yourself to the village in the gig, Miss Bertram. Our old cob, Bill, is perfectly safe.'

She gasped, pink infusing her cheeks, her green eyes sparkling with excitement. Was she so very eager to get away from the Hall? No sooner had the question formed in his mind than he realised its absurdity. Of course she would be eager to meet other people. What fun was it to be isolated out here with a two-year-old, an employer who barely spoke to her and a bunch of servants?

'That would be…but no. I…I do not know if I could. I am not used to horses.'

'Nonsense. Bill is an old hand. He knows the way to and from the village with his eyes shut and he never gets above a slow trot. I will teach you. You will cope admirably, I am certain.'

As he spoke, Miss Bertram smiled at Rendell with such pleasure Nathaniel's stomach twisted tight. He eyed the curate's clear, handsome countenance and experienced a sharp pang that no woman would ever again look at him in such a way.

No woman or Miss Bertram, specifically?

He surged to his feet and handed a dozing Clara to Miss Bertram, goaded by that snide voice in his head.

I am not jealous of Rendell. I merely do not want people here, in my house.

His reputation had kept visitors at bay for almost nine years and yet, less than a week after Miss Bertram's arrival, his home was already invaded. It was more than a man should have to bear.

See the effect of a pretty face on a man? You do right to keep your distance. Would Rendell be here if the governess was an old harridan?

He thrust aside the thought he was being unfair to Rendell. He was in no mood to be reasonable—he did not want people here. He preferred his animals and his birds for company.

'Thank you for calling.' He forced a pleasant tone. 'I apologise, but I have urgent matters needing my attention.'

Rendell stood and Nathaniel shook his hand.

'I am pleased to have made your acquaintance at long last, my lord. Dare I hope we might see you in church one of these Sundays?'

Nathaniel stared at him, then turned on his heel and stalked from the room.

Impudent devil!

Chapter Eight

'**M**rs Sharp.'

The housekeeper paused in the act of serving the evening meal. 'Yes, milord?'

'On Monday morning I shall require you to set aside an hour or two to watch Clara, if you please.'

'Yes, milord.'

He waited until Mrs Sharp left the room before saying, 'On Monday I shall instruct you on harnessing and driving Bill, Miss Bertram.'

He was tempted to relegate the task to Tam but, once the idea of teaching her himself had taken hold in his head, he could not relinquish it. She finished chewing her mouthful of food, then turned to look at him, her green eyes glittering. She was so beautiful, whereas he…he fought his usual battle not to move his head to hide his scars. Stupid, mindless reaction. She knew he had scars so what point was there in turning away?

'I am grateful, but there is no need for Clara to stay

with Mrs Sharp. She can come with us. She will not be in the way.'

'Clara likes Mrs Sharp. You need not think she will be unhappy staying in the kitchen with her. Besides, it will do Clara good to be watched by someone other than you, in case—'

'In case what? In case I leave her?'

Nathaniel put down his knife and fork to give himself time to think. Why had she almost bitten his head off? Her head was bent, a muscle twitching in her cheek as she pushed her food around her plate with her fork.

She flicked a glance at him. 'I apologise. I did not mean to interrupt.'

'If you had allowed me to finish my sentence, I was about to say in case you are ever ill or indisposed,' he said. 'Mrs Sharp may be a little…sharp, for want of a better word, but she is fond of Clara.'

'I am aware of that. It was not for that reason I spoke as I did. I should not have done so, but…'

She had begun speaking with such resolve, but now she hesitated, her eyes searching his, the golden flecks in her irises reflecting the light of the candles. Nathaniel's nerves jangled a warning that he might not care for what she was about to say. He waited for her to continue.

'When I first came here, you said Clara had faced enough disruption in her life.'

'You cannot believe that staying with Mrs Sharp constitutes disruption.'

'No, of course I do not. But…your inference was that Clara should not have to cope with losing any-one else from her life.' Her head tilted and she raised her brows. 'What about you?'

'Me?' His voice deepened into a growl. 'What the dev…deuce do you mean by that?'

Her indrawn breath sounded loud in the silence. 'Her parents died. She has been here only a few weeks, getting used to you, and then I arrive. Other than this afternoon, she has not set her eyes on her Uncle Nathaniel since last Tuesday.'

He liked the way she said his name. *Nathaniel.* He thrust that wayward thought aside and concentrated on her meaning. And, with a sense of shame, he re-alised she was right. That afternoon he had accepted he must change, but he still had not recognised the effect of his behaviour on Clara.

He recalled Miss Bertram's gentle rebuke: *'Clara is happy to see you, my lord.'*

In his efforts to shield himself he had failed to pro-tect Clara from the very thing she must fear—losing someone else she loved. No wonder she had been so delighted to see him earlier and no wonder she had clung to him later, when he had said goodnight to her as she was about to go upstairs to get ready for her bedtime.

Miss Bertram continued to eat her meal, but her attention did not waver, stirring...what? Not discomfort. Not any more. Already he was becoming accustomed to her presence. And he wasn't annoyed by her presumption. Rather, he was intrigued by her pluck and determination. He could not condemn her concern for Clara's happiness.

'I stand chastised,' he said. 'And I thank you for pointing out my dereliction of duty.'

Her eyes blazed, shooting golden sparks. *'Duty?'*

He stiffened. 'You forget yourself, Miss Bertram.'

She took no notice. 'A child does not require *duty* from those upon whom she is entirely dependent. She requires...*needs*...love. And...and *time*. And—'

Nathaniel held up his hands, palms facing her, fingers spread. 'Enough! I concede. It was poor phrasing on my part and you are right. I shall ensure I spend more time with Clara in future. In the meantime, I hope you can accept she will not suffer if Mrs Sharp cares for her on Monday. Bill is docile, but I do not think harnessing a horse to a carriage should be undertaken with a young child underfoot. She will be much better off in the warm kitchen.'

Miss Bertram bowed her head. 'Agreed.'

They finished eating in their now customary silence but, as Sharp brought in the brandy at the end of their meal and Miss Bertram stood to withdraw, an unexpected yearning for company beset Nathaniel.

'I shall take my brandy in the drawing room to-night, Sharp. And please tell Mrs Sharp to send in an additional cup with the tea tray.'

'Very well, milord.'

'Do you play chess, Miss Bertram? I have a fancy for a game.'

'I do not, my lord.'

'Would you care to learn?' He easily interpreted the doubt in those gold-green eyes of hers. 'There is no compulsion. I shall not dismiss you from your post if you refuse. We could as easily play a hand or two of cards.'

'I should like to learn the game. I have been told in the past that chess is a game the female mind cannot comprehend.' Her lips firmed, then she smiled, raising her chin. 'I viewed that as a challenge, but had no opportunity to discover whether he spoke the truth.'

'He?'

Grace did not immediately respond. They walked side by side to the drawing room and a sideways glance revealed a frown line between her brows and a wash of pink across her cheeks.

'He was an old friend.' There was the slightest tremble in her voice. 'He went away to be a soldier.'

A suitor, perhaps?

She had told him the barest of bones of her life before she had come to Shiverstone Hall. Would she ever reveal the flesh of her past? He would not ask.

Why would he need to know about her life before? She was a governess. That was all he needed to know. That, and how well she cared for his niece.

They entered the drawing room.

Ah. He halted.

'The chess table,' he said. 'I forgot. It was stored away.'

There had been no need to keep it out: gathering dust, creating work for Mrs Sharp, reviving painful memories for him. David had been his only opponent since he had moved here after the fire. And now... with David gone...

He tamped down the stab of pain and regret, turned on his heel and strode towards the dining room, grabbing a candlestick from a table as he passed. A patter of feet followed him.

'I can manage,' he said.

'It will be easier with two of us,' she said, sounding a touch breathless.

Nathaniel shortened his strides and a gurgled laugh reached his ears. He glanced down at Miss Bertram, now by his side.

Her eyes twinkled. 'It is hard work to keep stride with you, my lord. You have very long legs compared to mine.'

Nathaniel grunted at that naïve remark, his imagination delving under her ugly brown dress to the slim legs he suspected were hidden beneath. It took no effort to recall that glimpse of shapely ankle on her first day here. He tried to empty his mind of such thoughts the second they surfaced, but it was too late—his pulse had already accelerated. And the picture his wayward mind painted was not easily dismissed.

He directed his thoughts to the whereabouts of the table in a room filled with numerous unrecognisable items draped in holland covers.

'There.'

He pointed to a shrouded shape near the window. He tugged at the sheet covering it, revealing the chess table, a gift from Hannah and David. He smoothed his hand across the cool surface of the chessboard, created from sixty-four squares of attractively veined Italian marble set into a fine rosewood surround. Memories of a very different kind flooded his brain, dousing that inappropriate surge of lust.

'It is beautiful.'

He started as she copied his action, stroking the table with reverence. The sight of her elegant hand, with its slender fingers and perfect oval nails, next to his ugly skin churned his stomach and he snatched his hand away.

He sensed her quick glance, but kept his eyes averted.

'How can you bear to hide such craftsmanship away?'

He bent to lift the table. 'It is not heavy. I do not need your help.'

'Where are the chess men?'

'Inside the table. The top is hinged.'

He carried it to the door, then hesitated, looking back. Miss Bertram stood stock still, gazing around the room, a speculative look on her face.

'Do not forget the candle,' he said.

She snatched up the candlestick and hurried after him.

He set the table near the window and dragged the two wooden chairs close so they could play. As he did so, Miss Bertram lifted the top of the table and peered inside.

'Draughts! We used to play draughts sometimes at the school, my friends and I.' At first delighted, her tone became wistful. 'Isabel taught us.'

'Isabel?'

'One of my best friends at school. There were four of us.' Her head snapped up, her eyes sparkling. 'May we play draughts? I do know how to play that game.'

'Are you backing away from that challenge you spoke of, Miss Bertram?'

She blushed. 'No, of course not.'

'Good. I shall teach you the basics tonight: what the pieces are called, how they may be moved and the aim of the game, which is to trap your opponent's king in such a way he has no safe square to move to.'

'And then you can kill him?'

She said it with such relish, he was startled into laughing.

'I trust you refer to the king and not your actual opponent?'

'For the moment.' She peeped saucily at him through her lashes, triggering a tug of response deep inside him.

How long was it since he had enjoyed a joke? He concentrated on keeping their conversation to the rules of chess.

'No, the king can never be removed from the board. It is sufficient to have surrounded him. Your opponent then surrenders his king and you have won the game. It is called checkmate.'

Her fine brows gathered into a frown. 'That seems very odd to me. I should rather kill the king. Then there would be no room for doubt.'

Nathaniel listed the different pieces on the board, explaining how each man could be moved and how important it was to plan several moves ahead and guard against losing the most valuable men.

'So…this one…' she reached out and picked up the black knight '…can move like so?' She put the piece on the wrong square.

'No, no. The knight's movement is the trickiest of all the moves to remember. He can move in an "L" shape. So—' he used his left hand to demonstrate

'—from this square, this knight can move to here… and here…and…'

'And here!'

Her hand darted out and, before he could withdraw his own, she grasped his hand and tugged, sliding hand and knight together across the board to the fourth possible position. Her skin was warm against his, her fingertips soft. Fierce concentration creased her brow as she studied the board.

She pulled his hand again. 'And here!' She looked up, beaming. Then her mouth opened. 'Oh!' She snatched her hand from his. 'I am sorry. I…' Her cheeks bloomed beetroot red.

'You were carried away with enthusiasm?'

'Yes!' Her lips stretched in a tentative smile. 'Do you think I am ready?'

Nathaniel swallowed hard. She was so young. Naïve. 'Let us leave all that information to sink in,' he said. 'If you have time tomorrow, you might come in here and try to remember what each man is called and how he moves and then, in the evening, we will play.'

Her face clouded.

'And now…I shall challenge you to a game of draughts,' he said.

Her expression cleared. 'Oh, yes. That will be fun.'

Fun. An alien word to use in connection with himself and his life. He cleared the chessmen away and set out the draughtsmen whilst Miss Bertram poured the tea, brought in several minutes since by Mrs Sharp.

'You talked of your school friends earlier.' Nathaniel moved his counter in his opening gambit. 'Are they also governesses?'

What happened to your 'I don't want to know'? Or does that only apply to former beaux? Nathaniel dismissed that sneering voice as Miss Bertram played her opening move and he replied. He owed it to Clara to know more of the woman who would be raising her.

Didn't he?

'Yes. I am longing to hear how they go on.'

Miss Bertram studied the board, the tip of her tongue playing with her top lip, stirring long-suppressed needs deep inside Nathaniel. He forced his gaze to the board, but time and again it drifted back to the woman sitting opposite him.

'I asked Miss Fanworth to pass on my address to them so I hope they will soon write to me.' She moved another man, before adding, 'Although Rachel's letter might take a long time to reach England.'

'She has gone overseas?'

'Yes. She went to be the governess to the children of a sheikh, in the Kingdom of Huria. It is in the desert.'

'That does sound exotic. Did you not hanker after a similar adventure?'

She hesitated. 'No,' she said, finally. 'I think the North Country is enough of an adventure for me. Rachel's parents travelled much of the time, leaving her behind, and I think that is where her dream of travelling to faraway places began. She loves teaching children, so I am sure she will be happy.'

Silence fell whilst Miss Bertram again studied the board. She reached out and moved a man, jumping one of Nathaniel's, and grinned triumphantly as she made great play of removing it.

The devil. He would have to pay more attention to the game and less to his beautiful opponent.

'Isabel,' Miss Bertram said, as Nathaniel contemplated his next move, 'was the only one of us who spent much time with her parents as a child. Her papa taught her to play draughts and she taught us. She has gone to a family in Sussex, and Joanna, my other friend, has gone to a place in Hertfordshire. She is... she has no family and was brought up by Madame at the school.'

'You must miss your friends.'

'I do.' There was a pause. 'Do you not miss yours?'

'No.' Nathaniel kept his gaze on the game during the ensuing silence. Finally, he looked up. 'I no longer yearn after that frivolous way of life and my former friends crave nothing else.'

Irritated as much by his compulsion to explain as by her question, he studied the board again. There. A move he had overlooked. He moved one of his men, putting two of Miss Bertram's under threat. She peered more closely at the board.

'Hmmph. I cannot save both but, equally, you cannot take both. So I shall do this.' With another triumphant smile she moved a third man, reaching Nathaniel's side of the board and earning a 'crown' to turn her man into a king. 'Now I can move it forward *and* backwards.'

Nathaniel secured one of her men and they played on, the conversation on the safer territory of the game. When they finished, Nathaniel found himself the target of a pair of accusing green eyes.

'You allowed me to win.'

He had not. He had been too distracted to give the game his full attention.

'I thought it only fair to give you a taste of what you will be missing once we embark upon our chess challenge,' he said, looking down his nose at her. 'I want you to recall the taste of victory even as the memory of it fades on your tongue.'

Miss Bertram laughed, revealing pearly white teeth. Nathaniel responded, but the stiff pull of the skin at the side of his face soon jerked him back to reality. What the hell was he doing?

'Come. The hour grows late.' He pushed to his feet

and scooped the draughtsmen from the board. 'Open the top, if you please, Miss Bertram.'

She did as he requested and he returned the pieces to their place inside the table.

'Will you…will you be joining us at church tomorrow?'

Nathaniel reined in the temptation to snap a reply. She meant nothing by it. She was young and new to his household. She would come to accept his decisions and Shiverstone Hall would settle into a new routine.

'No.' He had no need to explain. He crossed the room to the door and opened it. 'Goodnight, Miss Bertram.'

He held the door wide as she passed through with a murmured, 'Goodnight, my lord.'

Chapter Nine

On Monday morning Clara sat happily at the kitchen table, helping Mrs Sharp knead dough.

She barely looked up when Grace said, 'Goodbye, sweetie. Be a good girl for Mrs Sharp.'

Despite the wrench of leaving Clara, even for so short a time, anticipation for the morning ahead fizzed through Grace's blood. She hurried from the kitchen and promptly collided with a wall of solid muscle. She teetered backwards and two hard hands gripped her arms as the scent of shaving soap and musk weaved through her senses. Her heart leapt and her pulse skittered.

'Oh!'

'Steady.' A finger beneath her chin tilted her head up and two deep brown eyes studied her, provoking a flush of heat through her body and into her cheeks. 'I had not thought you quite so eager to commence with your driving lesson, Miss Bertram.'

'I am sorry, my lord.'

Her voice sounded shaky. She cleared her throat and stepped back, tugging her upper arm free of his other hand. His hand fell away and her pounding pulse steadied.

'I did not want to keep you waiting.'

He held her gaze for a long moment, then smiled. 'Well, you have not, so you may relax.'

They left the house and, as they walked to the stables, a howl rent the air. Grace stopped, scarcely daring to breathe. 'What was that?'

'Brack.' Ravenwell kept moving. 'He objects to being shut up with the other dogs. I thought you might concentrate better with only Bill to worry about.'

Grace hurried to catch him up. 'It is not my fault I am unused to animals. I shall become accustomed to them, I promise you.'

It was the Marquess who stopped this time. 'I am sure you will. And to the human inhabitants also, I trust.'

'Everyone has been welcoming. Except—'

'Except Mrs Sharp. Yes, I am aware and I have spoken to her. It is not that she dislikes you but, as you must accustom yourself to the animals, so she must become accustomed to new people.'

Grace darted a look at him. It was not only Mrs Sharp who must grow accustomed to newcomers.

Inside the barn, Ravenwell entered a stall, slapping

at the huge, rounded quarters of a grey horse who obligingly stepped sideways.

'Miss Bertram...' Ravenwell untied the horse and backed him from the stall '...meet Bill.'

Grace pressed back against the wall. Bill was not as tall as some horses, but he was wide and looked very strong. The head end was not as intimidating as the rear and Bill eyed her with a gentle eye and stretched his nose out, whiffling through his whiskers.

'Take off your glove, so he can learn your scent,' Ravenwell said.

Grace removed her glove, reached out a hesitant hand and stroked Bill's nose.

Ravenwell presented a chunk of carrot on his palm and Bill picked it up delicately with questing lips and then crunched, eyes half-closed in contentment.

'Here.' Ravenwell passed Grace another piece of carrot. 'Hold your hand flat, like this.'

He supported her hand underneath with one hand and with the other he straightened her fingers. A pleasurable shiver darted through Grace, and she had to force herself to concentrate on his words.

'Never bend your fingers or thumbs. He would not mean to bite, but he might easily mistake them for a carrot. And horses have strong teeth.'

Ravenwell showed Grace the harness and how to tack up Bill, who stood patiently whilst she fumbled with straps and buckles and struggled with the notion she must open his mouth to put a metal bit between those long, yellow teeth.

'You may never need to harness him on your own but, if you should wish to go out and the men are out on the fells, it will be useful for you to know how to do it.'

They led Bill from the stable and backed him between the shafts of the gig, Grace gaining confidence all the time. Bill was so docile, how could she be scared of him? But she took care to keep her feet away from his huge hooves.

'Why does he have such hairy legs?' she asked as Ravenwell handed her into the gig and passed her the reins.

'They are called feathers. They protect the horse's legs against water and mud.'

He climbed into the gig and settled beside her, his thigh warm and solid next to hers, producing, once again, a shiver of awareness. He was so big, so male. She felt safe by his side.

'Now...' he reached for Grace's hands '...you hold the reins like so and Bill just needs a small shake to get him moving.'

Bill walked forward and the gig jerked into motion.

'Keep a light contact with his mouth—that is how you steer him—but you will find he is so familiar with the way to the village, you will hardly need to do anything. We will drive as far as the ford, so you can drive across the river, and then we will return home.'

Grace's confidence increased as the lesson continued. Her nerves dissipated and she began to enjoy both Ravenwell's company and the scenery. The weather was mild for the time of year: the sky a bright blue with white clouds scudding across it, although there was little wind at ground level. This was now her home. The isolation and wildness of the landscape fascinated her and she was surprised by a sudden impulsion to take up her paints and attempt to capture its grandeur. At school, her skill and talent had been in portraits and miniatures and the art master, Signor Bertolli, had often despaired of her lack of aptitude in executing landscapes. Affection warmed her at the memory of her messy and disorganised but always encouraging teacher. It would be hard to find the time to paint, with Clara to care for, but she would enjoy the challenge of improving her skill and Clara would benefit in time, when Grace could use her knowledge to help her daughter acquire the accomplishments expected of a young lady.

'Thank you for teaching me to drive,' she said, on impulse. A skill was a skill, whether it was painting or driving. 'It will be agreeable not to have to rely on anyone else if I wish to visit the village.'

'Did you enjoy the church service?'

'Why, yes. As much as one ever enjoys being preached to.'

'I doubt Mr Rendell would appreciate hearing you say that.'

'Oh, he is not at all prosy, I assure you. He is just like any other young man. I told him you were teaching me to play chess and he said he might challenge you to a match one day.'

Silence. Grace peeped sideways. Ravenwell was frowning, his brow low and his mouth tight. She had thought he might be pleased—he must be lonely, living out here with no friends.

He has chosen to do so. You know he will not appreciate your interference.

She had spoken without thought and now the easy atmosphere between them had changed. She could not unsay those words, but she could smooth the moment with inconsequential chatter to distract him from his thoughts. From his fears. Although why such a powerful and wealthy man should fear anything was beyond Grace.

'Miss Dunn has invited me and Clara to call at the rectory next week. With your permission, of course, and if you think I can safely drive Bill?'

He glanced down at her, his frown lifting, to Grace's relief.

'I am sure you will cope, but I shall send Ned with you the first time to make sure.'

'Can you spare him from his duties?'

'Yes. Your and Clara's safety must take precedence. It will be pleasant for you to have a friend in the village.'

'Thank you.'

She sensed reservation behind his words. Was he concerned her visits to the village might result in callers at Shiverstone Hall? She could find no words to reassure him without openly mentioning his dislike of strangers. She still did not understand his choice to live this way. Was it embarrassment over his scars? He was a grown man and a lord. Could he not just brazen it out? Or was there something else. Something deeper? Sharp had hinted as much on her first night at the Hall. She vowed to find out more.

They had reached the river—Shiver Beck—and Grace drew Bill to a halt.

'Why do you not build a bridge? I got wet feet using those stepping stones on the day I arrived.'

She glanced at Ravenwell as she spoke and caught him biting back a grin.

'It is *not* funny.'

'Of course not.' His eyes danced, giving the lie to his words. 'No one normally *walks* from Shiverstone into the village. Drive on, Miss Bertram. You will not get wet feet in the gig.'

Grace shook the reins. Bill crossed the ford without hesitation but, as soon as they emerged on to the far

side, Ravenwell showed Grace how to turn the gig
for home. It was clear he had no intention of going
anywhere near the village.

Grace drove back to Shiverstone and Ned emerged
from the barn to unharness Bill and rub him down.

'Should I not learn to do that as well?' Grace asked.

'Very well. Ned, you may leave him to us.'

When they had finished, Grace looked up at Ravenwell to see him studying her with an amused smile.
He removed one glove and reached to rub gently at
her cheek.

Grace stilled at his touch, a *frisson* of awareness
skittering down her spine and setting her insides
a-flutter.

'You have a smudge,' he said.

His eyes wrinkled at the outer corners as he smiled
and Grace's knees seemed to weaken, causing her
to sway towards him. Horrified by her involuntary
response, she braced her spine, even as every nerve
ending in her body tingled and her breathing quickened.

'Now, as you have proved such an able pupil, I have
another challenge for you.'

Grace swallowed. Hard. It was not the thought of a
challenge that so unnerved her, but his intimate gesture and the way her pulse had leapt when he touched
her, and her sudden awareness of how lovely and

kind his eyes were when he smiled—not at all what one would expect from this normally terse man. Her response scared her a little. He was so very...*male.*

Ravenwell, in contrast, appeared oblivious to both his gesture and to Grace's reaction.

'I shall introduce you to the dogs,' he said.

Those words vanquished her embarrassment. A horse was one thing. Bill had stood obligingly still most of the time—he had been either tethered or in harness and thus under control. The dogs... She backed away a step.

'Come...you must not fear them or they will sense it. How shall you manage with Clara when she wants to visit the kennels?'

'Are they shut in? They will not be...' she swallowed, trying to quell her fear '...jumping around?'

Ravenwell laughed. 'I will not allow them to jump around.' He crooked his arm, proffering it to Grace. She hesitated and he raised one brow. 'The track up to the kennels is stony. I should not like you to turn your ankle. Come, you may meet them one at a time. They will make a noise, but they will not harm you.'

It felt odd, placing her hand on the arm of her employer. It was rock solid under her fingers and, again, she was reminded of his powerful build as his aura of masculinity pervaded every sense. She felt vulnerable and yet protected at the same time. A peculiar mix, but not unpleasant. Side by side they followed the path to the kennels.

'How many dogs do you have?'

'Nine, plus Brack. They are an assorted bunch—I use them mostly for hunting, except for Fly and Flash. They are collies and they work the sheep out on the fells. You can meet them first.'

Ravenwell and Grace headed back to the Hall some time later, Grace's head spinning with the names and purposes of the various terriers, spaniels, and the one pointer as well as the sheepdogs. Brack, sulking after being shut in the kennels, was at their heels.

'Why is Brack allowed indoors and not the other dogs?'

'I cannot imagine the chaos of living with that lot under one roof. No, they are happy enough in the kennels; they have known no different from when they were pups. Brack…his mother was a terrier—a big lass and a total hoyden she was. She went missing once for two weeks and, when she came home, she was in pup. Tam reckons she'd been visiting over towards Kendal. There's a pack of otter hounds out that way and when the litter came the pups had that look about them. And Brack certainly loves water. It might be hard to believe it now, but he was the runt of his litter. He failed to thrive and his mother rejected him. So I took him in and hand-reared him and he's lived in the Hall ever since. Eight years now.'

Grace reached out and patted Brack's rough head, aware that most men, given those same circumstances, would have destroyed the weak pup.

'What happened to his ear?' She fingered the ragged stump on the left side of his head.

'His mother bit it off when she rejected him. He may not be the most handsome dog in the world, but he is loyal and trustworthy.'

'Looks are not everything,' Grace said, opening the door to the kitchen, 'and he is very patient with Clara.'

A warm fug of air, filled with delicious smells, assailed them as they entered the room. Clara looked up, then scrambled from her chair as Grace removed her hat and her cloak.

'Ma Berm. Ma Berm,' she shouted, arms lifted as she ran to Grace.

'Miss Bertram,' Grace corrected, even as her heart skipped. It had sounded so like Mama. But she must never allow her guard to waver. She was Miss Bertram. Not Mama. She dropped her outer garments on a nearby chair as she lifted Clara and hugged her close. 'What have you been doing, little one?'

Alice looked up from her task of peeling potatoes.

'She's helped us with the baking, ma'am, and now Mrs Sharp has gone to the parlour to set out refreshments. She said as you'd both be famished after all that fresh air.'

'Uncle Nanniel!'

Clara squirmed in Grace's arms and then launched herself towards her uncle, arms outstretched. Grace, caught unawares, staggered with the shift of weight in her arms and found herself for the second time that day pressed up against the Marquess. His arms came around her, steadying her, whilst Clara's arms encircled her uncle's neck, hugging him tight, locking them into a three-way embrace. For a few wonderful moments Grace leant into Ravenwell's solid, muscular body. Her lids fluttered closed as his musky scent enveloped her and she relished the sensation of being held...of feeling safe. Then, aghast at the yearning such feelings invoked, she wriggled. After a couple of failed attempts, they eventually parted. Grace sneaked a glance at his lordship, to find him regarding her with laughter lighting his eyes.

'You will no doubt wish to refresh yourself before eating, Miss Bertram.'

A teasing note warmed his words, conjuring a silent *hmmph* from Grace. Whatever her instinctive response to his lordship, he clearly did not see her as anything other than an amusing diversion. Without volition, her hand lifted to her hair which had, she discovered, fallen from its pins. At that moment Mrs Sharp returned to the kitchen.

'There you are, milord. I have been to—'

Her mouth snapped shut and she raked Grace with a look of such suspicion Grace's cheeks fired up all over again. Then she raised her chin. She had done nothing wrong. What right did the housekeeper have to look at her as though she'd caught her in some misdemeanour?

'Alice was just telling us about the luncheon,' Ravenwell said into the sudden fraught silence. 'Thank you, Mrs Sharp. I am afraid Clara was a little over-enthusiastic in her welcome, so Miss Bertram is about to go and attend to her hair.' His lips twitched and Grace suspected him of holding back a laugh.

'You may leave this little miss with me, Miss Bertram, and we shall see you in the parlour when you are ready.'

Ten minutes later, having hastily washed her hands and face and brushed out and repinned her hair, Grace came downstairs, her steps slowing as an unfamiliar shyness at the thought of facing Lord Ravenwell came over her. She pressed her hands to her fluttering stomach as she reviewed the morning. What would his lordship think of her foolish reaction whenever they touched?

You are being ridiculous. He cannot know what you feel.

A high-pitched squeal sounded, quashing any remaining awkwardness, and she hurried to the parlour, where she stopped dead at the sight of Ravenwell crawling around the room, Clara perched on his back like a monkey, giggling as she wrapped her small fists in his hair, clinging tight.

Brack stood aside, tail wagging furiously.

'Ride Brack!'

'Ride Brack?' Ravenwell laughed, reared up on to his knees and reached behind to swing Clara from her perch. 'As you have asked so nicely, Miss Clara, you may ride Brack once around the room.'

He sat her on the dog's back, holding her and— Grace could see—supporting much of her weight.

'Miss Bertram, would you please lead Brack around the room?'

Grace started; she had not thought him aware of her presence. She came forward and took Brack's collar.

'Come, Brack.' She was thrilled when he moved at her command.

They completed the circuit, and Clara shouted, ''Gain! 'Gain!'

Ravenwell laughed, scooping her from Brack's back. 'You will tire Brack out and Miss Bertram and I are hungry.' He pulled a chair out for Grace. 'I shall think about buying a small pony for Clara next year. I am certain she will enjoy learning to ride. And you can learn at the same time.'

A simple statement to give so much pleasure. For the first time since she arrived at the Hall she truly felt she belonged. She had a settled place in the world and a family, of sorts. She sat, murmuring her thanks, her emotions welling as she resolutely ignored her earlier disquiet over the feelings stirred by his lordship.

Ravenwell plonked Clara on the chair next to Grace, handing her a slice of buttered bread.

'This will keep madam quiet whilst we eat,' he said. 'Oh, by the way…' he reached into his pocket '…Mrs Sharp gave me this after you left the kitchen.'

Grace took the letter from the Marquess and read her name on the front in a familiar hand. Isabel. It had been addressed to her at the school and the address scratched out and readdressed to her at Shiverstone Hall. She turned it over and on the back was a short note from Miss Fanworth, thanking Grace for her letter and promising to write very soon. Excited, Grace began to break the seal, but then stopped. She should not read the letter at the table. Besides, she wanted to savour every word in private, with no one watching and able to interpret her thoughts and feelings from her expression.

Grace spent much of the next half an hour trying to deter Clara from snatching a sample of every morsel of food upon the table and then discarding it after one nibble.

Ravenwell watched her efforts with a sardonic lift of his brow.

'And this illustrates perfectly why children should take their meals in the nursery.'

Grace bristled. 'She is just excited by being in here and eating with us.'

He laughed, holding his hands up, palms facing her. 'There is no need to leap to her defence, Miss Bertram. It was merely an observation. I am not about to chastise her for doing what children do.'

Grace bit her lip. She should not speak so boldly to her employer. 'I am sorry. And I concede your point. It does not make eating my own luncheon particularly easy.'

'At least you will not have to fret about the effect of Mrs Sharp's cooking on your waistline.'

Grace relaxed at the teasing glint in Ravenwell's eyes, then grabbed at Clara as she stood on her chair and prostrated her torso across the table in her determination to reach a plate of macaroons, despite the half-eaten one already on her plate.

'That is true.' Grace stood up, hoisting Clara on to her hip. Clara squirmed, protesting vocally but unintelligibly. 'Now, this little girl appears to have eaten her fill so I shall take her upstairs for her nap.'

Ravenwell had also risen to his feet and a warm

tingle flowed through her at his gentlemanly gesture to a mere governess.

'And you, Miss Bertram? Have you satisfied your appetite after your exertions?'

She smiled. 'I have had sufficient, thank you, my lord. Thank you for teaching me to drive—I shall be sure to take advantage of my new skill.'

He cocked his head to one side. 'And dare I think you are becoming used to our countryside? You appeared to derive some enjoyment from the views.'

Grace untangled Clara's fingers from her hair. 'Oh, yes. I confess I found it somewhat bleak and intimidating at first, but I very much enjoyed it today. In fact, it has awoken a desire in me to get out my sketchbook, although I doubt I have the talent to capture its full glory. I have also resolved to take Clara for a walk every day, weather permitting.' She smiled at him. 'I might even take Brack.'

'Well! Today has been a success already and it is only half over.'

Grace headed for the door.

'Do not forget your letter, Miss Bertram.'

Isabel's letter! How could I forget?

Grace turned and Ravenwell was there, very close, the letter in his hand. She looked up, past the broad expanse of his chest, into his smiling brown eyes and awareness tugged deep in her core as, again, her pulse leapt and her breath quickened. His eyes darkened and grew more intense, then Clara pressed her cheek against Grace's and the moment passed.

'Thank you.' Grace took her letter, forced a quick smile and left the room, the meaning of that exchanged look teasing her brain.

Chapter Ten

Clara eventually dozed off and Grace escaped to her sitting room to read her letter.

It was concise, almost terse, and the news it contained shocked Grace to the core. Isabel, married? Her happy, joyful friend—who had loved to sing and had long dreamt of the passionate love with which she would one day be blessed—trapped in a marriage of convenience with the son and heir of a viscount?

Her marriage to William Balfour was, Isabel wrote, a joining of '*two sensible people in exact understanding of each other*'.

How Grace's heart ached for her friend. The letter sounded totally unlike the lively girl Grace loved like a sister. How she wished she lived closer and could offer her support and comfort. The date at the top of the letter told her it had been written way back in August. Poor Isabel. Wed over two months and Grace had not even known. She wondered how Isabel had fared since.

She would write back immediately and hope Isabel would be bolstered by her support. Although... her burst of enthusiasm faded. How could she write and burden Isabel with the truth about Shiverstone Hall and Clara? Isabel asked in her letter if Grace had tracked down her baby and, if Grace wrote a reply, she must lie.

But to lie would be a betrayal of their friendship.

She would wait. She would write to her friend later—after a few more weeks, when she was more settled here at the Hall and hopefully Isabel would be in a happier frame of mind and Grace would have come to terms with her own deception.

That decision—really no decision at all, merely a putting off of the inevitable—fretted at Grace for the remainder of the day.

'You have been remarkably quiet this evening, Miss Bertram,' Ravenwell said as they sat opposite one another at the chess table after dinner. 'I hope your letter did not bring bad news?'

Grace's attention jolted back to the drawing room in which they sat. 'Not bad news, precisely. But unsettling.'

She gathered her thoughts and tried to focus on the game. She studied the board, then leaned towards it, peering at the chessmen as though a closer perspective might conceivably improve her position.

I know I'm a beginner, but how have I ended up in such a predicament after so few moves?

The Marquess was watching her, a small smile playing around his lips.

'Quite,' he said, as though she had spoken aloud. 'Your attention is clearly not on our game.'

'I am sorry.'

'No need to apologise. It takes practice, and one's full attention, to play well.' Ravenwell began to move the pieces back to their starting positions. 'We will play another night, when you are not so preoccupied.'

He pushed back his chair and stood up, brandy glass in hand. He was going. Probably to his book room to work on his ledgers. Her surge of disappointment shocked Grace as she anticipated a long evening alone with her thoughts.

Ravenwell, however, did not move away from the table.

'Would you care to talk about whatever is bothering you?'

Grace recognised the effort it must cost this private man to make such an offer—she had seen and appreciated his efforts to change since she had pointed out that his avoidance of her was punishing Clara. She was no longer intimidated by his brusqueness, which she now knew concealed a gentle man who loved his niece and was kind to his animals.

'Isabel's news seems to be all I am able to think

about. Mayhap saying it out loud will help me make sense of it.'

He gestured to the chairs by the fire. 'Come, then.'

Where to start? But the Marquess was—or once was—a man of the world in which Isabel now found herself. He might be able to ease some of Grace's worries.

She told him about Isabel and her arranged marriage with William Balfour.

'Balfour...I know of the family, but I cannot recall a William. He is no doubt younger than I. But why you are so worried for your friend? She has made an excellent match. She will be set up for life.'

'You do not understand.'

How could he possibly understand when he had never met the free spirit that was Isabel?

'Isabel's parents doted on her...she dreamt of singing in the opera and she thrives on being adored. How will she survive with a husband who does not love her?'

Grace cringed at Ravenwell's huff of amusement. *He thinks me a romantic ninny now.* 'You do not believe love is necessary in a marriage?'

'I do not. You, on the other hand, expose your youth and naivety in believing such poetical nonsense.'

If only he knew...

The veil had been swept from her eyes long ago. In her mind's eye she saw Clara's father, Philip, tall, lean

and handsome with his ready smile, charm personi-
fied, who had flirted with her sixteen-year-old self
and persuaded her of his love—Philip, whose imma-
turity sent him fleeing to join the army when Grace
had told him she carried his child. Philip, who had
been dead nigh on fourteen months, killed in action.

She felt the familiar wash of sorrow over Philip's
death on the battlefield, but she had long since accepted that what she had felt for him had been infatuation, fed by his flattery and her foolish pride that
such a handsome youth should take notice of her and
make her feel important. Every trace of her naïve,
youthful love had been wiped from her heart as she
saw him for precisely what he was: a self-serving
youth who thought sweet words were a sufficient
price to pay to get what he desired.

And he was right, wasn't he?

A shudder shook Grace at the memory of that terrifying period in her life when she had succeeded in
concealing her condition from everyone other than
her best friends but, despite everything, she would
not allow her experience with Philip to sour her.

'I cannot accept that love can be dismissed as mere
poetical nonsense.'

'You make my point for me. You have no experience of the real world. Indeed, how could you have?
You have been secluded at your school since the age
of…what…ten?'

'Nine.'

'Nine. Precisely. Naïve nonsense. You should do yourself a favour and rid your brain of such romantic drivel.'

He could not hide his bitterness. Was it because of his scars, or had he unhappy experiences of love? Well, she would not allow him to sully her opinion of the world. She had always—like Isabel—believed in true love.

'Your friend will do very well in her marriage,' he continued, 'and it is a waste of your time to be fretting about her.'

'That is—' Grace stopped.

'That is what, Miss Bertram?'

His eyes were dark and unfathomable. His jaw set.

Sad. But she did not dare say that. She must not be lulled by this new, friendlier Ravenwell. He still paid her wages and he could still dismiss her if she forgot her place.

'That is no doubt wise advice,' she said instead. 'There is nothing I can do to help Isabel. Besides, she has a strength and determination that I am sure will help her cope.'

Ravenwell stood. 'Now your mind is at rest, I have work to do. I shall bid you goodnight.'

He strode from the room, leaving Grace staring after him.

What is going on inside his head? He cannot be happy, living like this.

She switched her gaze to the fire, watching mindlessly as the embers glowed red, emitting an occasional tongue of flame and sending intermittent sparks up the chimney. Her heart went out to the Marquess. How lonely he must be. She would love to see him smile more often and relax. There and then she swore to do all she could to bring more light, life and laughter to his life.

'What have you been saying to put his lordship in such a tear, missy?'

Grace started. She had not heard Sharp come in.

'I am not sure. We were talking about love and marriage...concerning some news I had from a friend,' she added hastily, in response to Sharp's smirk. 'He told me to rid my mind of romantic drivel and thoughts of love, then said he has work to do and left.'

Sharp tidied their empty cups on to a tray, then picked up Ravenwell's abandoned brandy glass— still half-full—and drained it with a single swallow and a wink at Grace.

'Ah.' He placed the empty glass on the tray and shook his head. 'No wonder.'

'Why do you say that?'

Sharp tapped his finger against the side of his nose. 'I'm not one to gossip.'

'You are admirably discreet, Sharp, but you *under-*

stand his lordship and that is why I ask you rather than any of the others—'

'The others? They do not know the half of what I know.'

'I'm certain *they* do not know the real reason his lordship cuts himself off from his friends and family.'

'No, they don't.' Sharp sat in the chair opposite Grace and leaned forward. 'Only me and Mrs Sharp know the whole truth. We was all at Ravenwell then, living at the Dower House while the manor was being rebuilt. His lordship had been courting Lady Sarah before the fire, but when he went to London to see her, she'd have nothing to do with him. She wed someone else soon after.

'He came home, and never went down south again. Even at Ravenwell, the stares and the whispers were so bad he'd barely leave the estate, but he still suffered from the guilt.'

Guilt? Grace longed to probe, but feared if she interrupted Sharp now he might clam up.

'And then his mother took it into her head to arrange a marriage. To Miss Havers. Desperate for a title and money, she was. But the little bi—beg pardon, *witch*—took one look at his lordship and swore that neither title nor wealth were sufficient to entice her to wed a monster. 'Course, that was soon after the fire. His scars were still raw then. They look better now.'

Ignorant women! Scorning an injured man in that way, destroying his faith in love. If I could get my hands on them...

Sharp's gaze rested on Grace's hands—curled into fists on her lap—and he smiled. 'Now you see why my missus is so protective of his lordship,' he said softly.

'After that—' his voice was brisk again '—we came to live here and we've been here ever since.'

It was as Grace suspected. Ravenwell had cut himself off from society to protect himself from rejection. And yet...that didn't really explain it. A man such as he...if he wanted to mix with others, surely he was strong enough to withstand a few stares and pitying glances?

'And the guilt?'

Sharp's eyes narrowed. 'I've said too much. Never you mind, missy, 'tis none of your business.'

Grace halted the gig and tied off the reins, as Ravenwell had taught her, delighted and proud at having successfully accomplished her first drive to Shivercombe. They were in the lane outside the rectory and she looked round as the front door was flung open.

'Miss Bertram!'

Mr Rendell—tall, slender, and handsome—hurried down the path to the front gate, beaming. There had been a time, Grace realised, when the attention of such a man would have set her heart soaring but now, although she was pleased to see the curate again, her heart remained stubbornly unmoved.

In her mind's eye an image of a very different sort arose—dark, brooding, attractive in an altogether different way—the difference between a boy and a man. She tried hard to ignore the *frisson* of desire and need that trickled down her spine.

'Good afternoon, Mr Rendell.' She accepted his hand to assist her from the gig and then lifted Clara down. 'As you can see, I have braved my first drive to the village, albeit with Ned in attendance to ensure Clara and I come to no harm.'

Ned had ridden behind the gig and now came forward to take charge of Bill.

'In that case, I shall congratulate you upon the success of your first outing and express my delight in finding you both unscathed by the experience. The weather is currently kind and it would be wasteful not to take advantage.'

'It would indeed. Miss Dunn did invite us to call upon her, but—because of the weather—we did not specify a day. I do hope this is not an inconvenient time? We shall not stay above half an hour, but having a purpose for my drive made it all the more enjoyable.'

'Alas, I am on my way to visit a parishioner, but

Miss Dunn is at home and I make no doubt she will be delighted to see you. With your permission, I shall escort you to her and then I must be on my way.'

'Thank you, sir. Ned, we shall not be long.'

'Go round to the kitchen door when you have secured the horses, Ned,' Mr Rendell said, 'and Cook will find you some refreshments.'

The curate picked up Clara and led the way into the square, stone-built rectory. He showed Grace into a smart drawing room and went in search of Miss Dunn.

The first person to come into the room was the Reverend Dunn, his twinkly eyes creased into slits by his cherubic smile.

'Miss Bertram, what a pleasant surprise. Elizabeth asks if you will join her in the parlour where there are some little friends young Clara might like to meet.'

He winked at Grace, held his hand out to Clara, who took it without hesitation, and ushered Grace before him, indicating a door at the end of the passageway.

'It is not as grand as the drawing room and we would not normally entertain visitors in here, but I am sure you will take us as you find us.'

Grace pushed open the door and stepped into a much cosier, if somewhat shabbier, room. The thought flashed through her mind that here was a home in which one could feel comfortable, in stark contrast to the dark, unwelcoming reception rooms at the Hall. The idea of effecting some changes— sparked initially by the beauty of the chess table— grew stronger.

'Good afternoon, Miss Bertram.'

The voice shook her from her thoughts and she gazed around what appeared to be an empty room.

'Go on in,' urged the Reverend Dunn from behind her.

Grace walked forward and there, shielded from the door by a sofa, was Miss Dunn, sitting on a rug before the fire with two kittens scrambling over her lap whilst a third pawed at a length of string being dangled in front of its nose. A large tabby-and-white cat sat to one side, assiduously washing itself whilst keeping one eye on the youngsters.

Grace laughed as the kitten pounced on the string and tumbled on to its back.

'Good afternoon, Miss Dunn,' she said. 'I had for- gotten about the kittens you mentioned on Sunday. They are very pretty.'

'Please, call me Elizabeth, for I am sure we are destined to be bosom friends.' She gestured to a chair and bade Grace sit. 'I hope you do not object to being received in our family parlour, but Mama has banned these little ones from the drawing room. Quite rightly, given the havoc they wreak. Please forgive me for not rising but, as you see, I am serving the useful purpose of providing a soft lap for their play.'

'Of course. And you must call me Grace.'

Her spirits rose. How lovely it would be to have a friend so close to her new home; it would help to ease the pain of missing her school friends.

'Look, Clara. See the kittens? Are they not sweet?'

Clara ran forward, all eagerness, and the kittens scattered.

'You must take care if you are not to frighten them, Clara,' Miss Dunn said, gathering her on to her lap. 'Sit here with me and we shall see which of them is bold enough to come and meet you.'

An hour later, Grace tapped the reins on Bill's broad back and they set off on the drive to Shiverstone Hall, Ned riding behind. Grace waved goodbye to Elizabeth and to Mr Rendell, who had not long before returned from his visit and joined them in the parlour, along with Mrs Dunn and a tea tray. Watching her new friend and Mr Rendell together—catching the occasional shared glance and the resulting pink tinge of Elizabeth's cheeks—Grace suspected there was more to their friendship than they might wish anyone to suspect.

As they left the village, Grace glanced at Clara, sitting quietly for once, one hand clutching tight at the handle of a covered wicker basket wedged on the seat between them. Doubts surfaced. Had she presumed too much, accepting this gift for Clara? Then Clara looked up at her, shining eyes huge in her beaming face, and all doubts shrivelled.

Ravenwell loved Clara.

He would not begrudge her a kitten.

Would he?

Thinking about the Marquess set up those peculiar nervy sensations deep in the pit of Grace's stomach once again. They had plagued her ever since the moment he had wiped that smudge from her cheek. Ridiculous thoughts and longings flitted in and out of her mind, no matter how hard she tried to quell them. She did not need to concentrate on driving. Bill, as Ravenwell had promised, needed no guidance to find his way home. Instead, she diverted her wayward thoughts by admiring the beauty of the day and of the surrounding scenery, imagining in her mind's eye how she might capture it on canvas.

Chapter Eleven

Nathaniel trotted Zephyr steadily down the track that led through the forest towards the village as Brack ranged through the trees, nose to the ground. He was concerned about Clara's safety. That was the only reason he couldn't settle to anything this afternoon, after he learned that Grace had driven them both in the gig to Shivercombe. Never mind that Ned was there to keep them safe. That was his role. He would only go as far as the river and he would await them there, if he did not come upon them beforehand. Sharp had assured him Miss Bertram only intended to stay at the Rectory for half an hour before returning and they had already been gone an hour and a half.

He emerged from the forest and followed the track as it curved towards the ford in the river. Here, large slabs of rock—smoothed by centuries of erosion by the flowing waters of Shiver Beck—had been laid across the riverbed to create a place for carriages to cross. The only time it became impassable was after heavy rain when—although not very much deeper—the swiftness of the current rendered the ford treacherous. At least the water level fell as quickly as it rose, so they were never cut off from the village for long.

Nathaniel reined Zephyr to a halt as they reached the ford and slid from the saddle, pulling the reins over the horse's head so he could crop the grass whilst they waited. Brack, as usual, could not resist the lure of the water and swam into the deeper water, downstream of the ford. It was a beautiful, crisp November day, but Nathaniel was in no mood to appreciate either the weather or the natural beauty of his surroundings. He crossed his arms and tapped his foot, his attention fixed on the track that led from the ford and soon disappeared from view as it wound into the village.

Finally, as he was beginning to think the unthinkable—that he must go into the village and make certain they were safe—he heard the *clip-clop* of horses' hooves and the rattle of wheels. His heart returned to its rightful position in his chest as Brack exploded from the river and shook himself thoroughly, sending sparkling drops of water arcing through the air. Nathaniel mounted Zephyr, sending him splashing through the ford as Bill plodded into view, towing the gig, and he heard Miss Bertram say, 'Look, Clara. There is Uncle Nathaniel.'

'Uncle Nanniel! See kitty!'

Bill halted beside Zephyr. Clara bounced up and down on the bench seat whilst Miss Bertram...he focussed on the governess. Miss Bertram did not quite meet his gaze. She looked sheepish. Guilty, even. What had happened in the village?

'Ned, you may ride on ahead,' Nathaniel said. 'There is no need for us both to accompany the gig.'

Even while he was speaking, he was chewing over the meaning of her expression. Had she met with Rendell? Did she feel guilty for meeting him whilst she was meant to be looking after Clara? He tamped down the spiral of anger that climbed from deep in the pit of his stomach, knowing he could not begrudge her some independence or the opportunity to make friends. He might choose to live the life of a recluse, but he could not insist that others—even if they worked for him—follow suit.

Besides—he took in Clara's joyous expression—it was good for Clara.

He reined Zephyr around, called Brack—who appeared strangely eager to clamber into the gig—to heel and nudged the stallion back into the river. A glance behind showed Bill following behind, splashing through the crystal water that reached halfway to his knees as he negotiated the ford with the ease of long familiarity. Once they reached the other bank, Nathaniel rode alongside the gig.

'Did you visit Miss Dunn?' She had said they would visit the rectory, to call upon the vicar's daughter.

'Yes, indeed, and we agreed we are to be friends and I am to call her Elizabeth and she will call me Grace.' She threw a huge smile in his direction, but it did not distract him from the tinge of anxiety in her eyes or prevent him from noticing her hurried speech. 'We had an exceedingly pleasant visit and then Mrs Dunn joined us, and Mr Rendell, and—'

'Kitty!' Clara half-stood in her effort to interrupt Miss Bertram and gain Nathaniel's attention. 'Kitty!'

'Hush, Clara. Sit down. It is dangerous to stand up.' Miss Bertram scooped Clara's legs from under her and plonked her back on the seat. 'And it is rude to interrupt.'

'Uncle *Naaaaaanniel.*' Clara's appeal was a whine of frustration.

Miss Bertram shot him a wary look from under the rim of her bonnet, then reined Bill to a halt, her expression resigned.

'I had better confess this now, for you shall discover the truth soon enough.'

Every beat of Nathaniel's heart thundered in his ears. What was she about to tell him? Sudden fear gripped him, clenching his stomach. He couldn't lose her. Clara would be inconsolable.

Miaow.

Brack reared up on his hind legs, his front paws on the step as he thrust his head on to Miss Bertram's lap, whining.

'Brack! Get down, sir! My apologies, Miss Bertram, I cannot think what has possessed him.'

'I can.' She brushed at the damp patch on her brown pelisse with a rueful smile.

'Kitty!'

Miaow.

'Oh, heavens! There is no help for it. My lord, Elizabeth… Miss Dunn…gave Clara a kitten.' Her tone rang with defiance, but her expression was wary. 'I know I should have asked your permission first, but—'

'*Kitty.* Uncle Naffaniel. Kitty!'

A kitten! He forced down the relieved laugh swelling his chest. And he had feared—he did not allow that thought to develop. It did not matter what he had feared. He was in danger of allowing his imagination too free a rein when it came to Miss Bertram. Their conversation the other night about romance should be enough to convince him to keep his distance. If she *had* developed a *tendre* for Rendell, so much the better.

'No wonder Brack is so interested in the gig. I assume it is inside the basket?'

Grace nodded.

'See kitty?'

'Not now, poppet. If he runs away we shall never find him. Besides, Brack might eat him for supper.'

'Oh, no. I did not think…might Brack hurt him?'

'Come, let us get home.' The horses began to move again. 'And I do not know, is the honest answer. We have never had cats at the Hall, but he is a hunting dog, so…'

Her face was stricken. 'What have I done? Clara will be devastated if he should get hurt.'

'Then we shall make sure he stays safe.'

'Thank you.'

Her face, as always, lit up with her smile, her mercurial eyes shifting from green to gold and back again. They were as changeable as the play of sunlight through the first leaves of spring, the colour always shifting, reflecting the light, and… Nathaniel tore his gaze from hers.

'It remains to be seen what Mrs Sharp will say.'

Their gazes clashed again—this time with a conspiratorial mix of amusement and trepidation.

'A cat? *Indoors?*' Mrs Sharp propped her hands on her hips. 'It will run riot, up and down the curtains, scratching the carpet. And the *mess*…'

'I am sorry, Mrs Sharp, I did not think of that. But…look at Clara's face…how could you deny…?'

Miss Bertram cast an anxious look at Nathaniel.

'The decision is made, Mrs Sharp. How hard can it be for five adults to keep control of one small kitten?' Nathaniel set the basket on the table as he spoke and unbuckled the strap that held the lid in place.

'My lord! Not on the *table*.'

'I shall not put the cat on the table, Mrs Sharp. I am merely removing it from the basket.'

Sharp—who had jumped guiltily from his favourite chair in the corner as Nathaniel, Grace and Clara had come into the kitchen—peered into the basket as Nathaniel lifted the lid. A reedy *miaow* issued forth, followed by a black-and-white face, whiskers quivering.

Sharp reached in and picked up the kitten. 'You look like you've been a-sweeping the chimneys.' He grinned at Grace. 'Is that his name? Sweep?'

'Sweep!' Clara reached up for the kitten.

'There, little miss.' Sharp put the kitten down and it shot across the room and underneath the large dresser at the far end.

'Causing havoc already,' Mrs Sharp grumbled as Clara let out a wail and toddled after the kitten.

'Oh, dear. I am sorry, Mrs Sharp.' Grace went to the dresser and knelt down to peer underneath.

Nathaniel's eyes were immediately drawn to the shapely round of her bottom, suggestively outlined by her woollen dress. He wrenched his gaze away, irritated he should even notice.

'Allow me, Miss Bertram.'

He crossed the kitchen to kneel beside her and reached under the dresser. Needle-sharp claws raked his hand and he bit back his curse as he scooped up the kitten and dragged it from its hiding place.

'Take the kitten up to the nursery where it is quieter.' He thrust the kitten at Miss Bertram. 'It will be your responsibility to clean up after it and to train it. Is that understood?'

'Yes, my lord,' she said, her eyes downcast.

He felt an ogre, snapping at her like that, but at least no one would suspect the truth of his wayward thoughts—they would blame his sour mood on the kitten.

He hoped Brack would accept it—he made a mental note to introduce them as soon as possible. It was a pretty little thing, with a fluffy coat that was mostly black, with white on its face, stomach, paws, and tail. Sweep. The name suited it, with its white face marred only by a black smear across its upper lip and another around one eye.

He watched Miss Bertram leave the kitchen, the kitten cradled in her arms. Clara bounced alongside, clearly delighted with her new friend.

She would not be intimidated by him. She had moved beyond that stage. She could see past his brusqueness. He would grow to accept Sweep as soon as he saw how much Clara loved her kitten. He would do anything to make Clara happy. Grace brushed out her hair and twisted it into a chignon as she prepared for dinner. Clara was already asleep, exhausted with all the excitement of the day, and Sweep sat on Grace's bed, watching her from wide green eyes.

'You will have to stay in the kitchen at night,' she told him.

She'd thought long and hard about it, but she could not have Sweep disturbing Clara at night, neither did she want him in her bedchamber. Cats, she knew, were often active at night and likely to disrupt her sleep. Now she had only to persuade Mrs Sharp to agree. She smoothed her dress over her hips and scooped Sweep off the bed.

'Mrs Sharp…' she said as she entered the kitchen.

'What is that cat doing here?'

'Now, now, missus.' Sharp came to Grace and took the kitten from her. 'Miss Bertram can hardly leave Sweep upstairs with Miss Clara asleep, can she? And you were complaining about mice only t'other day.' He winked at Grace. 'He'll do grand in here of an evening and Miss Clara can play with him during the day.'

'Hmmph. Just you keep it from under my feet. I'm too busy to have to watch where I'm stepping all the time.'

Grace handed Sweep to Sharp, smiling her thanks, and headed for the parlour. That was her first challenge accomplished and more easily than she had anticipated. Now for the second.

She waited until they had withdrawn to the drawing room, and Mrs Sharp—still grumbling under her breath about *that cat*—had delivered the tea tray. The Marquess, as was now his custom, had carried his brandy glass through from the parlour. Grace poured tea for herself and, ignoring the chess table, she settled into one of the two fireside chairs. Ravenwell hesitated, raised a brow and then joined her.

'Do I detect a desire to talk rather than play?'

'Yes, my lord.' She was committed now. She must do this, for Clara's sake. The worst he could do was refuse. 'When I first came, you said I might make changes to the nursery wing.'

He inclined his head. 'I did indeed. And have you done so?'

'I have, with help from Alice.'

'And did you find everything you need?'

'Yes...'

Grace sucked in a breath, but before she could continue, he said, 'I sense a question coming.'

Grace bristled at the smile teasing the corners of his mouth. He thought her amusing. Someone to be indulged.

'I am only asking for Clara's sake,' she said stiffly.

'I want her to have a home here.' She waved her arm, indicating the room in which they sat. 'The nursery and her bedchamber are now comfortable and cosy, but what about here?'

His brows snapped into a frown. 'Here? This is a drawing room. Not a place for children.'

'Children?' She leant forward. 'We are speaking of your niece. Do you intend for her never to come in here?'

'She does come in here,' he growled.

'Precisely.' Satisfied she had made her point, she sat back. 'Look around you. I am sorry if I speak out of turn, but there is nothing welcoming or homely about this room. And what about Christmas?'

'Christmas?' His brows shot up. 'What about Christmas?'

How could she explain without sounding full of self-pity? She did not want Clara's memories of her childhood Christmases to echo hers.

'What did Christmas mean to you as a boy?'

Understanding dawned in his eyes, and he smiled. 'Stir-up Sunday, delicious smells from the kitchen for days on end, gathering greenery and bringing in the Yule log, going to church on Christmas morning, exchanging gifts.' He gazed into the flames, a wistful look on his face, as he listed his memories. 'Twelfth Night and the Lord of Misrule. Family gatherings with pantomimes and charades...'

He fell silent. He looked…lost and vulnerable. It was the only time Grace had ever seen him with his guard down and her heart went out to him. It had been his choice to live this isolated life but he had been forced into it by the reactions of others. He had only been twenty-one. Such a young man.

He appeared to recollect her presence and his lips firmed. 'It is not the same now. I am happy with the house the way it is.'

'You may be content and you may not relish the thought of celebrating Christmas, but…do you not see? It is our responsibility to make sure Clara's childhood memories are as happy as yours.'

Ravenwell tilted his head as he focussed on Grace. 'And as happy as yours?'

'Some of them,' she admitted. 'The later ones. The Christmases I spent at school, with my friends, are some of my happiest memories.'

'And were your early Christmases *un*happy?'

'Not unhappy, precisely, but then I knew no different. My uncle and aunt were extremely devout and they eschewed anything that smacked of pagan tradition. For them, it was all about church and charity. Laudable, I know, but…for a child…'

She rose to her feet and walked away from the fireplace, away from the warm glow of the flames and the candles on the mantelshelf, to the dark end of the room, then stopped and faced him.

'This room should be the heart of the home and the focus of Christmas.' She waved her arm, encompassing the unlit fire and the bareness of the rest of the room.

Ravenwell looked around the room as if seeing it for the first time. 'I see what you mean. For Clara's sake.'

She smiled. 'For Clara's sake.' She returned to her chair. 'I should like to move some of the furniture back in here, with your permission.'

'I shall not object, as long as Mrs Sharp is agreeable. We kept the furniture to a minimum to lighten her chores. It has never bothered me in the past.'

'She has Alice to help now. And if the work should still be too much, I am sure Annie would be happy to earn a little extra.'

'You may do as you think fit.'

She had not expected enthusiasm; his grudging approval was a step in the right direction. She had vowed to turn this bleak house into a happy home for Clara. Now that vow had widened to include Lord Ravenwell.

Chapter Twelve

Three days later, Clara woke with a runny nose and a sore throat. She was listless and touchy all morning and Grace could do little other than sit and cuddle her next to the nursery fire. Even Sweep was unable to raise a smile or a spark of interest and the morning dragged as Grace remained on tenterhooks, constantly alert for signs of a fever developing. The only bright point was a letter from Rachel, sent all the way from Huria—via Miss Fanworth—which Ned brought back from the village.

Rachel's letter described a very different world to Shiverstone Hall. She wrote of the luxury of the palace she lived in—a *palace!*—the vastness of the surrounding desert and the beauty of the verdant oasis. She had three children in her care—eight-year-old Aahil, his sister Ameera, six, and his brother, Hakim, four—who were slowly growing to trust her. Grace could read her love for the children in the words she had penned. About her employer, the majestic-sounding Sheikh Malik bin Jalal al-Mahrouky, she said but little. There was caution in her words and Grace thought he must be most intimidating.

A little before eleven Mrs Sharp sent Alice upstairs to offer to sit with Miss Clara for a spell whilst Miss Bertram went to the kitchen for a cup of chocolate. Grace took Sweep with her, putting her next to Brack who, unusually for this time of day, was curled up near the kitchen range. After a hesitant beginning, the two animals had become friends.

'How is she?' Mrs Sharp handed Grace a cup of warm chocolate.

'Tetchy. And most displeased at being left with Alice,' Grace said, sitting at the table. 'Thank you.'

'It is to be hoped you do not succumb to the cold as well. You look pale.'

The housekeeper's concern was unexpected, endearing her to Grace, who cradled the cup between her hands and sipped, then tipped her head back, heaving a sigh, watching mindlessly whilst Mrs Sharp chopped carrots.

'I cannot believe how exhausting it is, sitting and doing nothing other than nursing Clara.'

'Has she slept at all?'

'Not yet.' Grace finished her chocolate and stood up. 'I must return and relieve Alice. Poor Clara, she is so miserable. She does not know what she wants, but she wants it *now.*'

'I have mixed up a remedy for her, to help ease her throat.' Mrs Sharp often treated common ailments within the household with her remedies. 'Give her a spoonful and then, when she does fall asleep, I will sit with her. You'll be bound to have a disturbed night with her and you have missed your walk today. You should go outside for some exercise whilst you are able to. It is a beautiful day.'

Startled by the housekeeper's unusual solicitude, Grace thanked her and, when Clara dozed off shortly after luncheon, Grace took her up on her offer.

Ravenwell had been out since first light, according to Sharp, sitting in his favourite overstuffed armchair in the corner as he sucked on his pipe. Grace lingered, hoping to learn a little more about her puzzling employer.

'Likes to keep himself busy, see. Stops him from brooding.'

'Brooding?' Grace busied herself folding Clara's freshly laundered clothes, as though any answer was of no consequence and she asked merely to be polite. The best way to wheedle information from Sharp was to pretend disinterest.

'Oh, aye. He exhausts himself every day, to stop him thinking about his father. It's the guilt.'

Guilt. Sharp had mentioned guilt before, but always refused to explain.

'Oh, I cannot believe his lordship has anything to feel guilty about.'

'Well that's just where you'd be wrong, missy.' Sharp tilted his head back and, eyes half-closed, blew a perfect smoke ring into the air. 'So you don't know ever'thing, for all yer education.

'No,' he went on after a pause. 'He'll never forgive himself. Feels it here—' and he thumped his chest in the region of his heart '—he does. He ain't the hard man you think he is.'

I don't think him a hard man at all. But she had more sense than to say so to Sharp.

'We tried to stop him going back into the fire, but three of us couldn't hold him back, he was that determined.'

'Was that the fire at Ravenwell Manor?'

'If'n only we could've stopped him, but he were like a man possessed. And his mother. It fair curdled the blood to hear her screams.'

'But…' she had to ask and hope Sharp wouldn't clam up '…why did he go back into the fire? Is that when he got burned?'

'Aye. 'Twas his father. He couldn't walk so well and he was upstairs when it broke out. His lordship… the Earl of Shiverstone as he was then…tried to rescue him. He got as far as the bedchamber, but then the roof caved in and his father was gone. Lord, the nightmares he suffered afterwards. Not to mention the pain. If'n you've ever burned your hand with a candle flame, missy, you'll know the agony. Only multiply that a hundred...a thousand...fold, and you might get nearer the truth.'

Poor Nathaniel. A hard lump of misery lodged in Grace's throat as she imagined his suffering, at only twenty-one years of age. Two years older than she was now. Another piece of the puzzle that was Lord Ravenwell slotted into place. The guilt, as well as the scars, must have been an intolerable burden to one so young.

She donned her pelisse and set off to walk up the hill behind the Hall, her sketchbook under her arm, hoping to capture the wildness and beauty of the landscape with her pencil. She had never ventured up on to the fells before—it was too far for Clara to walk—and she looked forward to exploring this area of her new home.

Her breath grew short as she plodded up the path, determined to reach Shiver Crag, jaggedly silhouetted against the blue of the sky, but she found she had to stop long before then to catch her breath.

She gazed back the way she had come. The day was clear and sharp, and the land fell away below her to flatten into the dale, with its woods and pasture. There was the river she had to drive across to reach the village and…she searched, her hand shielding her eyes…yes, there was the church tower, jutting out amongst the jumble of rooftops. Her chest swelled as she breathed in the cold air, refreshing her lungs and making her blood sing with energy.

She would walk a little further and sketch a little before going back. And she would hope that somehow, miraculously, her nap had restored Clara to full health. Her attention was caught by a huge, golden-brown bird circling lazily in the sky. *Good heavens.* She had thought the bird she saw when she first arrived at the Hall was big, but…this one was gigantic. She watched its mesmerising, effortless glide and marvelled at the span of its broad wings, tipped by feathers that resembled splayed fingers.

She looked back up to the crag. It was further than she first thought. She would have no time to reach it today, but it would be an imposing focal point for her sketches if she walked just a little further, to where the terrain levelled out ahead.

She trudged on until she reached the grassy plateau and there he was.

Ravenwell.

He had not seen her—he stood to her right, half-facing away from her as he delved inside a bag on the ground. What was he doing up here, all alone? Was he…as Sharp had said…brooding? It was odd there were no dogs with him. Nor was there a horse in sight. Did he come up here to this wild, solitary place to think about his father and the night of the fire? Would he welcome company, or would he send her away? The temptation to retreat before he saw her was powerful. She could disappear back down the path and he would never know she had been there.

But…this was her first opportunity to sketch this stark but beautiful landscape and she was loath to waste it. Making her mind up, she tucked her sketchbook more securely beneath her arm and headed towards the Marquess, picking her way across the springy tussocks of grass.

As she drew near to Ravenwell, he raised his left arm, clad in a massive gauntlet, straight out in front of him and let out a shrill cry. Grace's steps faltered. Was it some sort of ritual? A movement caught her eye. The bird—that monstrous bird—had stopped circling. It swooped purposefully and then flew straight at Nathaniel.

It's attacking! No!

Grace ran towards Ravenwell, waving her arms and her sketchbook, shouting as loudly as she could. The bird—surely as big as Grace herself—veered at the last minute, beating its powerful wings as it rose up into the air, its curved claws just missing Nathaniel's head.

Grace grabbed Nathaniel's hand in both of hers, her sketchbook dropping unheeded to the ground.

'Are you all right?' Her breath came in short, heaving bursts.

'What the *devil* do you think you're doing?'

Grace quailed at his fury. He tore his gaze from her and followed the bird's flight.

'Have you any idea how long I…?' He paused.

Hauled in a deep breath.

Looked back at Grace.

Narrowed his eyes.

'Did you ask if I was *all right*?'

Before she could reply, he threw back his head and howled with laughter.

She glared. 'What is so amusing?'

'You!' He gasped for breath. 'Were you trying to *save* me?'

'Well, I did, did I not? That monster attacked you. I frightened it away.'

His chest heaved as another peal of laughter rang out. 'That monster, as you describe her, is an eagle. And she has enough power in those talons of hers to do you some serious damage. And you thought to…'

Their gazes fused, and his words faded. Grace trembled as longing curled through her body and she lost herself in the molten depths of his eyes.

'I…'

At that single word, his gaze, soft as a caress, drifted down to settle on her lips.

* * *

Nathaniel's initial burst of rage was, within seconds, quashed by his mirth that this dainty, feminine girl had thought to rescue *him*. Her eyes, glinting in the sunlight, flashed her annoyance and he was drawn into their gold-green depths. And his laughter died. And then her lips parted and, without volition, his gaze dipped to trace their delicate shape and admire their soft, pink fullness. And to wonder how they would taste…

'I…' she whispered again.

Then he was jolted from his entrancement as shock flashed across her face and red infused her cheeks, and he felt the wrench deep inside as she released her grip on his hand. His right hand. His damaged hand, with its coarse and ugly puckered skin. He snatched it away, thrusting it behind his back, out of sight.

'I…I am sorry, my l-lord.' She would not meet his eyes now. 'W-was it meant to fly at you like that?'

She was so pretty. Too pretty, too delicate, for a beast like him. He found the strength to thrust aside his humiliation in order to smooth over their mutual embarrassment.

'Yes, but it is not your fault.' He occupied himself pulling the leather gauntlet from his left hand. 'You meant well.'

He conjured up the image of Ralph Rendell. Now there would be a suitable pairing: the same station in life, both of them young and attractive. Unscarred. That thought had the same effect on his lust as falling in Shiver Beck on a winter's day—something he had done once and never wished to repeat.

'Will it come back?'

He scanned the sky. Amber was very close to being fit enough to return to the wild. Would she return after her scare?

'There. See.' He pointed at the bird. 'She has not gone away. Not yet.'

'How...? Is she tame? Is she yours?'

He told her the tale of how Amber came to his care.

'Her wing is healed now. I've been releasing her for longer each day to strengthen it. She comes back for food, even though she has begun to hunt for herself. One day, she will simply not return and hopefully she'll head north, back to the Highlands where she was born.'

'It sounds so romantic, the Highlands.' Her voice was wistful.

'More romance, Miss Bertram?'

Her lips compressed and a light flush crept over her cheeks. Not the most sensitive comment, following their difference about romance the other evening, and that interlude just now, when he had thought...

What had he thought? For one moment, he had forgotten who he was. *How* he was. He had been a man, looking into the eyes of a pretty girl. It had been a mistake, not to be repeated.

'Have you ever been to Scotland?' he asked.

'No, but I have seen paintings. It is like this but... more so.'

Nathaniel looked around. More so indeed. Very much more so.

'Where is Clara?'

'She is unwell. I have left her asleep, with Mrs Sharp watching over her, whilst I take some exercise.'

'Does she need a doctor?'

'No. We both agree it is only a cold; there is no sign of fever. But she is very miserable, poor mite.'

'I shall come and see her when I go home.' Something caught his eye and he bent to pick it off the ground.

'Is this a sketch book?'

'I thought I might have time to capture the view. I have never been up here before. It is too far for Clara.'

Nathaniel riffled through the pages. 'There aren't many landscapes here.'

'No.' She put out her hand and he whisked it out of her reach so he could continue to look through it.

'They are mostly portraits,' she said repressively, 'and they cannot possibly be of interest to you as you do not know any of the subjects.'

'Oh, I don't know. Here.' He held up a watercolour of three young women and grinned. 'I could be interested in these three beauties. Are they the friends you told me about?'

A light flush stained her cheeks. 'Yes.'

He looked at the painting. It showed skill. 'This is very good. Which one is which?'

She named the three and he said, 'Would you paint Clara for me, when she is better? I should like to have a portrait of her at this age.'

'Yes, of course.'

'Thank you.' He handed her the sketchbook. 'Perhaps you would like to sketch whilst we wait to see if Amber returns?'

Grace perched on a rock and Nathaniel stood behind and off to one side, watching her work. He could watch her all day: her frown of concentration, the pull of her bottom lip through her teeth, the blonde strands of hair that had blown loose and glinted in the sunlight. Rendell was a lucky man, if she had set her sights on him.

All too soon, it seemed to Nathaniel, she closed her book and stood up.

'I must get back to Clara. Oh!' She pointed. 'Amber has come back.'

Sure enough, the eagle was circling out over the dale. Nathaniel hadn't even noticed.

'Stand back,' he said, pulling the gauntlet on to his left hand. 'And for God's sake stay still this time. We don't want to spook her again.'

He waited whilst she retreated several paces, then took a morsel of rabbit from his bag and called as he turned his left side to Amber and extended his left arm, the meat held between his forefinger and thumb. There was the swish of wings, the jolting impact of the landing and the squeeze of the eagle's talons through the stout leather of his gauntlet.

'May I stroke her?'

Nathaniel took a hood from his pocket and slipped it over Amber's head. 'You may now.'

He glanced down at her profile as he spoke. Her brows were bunched across the bridge of her perfect little nose as she stroked Amber's feathers.

'But she would not hurt me. You laughed at me when I thought she was attacking *you*.'

'I laughed at your bold conviction that *you* might protect *me*. I probably should not have laughed, for you showed courage, but please take more care in future, particularly if you have Clara with you. The hood is to keep Amber calm. She is still a wild creature at heart—can you imagine the damage that beak could inflict on a person's face?'

Grace peered at Amber and shuddered.

'It looks so cruel.'

'It is efficient. It helps her survive. Cruelty does not come into it. But she is a powerful predator and should be treated with respect. Come. It is time I returned her to her mew.'

They headed down the hill, to the stable yard.

'Would you care to see my other birds? They are smaller than Amber, but tame. I use them for hawking, as men have done for centuries.'

She hesitated before saying, 'I should love to see them, but maybe another day? I must return to Clara.'

'I shall come and see her once I've put Amber away.'

Nathaniel watched Grace walk away, conflicting emotions churning his insides as he thought back to that moment up on the fell.

That look.

It had fired all sorts of longings deep within him. And she responded—her eyes had not lied. She had been all too aware of that *frisson* that passed between them.

It had been so very long since he'd experienced feelings for a woman—not just the physical need for a woman, but the longing for...more. That most dangerous of random thoughts had taken root in his heart: *What if...?*

She had held his hand without flinching, without even seeming aware... With a harsh sound, he quashed the bud of hope that formed deep inside his heart before it could begin to unfurl.

A beautiful girl like Grace would never want someone as damaged as him.

This yearning inside...it had been stirred up by

Hannah and David's deaths…by the realisation that, now, apart from his mother, he was truly alone.

I will adjust to this new reality. I still have Clara. No one can take her from me.

He returned Amber to her enclosure, working without conscience thought, his heart heavy, aching with the burden of loss.

When he reached the house, he found Clara inconsolable—the only place she would settle was on Grace's lap and consequently he saw little of either of them for the rest of the afternoon or the evening. Bored with his own company, Nathaniel went to the book room to work on his ledgers, but he could not concentrate, his wandering thoughts returning again and again to that moment on the fell when their gazes had clashed. Finally, he admitted defeat and, as the clock in the hall struck eleven, he climbed the stairs to bed.

On the landing, a whimper and a cough reached his ears. Praying Clara had not taken a turn for the worse, he headed for her bedchamber.

It's a cold. Nothing to fear. She will recover.

But cold dread gnawed at him. Childhood was precarious; so many died in infancy. He could not bear… Clara was all he had left of his beloved Hannah. He could not lose her as well.

He must set his mind at rest. He entered her bedchamber quietly, his gaze drawn to the bed, dimly visible in what remained of the firelight.

Clara was asleep, spreadeagled on her back, mouth open as she snored gently. Love for the tiny girl filled his heart. So very precious. A pale shape on the far side of the bed caught his eye—a hand, resting on the coverlet, mere inches from Clara. He tiptoed around the bed, his wavering shadow preceding him, and gazed down at Grace, fast asleep in a chair by the bedside, her head tipped back, the white curve of her throat both seductive and vulnerable. Even in sleep, she was graceful, her lashes fanned against her delicate cheekbones, her honey-blonde hair lying in a loose plait over her shoulder.

Grace. The name suited her to perfection. Ever since that afternoon, Nathaniel had found it impossible to think of her as Miss Bertram.

Grace.

She was clad only in a thin white nightgown that clung to her, softly draping petite breasts and clearly outlining the hard buds of her nipples. Blood surged to his loins. He forced his gaze from her breasts, quelling his inappropriate lust.

She was cold.

A blanket pooled around her feet. He crouched to gather it up and then softly settled it over the sleeping woman. A faint line creased her brow and she turned her head against the back of the chair and shifted her hips. She murmured…a soft, indistinct sound…and then stilled, her brow smoothing over, her lips relaxing, as she sank once more into sleep.

Nathaniel—breath held—tucked the blanket around her so it wouldn't slip again and then carefully, silently, refuelled the fire.

Then he tiptoed from the room and quietly closed the door.

Chapter Thirteen

'What do you think, Alice?'

The young maid stood back. 'They look better, miss. They make the room lighter. More...more happy, somehow.'

'I think so too,' Grace said, admiring the new curtains at the windows of the drawing room.

She had found them in a huge old linen press in a spare bedchamber during one of her searches for items to bring a more homely touch to the Hall. The original heavy deep green curtains had deadened the room, sucking the light from it. These, in contrast, were patterned in white and gold and instantly brightened the room. The gold echoed the yellow veining in several of the 'white' squares on the chessboard and in the marbled panels set into the doors of a small decorative cabinet Sharp had carried into the room at her behest.

Thinking about chess set Grace's thoughts in the direction they had taken ever more frequently since her chance meeting with Lord Ravenwell up on the fells three days before. He *had* changed since her first week at the Hall, when they had only met at dinner-time in the evening. Now, he regularly visited Clara in the nursery—where yesterday he had surprised them both with a dolls' house he'd had sent from York—and he spent every evening after dinner with Grace in the drawing room: playing chess or cards or reading, sometimes aloud, whilst Grace applied herself to mending or embroidery. However much Grace adored spending time with Clara during the day, she anticipated the evenings, and Ravenwell's company, with increasing pleasure.

She hoped he would approve of the changes she was making today. She had uncovered the pianoforte and also a pale gold sofa, which she had grouped with the two wing-back chairs near the fireplace, and Sharp and Ned had brought in two more uphol-stered chairs that she had found stored under covers in the dining room. All it needed now was a few or-naments on the mantelshelves and it would be done.

'There's another rug, miss,' Alice said, eyeing the small rug set before the fire where Clara—still a bit snuffly after her cold but with her energy restored—sprawled with Sweep. 'It's nicer than that dull thing, so Mrs Sharp says, with pretty colours in a pattern.'

'Clara. Take care with Sweep's claws, sweetie.'

Grace cocked her head at Alice. '*Mrs Sharp* told you that?'

The housekeeper was slowly warming towards Grace, but her reaction this morning when Grace told her she was moving some furniture into the drawing room had been unpromising. Grace had feared a return to their former frosty relationship.

'Yes, miss. She came in when you was out with that cat.'

The entire household, apart from Grace and Clara, referred to Sweep as 'that cat'. Clara was besotted with her kitten, who was running the household ragged, and Grace tried to forestall as much of his mischief as possible. She took him outside several times a day to keep the house clean and in the vain hope of wearing him out. As he grew, he would become easier to cope with. She hoped.

'Did Mrs Sharp tell you where the other rug is?'

'No need, miss. Sharp's gone to fetch it.'

With that, the door opened and Sharp staggered in, a rolled-up carpet—for it looked too big to be called a rug—on his shoulder. They moved the furniture, rolled up the old dingy rug and unrolled the new one, with its symmetrical pattern in white, yellow and green.

'I've given it a good beating,' Mrs Sharp said.

Together, the four of them heaved the furniture back into place, then stood back to admire the effect.

'It looks beaut—' Grace stopped, her heart plummeting. 'Where is Clara?'

She had moved Clara to the other end of the room whilst they were busy, but now there was no sign of her. Or of Sweep. The door was ajar and, cursing herself for getting distracted, Grace dashed out into the hall.

'Oh, no!' Mrs Sharp clutched at Grace and pointed wordlessly up at the landing, her face ashen.

Nausea welled into Grace's throat, her stomach clenching in violent denial of the tableau on the galleried landing above: Clara, standing on a wooden chest and leaning over the balustrade, arms waving as she stretched to reach Sweep, who was strolling nonchalantly along the handrail.

'Sweep! Sweep! *Bad* kitty!' she shouted. 'Danjous!'

Before Grace could move, or speak, a dark shape streaked past the group clustered in the hall. Brack reached the landing, reared up on his hind legs and grabbed Sweep in his mouth. Clara's howl galvanised Grace into action and she tore up the stairs. By the time she reached the landing Brack was back on all fours and had retreated to the far side of the landing, the kitten clamped in his jaws, and Clara had clambered off the chest.

She ran towards Brack, shrieking, 'No! No! No bite!'

Grace swept Clara into her arms before she could

reach the dog and turned away, pressing her face, eyes tight shut, into the sweet-scented skin of her daughter's neck, sickened by what had so nearly happened and also by the sight she might see if she looked at Brack. Clara would be devastated if Sweep was injured. The others had followed her—she had heard them pounding up the stairs behind her. Let them deal with the tragedy.

A hand gripped her shoulder, and tugged her around.

'It's safe to look,' rumbled a deep voice.

His lordship. Nooooo. I'll lose my job...no more than I deserve... Clara could have been killed! But, oh, how can I bear...?

Her panicked thoughts steadied. *Safe.* He said it was safe to look. Gingerly, she lifted her head and opened her eyes. A squealing Clara was plucked from her arms. Her gaze darted to Brack, lying by the wall, forelegs outstretched. And Sweep. On his back, between Brack's legs, paws waving in the air as he tried to bat the dog's nose. As Grace watched, Brack lowered his head and swept his tongue along the kitten's exposed stomach.

No blood. No disaster.

Her heart slowed from its frantic gallop to a trot and she breathed again. There was no one else on the landing. Those feet she had heard behind her had been Ravenwell.

'How...?'

'I was in the hall. You dashed past without even noticing me. It was I who sent Brack to fetch the cat.'

Grace dropped her chin to her chest. Sucked in a shaky breath. 'I am sorry. Clara should not...I allowed myself to be distracted.'

'By what, may I ask?'

How could she admit she had been distracted by making changes in his house? How could this be worse?

It would be worse if Clara had fallen. Her knees trembled at that thought and she squeezed her eyes shut again, her neck and shoulders tight with the effort it took not to collapse in a wailing heap.

I have made a mess of everything.

'Well?'

That single harsh word forced her eyes open and her gaze to his. His dark eyes bored into her.

'Alice?' His voice rose, calling down to the hall below. 'Come up here. Take Miss Clara to the nursery. And take that infernal cat with you.'

He raised a brow. 'I'm waiting.'

Grace gripped her hands together. 'We were making a few changes in the drawing room.'

His brows snapped together. 'What changes?'

She forced herself to hold his gaze. 'You did say I might.'

A look of scorn crossed his face. She could not

blame him. What happened was inexcusable. Clara had been in her charge.

'I am sorry,' she said. 'I am not trying to excuse myself. We were moving furniture. One minute Clara was playing at the other end of the room with Sweep, the next she was gone.'

Fear shivered through her as she relived the terrible moment when she had run out into the hall and seen her little girl… She bit back a sob.

'We?' That quiet voice bristled with menace. 'You mean to tell me my entire household was present and not one of you noticed Clara leave the room?'

'It was n-nobody's fault but mine, my lord.'

'At last something we can agree upon.' His eyes flashed with anger.

'Wh-what will you do?' Her voice wobbled as the next sob broke free. 'P-please…do not dismiss me. I l-like it here.'

'You cry at the thought of losing your position here, but what of the fact my niece could have been *killed*?'

'I d-do not cry for myself! That picture is burned into my mind…she's so small…so vulnerable…I cannot forget the horror of seeing her…'

Her hands twisted painfully as she tried to interpret his expression through blurred vision.

'The only reason you are here is to look after my niece.' His voice was harsh and uncompromising. 'Yet it appears to me you are more interested in altering your surroundings—*my home*—into your idea of suitably luxurious surroundings for yourself than in Clara's welfare.'

Stung, Grace glared at him. 'That is unfair. And untrue. You *know* my reasons for those changes. You *agreed*.' She hauled in a breath. 'I only wish to make a comfortable and happy home for your niece. She is a *child*. You may choose to live in these cold cheerless surroundings, but Clara deserves better! She deserves a home and a loving family.'

'Instead of which she has me. And a houseful of servants.'

Bitterness infused his words and shame coursed through Grace. She had not intended to wound him but, before she could try to repair the damage, Sharp called urgently from the hall below.

'Milord! Milord!'

'What is it?'

'It's her ladyship, milord. Her carriage is coming up the track.'

Ravenwell's jaw clenched. He shot a hard look at Grace. 'This matter is not resolved.' He reached into his pocket and pulled out a letter. 'Here. Ned brought this back from the village. It is a happy chance that brought me indoors to give you your letter immediately. Had I delayed, Clara might well be dead by now.

'Go. Make Clara presentable and bring her down

to greet her grandmother in twenty minutes. And, for God's sake, keep that cat out of the way.'

He ran down the stairs, Brack at his heels, and Grace turned to walk slowly towards the nursery wing, her eyes burning with shame.

'Had I delayed, Clara might well be dead by now.'

He was right. She had never seen him so furious, nor so scathing. What if he persuaded his mother to take Clara home with her? If he did not think Grace a fitting person to care for her, he might very well do that. She must work hard to impress her ladyship. If *she* thought Grace suitable, she might persuade Ravenwell to keep her as Clara's governess.

Before she went to the nursery room to get Clara ready, Grace slipped into her bedchamber, needing a moment of quiet to settle her nerves. She perched on the edge of the bed, still shaken, sick dread swirling through her.

She opened her letter, seeking distraction. It was, she saw with a glad heart, from Joanna. Eager to find out how her friend was faring in her role as governess to the Huntford family in Hertfordshire, Grace began to read, her jaw dropping at Joanna's amazing news: the newborn baby who had been abandoned on the doorstep of Madame Dubois's School for Young Ladies was, in reality, the granddaughter of a marquess. And not only had her grandfather publicly acknowledged her and introduced her into society, but Joanna had also met and fallen in love with Luke Preston, the son of the Earl of Ingham, and they had recently married.

Her happiness shone through every word she had penned.

Pleasure for her friend warred with envy in Grace's breast. Yes, she was excited and thrilled for Joanna, for she knew how Joanna had longed to know about her real family, but she could not help but compare Joanna's happy future to the uncertainties of her own. She did not want to leave Shiverstone. She *would* not leave Shiverstone. She did not know how but she must, somehow, persuade his lordship that he could not manage without her.

Putting the letter aside, she hurried to the nursery to make Clara presentable to meet her grandmother.

Ten minutes later, Grace drew in a deep breath, smoothed a nervous hand over her hair and tapped on the drawing-room door before entering, Clara's hand firmly in hers. The Marquess stood before the fireplace, hands clasped behind his back. His eyes were hard, anger still simmering. She swallowed and crossed the room, surreptitiously towing Clara, whose steps had suddenly lagged. An elderly lady— stoutly built, with the same deep brown eyes as her son—watched them cross the room.

Grace bobbed a curtsy.

'Mother, this is Miss Bertram. Miss Bertram, my mother, Lady Ravenwell.'

'Good morning, Lady Ravenwell.'

Every inch of Grace passed under her ladyship's inspection before, finally, she inclined her head. Her expression indicated neither approval nor disapproval. It was hard not to squirm under such scrutiny, which revived uncomfortable memories of various summonses to Madame Dubois's study for some infraction of the rules.

Her ladyship's expression softened as she switched her gaze to Clara. She held out her arms. 'Come to Grandmama, Clara.'

Grace urged the little girl forward, worried she did not remember her grandmother, but Clara's initial reluctance turned to eagerness and she rushed forward, releasing Grace's hand.

'Ganmama.' Clara allowed herself to be hugged and kissed, then wriggled free. 'Ganmama. I got Sweep.'

'Oh! She is talking again. Oh, Nathaniel, you have worked wonders with her.'

The Marquess cleared his throat. 'I believe you must credit Miss Bertram with Clara's progress.'

'Then I shall. Thank you, Miss Bertram.'

Grace smiled at her ladyship and was once more subjected to a sharp appraisal. Had Ravenwell told his mother about Grace's dereliction of duty? A glance at Ravenwell's rock-like expression revealed no clue. She hovered a moment, unsure for the first time of what was expected of her. She had begun to feel like part of the family, with an established position in the household, but Lady Ravenwell's arrival had underscored her true position. She was neither family nor servant, but somewhere in the middle, and she now felt awkward and out of place. She retreated to a chair by the window whilst Clara remained by her grandmother, pleading with her to come and see her kitten.

The same thought bombarded Grace's head without pause: she had forgotten her place and had crossed that boundary between staff and family. Lord Ravenwell was right to be furious. Furtively, she scanned the room. Her changes might have improved the room, but she understood how they must appear to him. She had been presumptuous, both in accepting the kitten without consulting him first and in initiating changes in *his* home. She was meddlesome and an irritant and she had compounded her error by embroiling the rest of his staff in—

'Miss Bertram!'

His voice, exasperated, penetrated her silent scold. She jerked to her feet. He stood directly in front of her and she was forced to crane her neck to meet his gaze.

'You had better go and fetch that infer... Sweep,' he growled. 'Clara will not rest until Mother has made its acquaintance.'

Chapter Fourteen

Dinner with Lady Ravenwell was an ordeal. Her ladyship—resplendent in a green satin gown, a matching turban and emeralds—barely acknowledged Grace's presence, talking to Ravenwell about mutual acquaintances in whom he clearly had no interest. It was a relief when the meal was over but, before Grace could excuse herself and disappear upstairs, Lady Ravenwell made clear her expectation that Grace would join her in the drawing room whilst her son remained in the parlour with his brandy.

'You may pour the tea,' the Marchioness commanded as she swept from the room.

Grace glanced over her shoulder at Ravenwell, hearing the scrape of his chair on the floor. It had become his habit to drink his brandy in the drawing room, over a game of chess or a hand of cards, but he had merely pushed his chair away from the table. He leant back, stretching his long legs straight. He caught her eye and, for the first time since that afternoon, she caught a glimmer of humour in his expression. She pressed her lips together and stalked from the room. She had no trouble interpreting his amusement.

She was the lamb to be sacrificed on the altar of his mother's chatter.

It was worse than she feared. His mother did not wish to converse with Grace. Neither did she wish to talk at her, as she had talked at Ravenwell throughout their meal. Her intention became clear as soon as Mrs Sharp had deposited the tea tray and left the room. Grace had barely begun to pour when the interrogation began.

Where was she from? Who were her family? *Where* had she gone to school again? What were her qualifications…if any? Lady Ravenwell's tone clearly expressed her doubts on that last one. And the question that recurred time and again: how, precisely, had Grace found out about the position of governess at Shiverstone Hall?

'The post was advertised in the *York Herald* which is not, to my knowledge, read in Salisbury. How did *you* discover it?'

'My teacher at the school, Miss Fanworth, was told of the vacancy by a friend of hers.'

Grace's hand was tucked down by her side with crossed fingers. A lie was not really a lie if you had your fingers crossed—or so she and her friends had told each other when they were young. Besides, it was very nearly true. It was Miss Fanworth who had arranged Rachel's position in Huria—she could quite easily have done the same for Grace.

'What is the name of this friend?'

'I do not recall.'

'Have you ever been to Harrogate, Miss Bertram?'

'No, my lady.' That, at least, was no falsehood. The stagecoach in which she had travelled to Ravenwell Manor had put her down before they reached Harrogate.

By the time the Marquess came through, close to an hour later, Grace's nerves were in shreds and, as her ladyship's focus shifted to her son, she begged to be excused.

'Do you customarily retire at such an early hour?'

'I am concerned Clara may have trouble sleeping tonight with all the excitement of your arrival, my lady, particularly after her recent cold. From my sitting room upstairs, I shall hear if she wakes.'

Visions of Clara wandering out on to the landing—even though she knew that chest had been removed—had plagued Grace all evening.

'Very commendable, I am sure. I believe in bestowing praise where it is due, Miss Bertram, and I confess that, despite your youth, you have impressed me with your attention to duty. I thank you for taking good care of my granddaughter.'

Grace blushed as, without volition, her gaze flicked to Ravenwell and fused with his. They both knew that to be a lie.

As she mounted the stairs, the certainty he would now tell his mother the truth churned her insides until she felt sick. Lady Ravenwell's clear suspicions about Grace were troubling enough, but if she should learn of Grace's neglect, Grace would surely be dismissed and then what would she do? She peeped into Clara's bedchamber. Her daughter was sound asleep, on her back as usual, with the blankets kicked askew and her thumb jammed into her mouth. Grace crept in and stood by the bed, love for her child flooding her. Finally, she straightened the covers, bent to kiss Clara's forehead and then retreated to her sitting room.

Grace pondered her uncertain future as she stared into the flames. That future was entirely in the hands of Lord Ravenwell and never had she felt more keenly the divide between her station and his world—a world to which, she realised, both Isabel and Joanna now belonged. She did not begrudge them their good fortune, but how she wished a small piece of their luck might rub off on her.

What could she do? What power did she have?

The answer was none.

She could only wait, impotently, for his decision

and then, if he decreed she must go, she must be prepared to fight. For one thing was certain: she would *never* leave her daughter.

We could run away. I could take Clara and go.

For a few minutes, she indulged that fantasy, before reality crashed over her. It was not even remotely possible. Snatch the ward of a nobleman? And how could they live? And then an even greater truth struck her—an insight so startling it near stole her breath. With a gigantic thump of her heart, she understood she would not leave even if she could.

Because taking Clara away from Shiverstone Hall would mean leaving Lord Ravenwell.

Nathaniel.

And not only could she not bear it if she were never to see him again, but she would never, ever—*could* never, ever—hurt him in that way.

Shaken to her core by that revelation, Grace stumbled to her feet and returned to Clara's bedchamber. She stood and gazed at her beautiful daughter, battling against the sick realisation that, somehow, she had fallen for Nathaniel. She had seen beneath the scarred, irascible and reclusive façade he presented to the world to his kind, loving, intelligent heart.

But... Caution screamed through her head. *Remember Philip. You thought you were in love with him and you were wrong. Don't make the same mistake.*

Nathaniel is a marquess, far above your touch. And right now he does not even like you.

Finally, lids heavy and stifling a yawn, she knew she must go to bed. She bent over Clara and smoothed her curls gently from her forehead.

'Sleep well, my beloved little girl, and sweet dreams,' she whispered. 'Mama is watching over you.'

A sudden sound from behind her sent her spinning to face the door.

Nathaniel froze.

All he could take in was the guilt written all over Grace's face.

Mama?

He pushed away from the doorjamb, against which he had stumbled when he heard her words. Her eyes were huge and he saw the movement of her throat as she swallowed. And then she moved, gliding towards him, one finger to her lips, her eyes…her beautiful, gold-green eyes—the image of Clara's, and how hadn't he seen the resemblance before?—stricken.

He barely moved aside and she brushed past him, out into the passageway. The hairs on his forearms rose at her touch and her clean, sweet lily-of-the-valley scent pervaded his senses.

Mama.

He followed her out of Clara's room on to the landing.

'Explain yourself.'

Anger flared, boosted by the vision of Clara in danger that afternoon, and his panic when he had seen her. How very precious she had become to him. What would he do…how would he survive…if he lost her too? His very vulnerability terrified him. And now… what would this new revelation mean for the future for all of them?

Grace had paused to close Clara's door.

'Well?'

She was trembling. He hardened his heart and strode to the door of her sitting room. He held it wide and beckoned. Inside, he stoked the fire and added more wood, willing his temper under control before trusting himself to look at her.

Grace stood inside the door, fingers interlaced, knuckles white. 'Why did you come to Clara's room?'

'Am I not allowed? She is *my* ward. I needed to ensure she is safe after the danger she was put in this afternoon.'

She flinched. 'You cannot know the guilt I feel over my neglect.'

'I am still awaiting an explanation. Do not make me ask again.'

'Clara is my daughter.'

That simple statement crushed any residual

hope that he had misheard. The agony in her voice wrenched at his heart, but he could not quash his anger, or his hurt, over her betrayal. He had begun to trust her. Since her arrival, his evenings had changed from something to dread to a time keenly anticipated. How, and when, had the barriers he had built against the rest of the world been breached?

'Why are you here? Did you intend to snatch her away from me?'

Her mouth fell open and yet her gaze skittered from his. 'No! I would never do that.'

'But the thought crossed your mind.'

He watched her intently, noting a blush creep up her neck to her face.

'Only once. You were so angry with me…earlier… but I would never do such a thing. It was a fleeting thought, soon exposed for an idle fantasy. I could never take her from you, nor you from her. I am not so cruel.'

'You said this afternoon that Clara deserves a home and a loving family. You said she deserves better than me and a houseful of servants.'

Her eyes flashed and she crossed the room to glare up at him.

'You twist my words, my lord. It was you who said she only has you and a houseful of servants.'

'But you believe it is the truth.' He grabbed her, his fingers biting into the soft flesh of her upper arms.

'You think she deserves better. That I am incapable of giving her a happy childhood.'

'No!'

She squirmed to free herself and he released her, taking a step back, ashamed he had allowed his anger to prevail. Yet she did not retreat. She moved closer, her gaze searching his.

'Clara adores you.' Her scent enveloped him and her breath was warm upon his skin. Her fingertips caressed his cheek with a featherlight touch. 'You do not see how her eyes light up when she sees you. She has settled here. She is happy.'

Her eyes darkened and her hand slipped to rest against his chest. Without volition, his head lowered and he brushed her sweet, silken mouth with his. His blood quickened, together with the compulsion to sweep her into his arms and taste her again. And again. But doubts nipped at the heels of that compulsion.

Why now?

She must be desperate indeed to contemplate seducing a man like him—desperate to stay with her daughter.

Nathaniel spun away and faced the hearth, propping both hands against the mantel, gripping the wooden edge, grounding himself. She sounded sincere, but could he trust his instincts? He silently berated himself for a fool. He should dismiss her immediately.

There was no excuse for her deceit. But he could not utter the words. God help him, he *wanted* to understand. More, he wanted to forgive. He did not want her to go. His very neediness infuriated him, but it was a fury directed against himself, not her.

'That should not have happened.'

'I am sorry.' He had to strain to hear her whispered response.

'Why *did* you come here, if not to reclaim your daughter?'

'I p-promised myself, when she was born, when I gave her away that, one day, I would find her and make sure she was loved and wanted.'

'She was. My sister and her husband doted on her. And now—'

'And now, you dote upon her.'

'Yes,' he said gruffly. 'So why this charade?' He turned to face her. 'Why did you apply to be her governess?'

She hung her head. 'I did not. Not precisely.' A puff of air escaped her and her shoulders slumped. 'I shall tell you the whole story. M-may I sit?'

'Of course.' He waited until she sank on to the armchair by the fire, then dragged over a wooden chair to sit opposite, swinging it around to straddle it, resting his arms across the back.

She told him a tale that was not unique. It happened too frequently: a young girl, her head turned by romantic words and enticing kisses, and a green youth who did not consider the repercussions of his persuasions.

'Seventeen years old.' If such a thing happened to Clara, when she was so young and innocent, he would be after the culprit with a horsewhip. 'What did your uncle have to say about it?'

Her head jerked up, her expression one of horror. 'My uncle did not know. He and my aunt are very devout...they would not...nobody knew, only my three best friends, and I swore them to secrecy.'

'But...surely your teachers must have realised.'

'I managed to hide the change in my shape. My clothes were always loose on me—my cousins are bigger than I and Aunt refused to alter the dresses too drastically. She said I would grow into them and it was not worth altering them twice.'

Compassion blossomed for the child unwanted by her own family. No wonder she needed to ensure Clara was loved and wanted.

'When the babe came...' She fell silent, leaning forward, her elbows propped on her knees, staring at the floor. 'Well...' She hesitated again, then she looked up at him, a blush staining her cheeks but with a look of resolve. 'It was worse than any of us thought it would be. My friends went to fetch Miss Fanworth and afterwards she...'

Her voice had started to wobble and tears brimmed. Wordlessly, Nathaniel passed her his handkerchief.

'Thank you.'

She mopped her eyes before resuming her tale.

'Miss Fanworth thought it best to find a family who would adopt the baby. She knew my own family would not stand by me, so they were never told.'

'But...the principal of the school. Madame Dubois. She must have known. I am surprised she did not expel you.'

'I have no doubt she would have, but she never knew either.'

'And you knew Clara had gone to Hannah and David?'

'No. I did not know who her new parents were until my last day at school. Miss Fanworth told me their name and that they lived in Gloucestershire. That was all I knew. By the time I tracked them down, it was too late and Clara had gone. I was told you were her new guardian and I was even more determined to make sure she was happy. And that you wanted her here with you.'

'Unlike you, with your uncle and aunt.'

'Unlike me.'

She paused, staring down at the handkerchief she kneaded in her fingers, nibbling at her bottom lip. Then she shook her head and looked up, a mischievous glint in her still-watery eyes.

'Those stories I was told about you, in the village...
well, suffice it to say they were wild enough to drive
me on to come here. I even braved walking through
that horrid wood. And then, when I arrived...I was
so petrified by the dogs...and then you growled at
me that I was late and before I knew it the idea of
staying on...of seeing Clara every day...'

She choked on her words, then hauled in a ragged
breath.

'Don't send me away. *Please* don't. I know I let you
down today and I still feel sick at what might have
happened, but I swear I shall take more care in future, only I *cannot* go...I simply cannot. I'm sorry I
did not tell you the truth but, once I was here...how
could I?'

Nathaniel held up his hand, hating to hear her beg.
Although she had lied, he could not condemn her. She
had been driven only by concern for Clara's welfare.

But what about that kiss? She ought to go.

I know. But I do not want her to go.

Then you must confront it. Now.

'I cannot condone what you have done, but I shall
not send you away. I, too, am not so cruel. There was
no need to try to entice me with...with...'

Dammit. I can't even say the words.

'Understand this, Miss Bertram. If you stay, you
stay on as Clara's governess. Nothing more. And no
one—ever—must know the truth. Were the truth to

get out, it would be too shocking. You must realise the damage such a scandal would do to Clara in the future.'

'Yes. Of course. I understand.' Grace slumped back in her chair, hand to her face, still clutching Nathaniel's handkerchief. 'Thank you.'

Her voice was muffled, her shoulders quivered and he heard a distinct sniff. He suppressed his urge to comfort her. Instead, he stared into the fire, waiting for her to regain her composure. The wood had caught well and tongues of orange, yellow and occasional green reached for the chimney. Eventually, from the corner of his eye, he saw her hands leave her face and she straightened in her chair.

'So,' he continued their conversation, 'the secret will remain between the two of us. No one else must know. I—' A thought struck him. 'Have you told your friends?' He could not recall franking a letter for her, other than the two she wrote on the day she arrived. 'Or your teacher?'

'No. I was too ashamed to admit what I had done and neither do I wish to lie, so I have not yet written to them. I merely told Miss Fanworth that I had tracked Clara down and that she was happy and that I had secured a post here as governess. She does not know the truth.'

Relief, doubt and the still-present anger combined in a stomach-churning mix.

'And, most particularly, my mother must never know.'

'D-did you tell her what happened this morning?'

'No. I did not wish to worry her.'

'That is a relief.'

Her lips quivered in a tremulous smile, prompting a surge of blood to his loins. How he craved a further taste, but he could not take that risk—a beautiful woman like Grace could never truly desire a damaged man such as him.

What about when you met on the fell? There was a spark between you then.

He dismissed that thought with a silent curse. He had not known at the time that Grace was Clara's mother, but Grace knew the truth and she would know the one certain way of remaining with her child was by making herself indispensable to her employer by whatever means necessary. No wonder she felt entitled to alter his home to suit her own needs.

'Where is her father now? Are you still in touch with him?'

'He is dead.'

'I am sorry,' he said.

'I have no need of your sympathy. What I believed to be love was, in truth, infatuation. I was filled with longing for romance and I fell for his sweet words. I am older and wiser now.'

He raised a brow. 'You are? Our recent conversations suggest otherwise.'

Her cheeks bloomed pink. '*I* have not allowed *my* experience to sour me, or to turn me into a cynic about love, if that is what you mean.'

Touché, Ravenwell!

There was nothing to say that would not sound defensive. What if he was a cynic? Did he not have good reason?

'I bid you goodnight, Miss Bertram.' He bowed and left.

Chapter Fifteen

'I have concerns about that young woman, Nathaniel.'

Nathaniel took a second to compose his expression before looking at his mother, ramrod straight on the other side of his desk. He laid his pen aside, rose to his feet and rounded the desk to pull a chair forward for her. Then he crossed the book room to shut the door.

'What are your concerns, Mother?' he asked as he settled back into his own chair, elbows on the armrests and fingers steepled at his chest.

'I am far from convinced of the reason she has come this far from her friends and family to take up a position as a governess. Why would she not choose to stay—?'

'Mother, please do not interfere in my domestic arrangements. Miss Bertram is good with Clara. I do not want to lose her.'

'But it makes no sense, quite apart from the recklessness of a young woman travelling *alone*, from one end of the country to the other, to attend an interview with no guarantee of employment at the end of it. She is hiding something. I am convinced of it.'

'You are allowing your imagination to conjure up unwarranted suspicions.' It was hard to allay his mother's doubts and suspicions when Nathaniel was still plagued by his own. 'I understand her teacher knows someone in the county who read my advertisement.'

'I have a mind to write to this Madame Dubois and—'

'There is no need. I have already done so and have received a satisfactory report of Miss Bertram's time at the school. There is nothing for you to worry about.'

'I am your mother. I am allowed to worry about you.'

'About me?' Nathaniel felt his brows bunch in a frown. 'I thought this conversation was about Clara's governess?'

His mother ignored him. 'I cannot be easy in my mind about Miss Bertram. Fish heard gossip in the village that a young woman had been snooping around, asking questions about Hannah and David and what had happened and whether Clara was at the Manor. What if it was Miss Bertram?'

'Fish should mind his own business.' The butler at Ravenwell Manor had always been a busybody. Nathaniel pushed his chair back and went to crouch by his mother's side. 'There is nothing to worry about. Miss Bertram is good for Clara and she has settled in here well. Why, even Mrs Sharp is warming to her and that in itself is a miracle.'

'Mrs Sharp worries about you too.'

Nathaniel surged to his feet. 'It is neither her place nor yours to worry about me. I am a grown man and I am perfectly capable of managing my own household.'

He stalked back around his desk and threw himself on to his chair, furious he had allowed his mother to rattle him.

His mother's lips thinned and her nostrils flared as though in response to a bad smell.

'She is very young. It would surely be better for Clara if her governess was a more mature woman. Someone more experienced.'

'Better for whom? I believe Clara will benefit from having someone young and lively. And Miss Bertram is schooled in all the accomplishments required for a young lady. She will be an excellent teacher for Clara as she grows up.'

'She is also exceedingly pretty.'

Ah. So now we get to the crux of the matter.

Nathaniel met his mother's scrutiny with a raised brow. Lady Ravenwell sighed.

'Very well, I shall say no more for the time, but I

shall keep a wary eye on Miss Bertram whilst I am here.'

Heaven forbid his mother should discover the truth. Or that she might suspect his growing attraction for Grace, or that they had kissed—albeit just a brush of the lips—last night. Nathaniel had lain awake half the night fretting over whether he was right to allow Grace to stay but, in the end, he accepted he could do nothing else. He could not part mother and daughter. And he did not want to lose Grace for his own sake as well as Clara's. He enjoyed her company. She had brought light and hope into his life, just with her presence.

That kiss had been a moment of madness, when both of their passions were roused.

It must not happen again.

'There is no need but, if it will help set your mind at ease, then by all means do so,' he said. 'I am confident you will see that Miss Bertram is very fond of Clara and has her best interests at heart.'

'If you say so, Nathaniel. Now, I must also speak to you about Christmas.'

'Christmas?'

First Grace, now his mother. How he wished the festive season would pass Shiverstone by without any fuss. He'd had no appetite for celebrating since the fire but, last year, Mother, Hannah, David and, of course, Clara, had come to Shiverstone for the full twelve days, refusing to allow Nathaniel to spend another Christmas alone. Now, the happy memories of last year were yet another painful reminder of his beloved sister.

'I wish you and Clara to come to the Manor for the Christmas season as I find I am unable to come here.'

'May I ask why you are unable to come to the Hall?' Would Mother, like him, find the memories of last Christmas too painful?

His mother grimaced. 'Uncle Peter has invited himself and his family to stay at the Manor. He stopped for a few nights on his way up to Scotland and, before I knew what had happened, it appears it was all agreed.'

Her obvious vexation made Nathaniel smile. His father's younger brother was a slippery fellow and, as the years passed and Nathaniel showed no sign of marrying, his uncle's sense of entitlement to the Ravenwell title and estates had grown.

'Oh, no. Poor Mother. What a sorry Christmas you will have, with that flock of vultures eyeing up the furniture. I've a mind to marry simply in order to put his nose out of joint.'

'Oh, how I wish you would, Nathaniel.' Mother leant forward in her eagerness. Then she visibly subsided. 'But I fear you will never give yourself a chance of happiness. I could throttle both Lady Sarah and Miss Havers for the way they behaved.'

'They did me a kindness. Would you really want such shallow sorts as either of them to become my Marchioness?'

'I would like *someone* to have the opportunity. I fear you will never meet anyone out here in this wilderness. Please say you will come to Ravenwell for Christmas, Nathaniel. We could have a Twelfth Night party as we used to.'

He hated to deny her, but he simply could not face it. He did not have to say so; his expression must make his refusal plain.

'Please, Nathaniel? I cannot bear to think of you here, all alone—'

'I am not alone,' he said, more sharply than he intended. 'I have Clara.'

And Grace.

'And do you not think Clara would benefit from seeing her relations?'

'No, I do not. Hannah told me about the first time my uncle saw Clara. He called her a...well, you may guess what term he used. He made no attempt to disguise his disapproval. No, I shall not subject Clara to my uncle's insults. I am sorry, Mother, but we will spend Christmastide at Shiverstone Hall.'

His mother stood. 'Do not think this is the last word on the subject, Ravenwell, for it is not.'

Blast, he'd annoyed her now. She only ever called him Ravenwell when she was angry with him.

* * *

His mother stayed a week. By her last day, Nathaniel's patience was stretched to breaking point. Every day had seen a repeat of their conversations about Grace and about Christmas. Finally, his mother had accepted he meant what he said. He would not send Grace away and replace her with an older governess and he and Clara would not be going to Ravenwell Manor for Christmas. The only good part of his mother's visit was that her presence masked the inevitable awkwardness between Grace and him and made it easier to avoid being alone with her.

His final conversation with his mother took place in the drawing room—which, if he was honest, *had* improved beyond all recognition since Grace had changed it. Even his mother had commented on its pleasant appearance in comparison with her last visit. Lady Ravenwell had already visited the nursery to kiss Clara farewell and Nathaniel and his mother were alone, awaiting her carriage.

'Nathaniel.'

His heart sank. He knew that look. 'Yes, Mother?'

'Do not look so hunted. Even I must accept defeat at some point. I shall not mention Christmas, nor try one last time to persuade you to appoint a different governess.' She crossed the room to peer from the window, then returned to stand in front of him, her expression resolute. 'I hope you will take what I am about to say in the spirit in which it is intended, son. I only ever have your best interests at heart. You do know that, don't you?'

He took her hands. 'Of course I do.' There was no escaping it. Let her say what she must. She would be gone soon. 'What is it you feel honour-bound to say?'

'Nathaniel! There is no need to take that tone of voice.'

'My apologies, Mother.' He deserved that rebuke. 'Please, do go on.'

'I urge you to take care with Miss Bertram. You already know my concerns about her and I shall not repeat them. But you are a wealthy man. A noble-man. You are a good catch for a scheming miss and what better way to inveigle her way into your affections than through your niece?'

Nathaniel's muscles turned to stone as his mother placed a gentle hand against his scarred cheek. Every instinct screamed at him to pull away, but he knew that would hurt her and might even lead her to believe there was some truth in what she said. He released her other hand and folded his arms across his chest.

'I am a grown man, Mother, not a green youth. I can take care of myself.'

'I have seen the way you look at her, Nathaniel, when you think yourself unobserved.'

He struggled to control his dismay as her words sank in. Was he so transparent that even his mother could see through him? What if the servants could see the truth? What if *Grace* could tell? He must take more care.

'Living out here, all alone…take care, darling. Please.' Her voice became urgent as the sound of wheels on the gravel outside heralded the arrival of her carriage. 'She is exceedingly pretty, but no good can ever come of getting embroiled with an employee. I make no doubt she is well aware of the luxuries and comforts that await the woman who ensnares you. From governess to marchioness would be quite an achievement for one such as Miss Bertram.'

No suggestion that Grace might like him for himself and not merely for what he could provide. Even his own mother thought him unlovable. He thrust down his pain.

'You have nothing to fear, Mother.'

Quite apart from the fact a beauty like Grace would never look twice at someone like me, she still visits the village regularly to see Rendell. If she is interested in anything other than being with Clara, it is not me.

'Miss Bertram is here solely to care for Clara.'

Grace put her lips to Clara's ear as she hugged her tight to her chest.

'Shh…' she breathed, willing Clara not to speak.

After Lady Ravenwell came to the nursery to say

goodbye to Clara, Grace had made the mistake of saying that Grandmama would be travelling in her carriage. Clara's eyes had widened.

'Wanna see horsies.'

She'd been adamant and Grace had finally succumbed. Although Lady Ravenwell had clearly not taken to Grace, surely she would be pleased her granddaughter had come to wave goodbye.

Now, Grace stood frozen outside the drawing room, absorbing what she had heard, her heart racing. The thud of booted feet approaching the door from within sent her scurrying to the front door. She would think about what she had heard later. For now, it was imperative Nathaniel had no inkling she had overheard his mother's words. The past week had been awkward enough, since that incident with Clara and since he had discovered she was Clara's mother.

And that kiss—she could almost cringe when she recalled how she had invited it.

It had been he who had resisted deepening that kiss. Not she.

Oh, but was her ladyship right? Did Nathaniel watch her? Did he think of her as a woman and not merely a governess?

But then why had he avoided being alone with her since that night unless he, too, suspected her of planning to ensnare him into marriage.

'Miss Bertram.'

She turned, willing her expression not to give her away. Nathaniel, his mother on his arm, approached across the hall.

'I did not expect to see you down here.'

Grace stretched her lips in a smile. 'I made the mistake of telling Clara that Lady Ravenwell was going away in a carriage. Clara is most eager to see the horses.'

'Ah.' He tweaked Clara's cheek, then smiled at his mother. 'Your granddaughter has developed a healthy obsession for horses. Here...' he reached out '...I will take her. You may go about your duties, Miss Bertram, and I shall send Clara to you later.'

Send. Not bring. It is not my imagination. He does avoid being alone with me.

There was nothing Grace could do but relinquish her daughter, drop a curtsy and return upstairs. She tidied the nursery, the conversation she had overheard repeating in her head until she could scream her frustration.

That Lady Ravenwell suspected her of having designs on Nathaniel was no surprise. His mother clearly thought the worst of Grace and her motives in coming to Shiverstone. Grace searched her conscience, but she could honestly say that, despite her own burgeoning feelings, she had never...*never*... dreamed of *catching* Nathaniel or of inveigling her way into his affections as his mother had so vulgarly put it. She had only ever followed her natural urges, inviting his kiss because she wanted him to kiss her, not because she planned to lure him into marriage. And now, with his mother's suspicions planted in his head, would Nathaniel also suspect her of being a scheming miss, out to seduce him for mercenary reasons?

But…his mother's words echoed again: *I have seen the way you look at her when you think yourself unobserved.*

Did he look at her in such a way? Or was it lust his mother saw? Would any red-blooded man not, on occasion, find his baser instincts come to the fore, such as happened that day out on the fell? Surely that was merely a man tempted to succumb to the moment? There had been other instances of tenderness—such as when he had wiped the smudge from her cheek—but his action had been that of a brother, not an admirer.

Images from the past darted through her memory and her stomach clenched. She must not repeat the mistake she had made with Philip. Now, more than ever, she wished her friends were here to talk to or that she could write to them and ask their advice. They would help her make sense of this tangle of emotions: Joanna with her calm good sense and her ability to accept whatever life threw in her path, fun-loving, independent Rachel with her healthy scepticism about love, Isabel, with her love of the dramatic, always ready to distract and entertain whichever of her friends was feeling blue.

Deep down, though, she knew what her friends would say. They would tell her to banish any dreams of Nathaniel as a man. He was her employer.

Nothing more. Two words that prompted an echo from that fateful night.

If you stay, you stay on as Clara's governess. Nothing more.

He could not have been more clear.

She must forget that overheard conversation. Clara would be her focus, no one and nothing else. She would fight her feelings by keeping busy. There was plenty to do with Christmas less than four weeks away. She had used her spare time during Lady Ravenwell's visit productively: knitting mufflers for Sharp and the outdoor men and mittens for Alice and Clara, as well as embroidering handkerchiefs with initials and edging them with lace for Mrs Sharp and Annie.

She had racked her brains for a present for Nathaniel and could think of nothing more interesting than also embroidering his initials on a handkerchief, but her brain was full to bursting with ideas for making Clara's Christmastide a time to remember. There were doll's clothes to sew, a bonnet to knit to match her new mittens and, best of all, a painting of Sweep to hang on Clara's bedchamber wall. Tam—who had a talent for carpentry—had agreed to frame it and Sharp had promised to paint the frame with gilt paint.

A soft knock at her sitting-room door drew her attention and she tucked the handkerchief she was currently embroidering down by her side, out of sight.

It was Alice, holding Clara by the hand. Brack had followed them upstairs and, with a flash of inspiration, Grace knew what she could give Nathaniel for Christmas. He had already requested a portrait of Clara but she could include Brack in the portrait, too, as a surprise.

He might not return her love, but that did not stop her from wanting to make him happy and to brighten his life. His smile would be her reward.

Chapter Sixteen

It did not take Grace very many days to realise that coaxing a smile or, indeed, any indication of pleasure, from Nathaniel was a task beyond her meagre efforts. Clara was the only person who could tease a pleasantry from her increasingly taciturn uncle on the very few occasions he visited his niece whilst she was in Grace's care. Most days, though, upon his return from a day spent outside, Nathaniel sent Alice to bring Clara to him in his book room, leading Grace to the conclusion that, knowing the truth of their relationship, he simply did not want to see her and Clara together.

Their former easy friendship was no more and Grace mourned its passing. After overhearing his mother's warning, Grace had feared she would analyse Nathaniel's every word, look and gesture for his true feelings but, in actuality, there was no mistaking his opinion of her. His rejection of her—even as a friend—resurrected all her old insecurities. Her uncle, aunt and cousins had not wanted her. Philip had not wanted her. Now Ravenwell could barely stand being in the same room as her. Clara's very existence confirmed Grace's lack of moral character and she supposed she should be grateful Nathaniel hadn't cast her out on her ear immediately.

Her life at Shiverstone Hall would be lonely indeed if not for Clara. Clara was a constant joy: the shining star around which Grace's life revolved. She gave Grace the strength to endure the shards of pain that pierced her heart every time Ravenwell looked right through her.

A week after his mother's departure, Grace and Clara returned from a visit to Elizabeth and, after handing Bill to Ned to unharness, Clara spied Tam.

'Doggies?' She ran up to him, her eyes beseeching. 'See doggies?'

He tweaked her cheek. 'Might I take Miss Clara to the kennels, Miss Bertram?'

'Yes, of course, Tam. I believe I might wait here for her, if you do not mind.'

Tam grinned. 'We'll not be long.' He knew very well Grace's dislike of facing the dogs all at once.

Grace could hear Ned whistling in the barn as he rubbed Bill down. She leaned against the barn wall, her mind drifting, thinking of nothing in particular. The ring of a boot heel on stone jerked her back to awareness and she straightened just as Nathaniel strode around the corner, coming from the direction of the mews where he kept his birds.

He stopped short, his brows bunching, and Grace's heart sank even as her breath caught at the mere sight of him. She could not bear this. How was she ever to mend this distance between them? It was as though he hated her. His mother could not have been further from the truth if she had tried. She stretched her lips into a smile.

'Good afternoon, my lord.'

'What are you doing here? Where is Clara?'

'She has gone with Tam to the kennels. I am waiting for them to return.'

'I see.'

He began to move away. There was a time when he would have teased her about her nervousness around the dogs. Now he could barely look at her. Rebellion warred with caution in her heart and won. How dare he treat her like a pariah?

'My lord, you did offer to show me your hawks. Might we go and see them now?'

He stared at her, expressionless. 'I am busy.'

She'd risked thus far. She would not back down. 'When might I see them, then?'

'When I invite you, Miss Bertram.' He lifted his hat. 'Good afternoon.'

He strode away before she had any chance to reply.

Following that encounter, Grace made no further

attempt to break through his reserve. She could not afford to alienate him. She was here, with Clara. That was the most important point of all. Any further tension between herself and the Marquess could only jeopardise her future at the Hall—a risk she must not take.

Her trips to the village—whether to visit Elizabeth or to attend church—provided some respite to the increasingly fraught atmosphere at the Hall, but even those were lost to her when day after day of heavy rain confined them all to the house.

Almost two weeks after Lady Ravenwell's departure, Grace pulled open the curtains in Clara's bedchamber and folded back the shutters. At last! The rain that had fallen incessantly for the past week had stopped and given way to the sun: pale and weak, maybe, as it hung in the washed-out blue of the sky, but without doubt the sun.

'Look, sweetie,' she said to Clara. 'Ned was right. It *has* stopped raining. We shall be able to go out today.'

And what a relief that would be. With everyone confined indoors, unable even to attend church on Sunday, tempers had begun to fray, with snapped remarks and frowning faces on everyone. She turned to Clara, who had scrambled from under the bedcovers and was jumping up and down on her bed.

'Clara. Do not bounce on your bed. I have told you before.'

'Sweep! Sweep!'

'Yes, we will go and find him, as soon as you are dressed and have eaten your breakfast. Come, quickly now, or your porridge will be cold.'

She dipped the washcloth in the warm water Alice had brought up and washed Clara's hands and face, then dressed her in a warm, woollen dress. She then uncovered the serving dish of porridge and served up a bowl each for herself and for Clara. They would need something warming inside them if they were to drive to Shivercombe today, as she planned. The thought of visiting Elizabeth buoyed her spirits.

Hand in hand, Grace and Clara went to the kitchen.

'Sweep!' Clara ran to her kitten, who promptly disappeared under the dresser—his favourite refuge.

'Clara. I have told you. You must move slowly and not shout. You have scared him.'

Grace laughed, looking at Mrs Sharp to share her amusement. She was busy slicing ham from a joint and had not even glanced up when they came in the room. There was a large basket on the table, half-full, and the set of her mouth suggested she was not in a good mood.

'His lordship wants food sent out,' she grumbled. 'I told him, I did, Ned'll have to come back after it. I haven't got time to spend traipsing all over the fells

a-looking for them and Sharp's rheumatics are playing him up, with all the wet weather.'

'Could I take it for you?'

Mrs Sharp paused, then shook her head and resumed slicing. 'No. You've got Miss Clara to watch
and I can't have her under my feet today. Alice is
helping Annie with the laundry. Got to make the
most of the weather while there's a chance of dry-
ing them sheets.' She shook her head. 'His lordship's
got no idea. He can only think about them animals.
Setting that bird to fly today, they are, then seeing
to the sheep. He doesn't understand what it takes to
keep this place running. And with Christmas just
around the corner, too.'

She wrapped the slices of ham in a clean cloth and
put the bundle into the basket, then wrapped thick
slices of bread and some hunks of cheese and piled
them on top.

Grace watched her in silence, chewing at her lip.
'Is there anything else I can do to help?'

She got the answer she hoped for. 'No. You're better off taking Miss Clara out for a breath of fresh
air. And take that wretched cat out of here too. Although…' she paused again to wipe her brow on her
sleeve '…he did take after a mouse this morning.
Didn't catch it, mind, but I dare say he'll get better
when he grows. At least then he'll be some use.'

Grace ignored the housekeeper's grumbles. It was

plainly one of those days and the less said the better. 'I thought I might drive to the village and call upon Elizabeth,' she said. 'If you are sure you do not need me.'

'That is a…oh, drat! I forgot to put in the pickles.'

The housekeeper rushed to the larder, returning with a jar of pickled beetroot and a bowl of apples. Grace didn't linger. Mrs Sharp was clearly preoccupied. She put on her cloak and bonnet, then helped Clara with hers and then they headed for the barn where Bill was stabled.

Some time later—hands chilled following her struggle with stiff straps and buckles—Grace climbed aboard the gig and gave Bill the office to proceed. She felt inordinately proud of herself. It was the first time she had harnessed Bill to the gig without help. She had checked and double-checked each fastening and she was confident nothing was amiss. She smiled down at Clara, tucked in by her side, a blanket around her legs.

'This is fun, is it not, sweetie? We are off on an adventure, after being stuck indoors for so long. It will be nice to see Miss Dunn again, won't it?'

'More kitties?'

Grace laughed, tilting her face towards the sun and breathing deeply of the clean, fresh air. 'No more kitties,' she said. 'I think one is enough, don't you?'

She drove the gig down the track and into the forest. It still gave her the shivers, but she felt much braver driving the gig than she had when she had walked through it all alone, scared of every sound and terrified of what might await her at Shiverstone Hall after the villagers' lurid stories.

Her confidence soared. She had been a town girl through and through, but now she had learnt about the countryside and the animals. She had climbed the fell and touched an eagle. She could harness a horse and drive a gig. She had even grown to like the dogs. Well… She liked Brack on his own. She was still wary when they all ran loose at once, leaping and barking. How her friends would stare at what she had accomplished and how brave she had become.

The only dark cloud in her life was Nathaniel.

She no longer deluded herself that he harboured feelings for her and she could only pray they might soon regain their former easy-going companionship, with its games of chess and cards, and accompanying smiles and laughter. Since his mother's visit all of that mutual ease had fallen away and, at dinner every evening, they each fumbled for the right words to say.

Heartsore. She had heard the word before, but hadn't known such pain could be real.

Bill plodded placidly on through the wood and, very soon, they emerged from the cover of the trees

and followed the curve of the track down to the ford.
Bill stopped. Grace frowned.

'Get up, Bill.'

She shook the reins. Bill took two steps, then jibbed
again, his front hooves at the water's edge. Grace
slapped the reins on his back, clicking her tongue
in imitation of Ned, but Bill would not budge. The
ford was wider than usual, but the water—murky
and brown instead of its normal crystal clarity—did
not look much deeper. Grace doubted it would reach
Bill's knees, let alone swamp the body of the gig.

She flicked the whip across the horse's broad back.
He laid back his ears and shook his head, setting his
bit jingling.

Stupid animal, frightened of a bit of water.

'Stay here, Clara, and do not move. I shall be back
in a minute.' Grace tilted Clara's chin so she could
look her in the eyes. 'Promise?'

The little girl nodded and tugged the blanket tighter
around her legs. Satisfied Clara would stay put, Grace
climbed from the gig and walked to Bill's head.

Nathaniel scanned the sky to the north. He had set
Amber free as soon as he had reached the high fell.
She had circled above him and his men for a long
time, waiting, he knew, for him to call her in with
a reward of food, but he had ignored her. Instead,
he and his men had concentrated on locating their

sheep after all the rain, rounding them up ready to drive them off the fells to the lower pastures for the remainder of the winter. Finally, Amber appeared to give up and she flew north in a steady line until now she was a mere speck in the distance.

Even though it was the right thing to do, Nathaniel was sad seeing the giant bird go. He hoped Amber would soon regain her mistrust of man—she had already successfully hunted for herself, so hopefully she would have no reason to seek out humans.

'Your lordship.'

'Yes, Tam?' Nathaniel answered absently, still watching that increasingly faint speck. They had stopped for a brief rest, on the edge of the fell above Shiver Dale.

'My lord!'

His interest caught by Tam's urgent tone, Nathaniel joined him on the edge, where he gazed out over the dale to the south.

'Look.'

Nathaniel followed Tam's pointing finger, down the slope to the dale where the beck flowed. A horse and gig had emerged from the wood, heading down the track that led to the ford.

'That's Bill,' Nathaniel said. 'And Miss Bertram.'

Grace. Off to visit that damned curate again.

Jealousy flooded through him, turning him rigid with anger even as his common sense reminded him he had done everything possible in the past two weeks to keep her at arm's length. Then his brain caught up with what his eyes were seeing.

'What on earth does she think she's doing? The river isn't safe to cross after all that rain.'

'Ay, but will *she* know that?' Ned said, from where he held their three horses. 'That's Miss Clara in the gig 'n' all.'

'Bill's sensible; he won't attempt to cross.' Nathaniel tried to believe it, but he knew how deceptive the beck was after rain. What if she persuaded the cob to go forward? The power of that current... Sick anxiety twisted his gut and he walked across to Ned and took Zephyr's reins, pulling his head up from the grass. 'I'll go down and turn them back.'

He tightened Zephyr's girth and mounted before looking down the hill again. Sure enough, Bill had planted his feet on the edge of the river and was refusing to walk on. He headed Zephyr down the slope, in a direct line to the ford, leaning back to help the horse with his balance. The ground was slippery and, more than once, Zephyr's hooves slipped and only the stallion's great strength prevented them tumbling. It took all of Nathaniel's concentration to pick out a safe path.

Then he heard a shout from behind him. He looked up and a spasm of fear clutched his belly. Grace had climbed from the gig and was pulling at Bill's bridle, trying to persuade him into the river. Nathaniel swore loudly and, heedless of the danger, he dug his heels into Zephyr.

The stallion responded gallantly and they bounded down the slope, his hooves skidding perilously as Nathaniel offered silent prayers for the surefootedness of the stallion and the continued stubbornness of the cob. They reached gentler ground and Zephyr transitioned into a gallop, but it was heavy going across the sodden ground. Then time appeared to slow as Nathaniel saw Grace try once more to tug Bill forward. Bill threw his head up, knocking her off balance.

'Noooooooooooo!'

Nathaniel crouched low over the stallion's neck, urging him ever faster, but there was nothing he could do to prevent the tragedy unfolding. He could only watch, helpless, as Grace toppled backwards, arms windmilling, into the water.

Chapter Seventeen

Five seconds later Nathaniel reined Zephyr to a halt as a black-and-tan shape streaked past and launched itself into the river. Bill again stood, statue-like, facing the water. The river swept on. No sign of Grace. Or Brack.

I must find them. He looked at Clara: eyes huge, huddled in a blanket in the gig. *I can't leave her alone.*

He wheeled Zephyr around, staring back across the dale. Tam had already reached the bottom of the hill; he would reach the gig in a matter of minutes. Nathaniel waved at Tam, then pointed to Clara. Tam raised his hand in acknowledgement, then leaned forward over his horse's neck, urging him faster.

'Do not move,' Nathaniel called to Clara.

No time for more. No time to stop and reassure her. Heart in mouth, he kicked Zephyr into a canter, following the beck downstream. He trusted the stallion to pick a safe path as he scanned the river, trying not to despair at the speed and strength of the roaring, churning mass once they left the comparative calm of the ford. They weaved around bushes and trees, always sticking as close as possible to the riverbank. Finally—he hauled on the reins—a flash of white, a face, two arms wrapped around a sturdy branch protruding from the beck.

Nathaniel leapt from the saddle and raced to the water's edge.

'Grace!' Her eyes were screwed shut, lips drawn back to bare clenched teeth. 'Grace!'

A tree had toppled into the beck, its trunk disappearing under the surface some ten feet before that branch emerged from the swift rush of mudcoloured water. Nathaniel shrugged out of his greatcoat, pulled off his boots and clambered on to the trunk. He cursed freely at the rough bark that cut into his knees as he crawled along and again when he reached the place where the trunk sank from sight under the frigid water. The tree's bulk helped steady the rush of the beck at this point, but it was still fierce enough to knock him off balance. Nathaniel manoeuvred around to sit astride the submerged tree, then steadily pulled himself closer to Grace.

'Grace! Hold on, sweetheart. I'm coming.'

Her eyes opened. *Thank God.* They stared uncomprehendingly. Her lips were blue and now he could see her teeth chattering. He must get her out of this and fast. He pushed himself to go quicker, aware—even as he neared her—that she was rapidly weakening. Her head lolled on her neck and her arms were losing their hold, gradually slipping.

'Hold on! Think of Clara! You can't leave her!'

She made a visible effort to rouse, forcing her head up and opening her eyes. Nathaniel dragged himself along the submerged truck, ever closer.

You can't leave me.

His father's face… Hannah's… David's…they floated through his mind's eye and his throat thickened.

'Stay with me, love. Hold on. I'm coming.'

I cannot lose you as well.

A sob erupted from his chest. He clamped his teeth against the next.

No time to fall apart, Ravenwell. Get on with it. Get her.

She was so close. Just like his father. He had seen him, through the flames, but he could not save him. He had failed his father. Left his mother a widow. He would not fail Grace and leave Clara an orphan. As if in a nightmare, he saw Grace's head slump and in a final, desperate lunge, he reached her at the moment her hold on the branch slipped. He hauled her into his chest with one arm and snatched at that same branch with his free hand. Immediately, the power of the flow lifted him and tugged at his legs until he was stretched out, feet pointing downstream. He fought the greedy suck of the river, gritting his teeth against the screaming agony of his arm and shoulder, hauling them both against the current until he was close enough to link his arm around the branch.

Gasping, he stared at the bank. So near and yet so far. But failure was not an option. Clara needed them both. He kicked out with his legs, struggling to bring them back under him until, at last, he could feel the trunk beneath his feet. He could not risk turning to face the bank. Sending a heartfelt prayer heavenwards, he shifted Grace into a more secure hold and dropped into the water, one leg each side of the trunk again, gripping it with muscles honed from years of riding. He inched backwards along the trunk, desperation fuelling him, until he reached the bank. Near-exhausted, he dropped to the ground, Grace's inert form cradled in his arms, and staggered away from the river.

Six feet from the water's edge, his knees buckled and he collapsed, cushioning Grace against the fall. He set her down and she immediately rolled to her side and began to cough, water dribbling from her mouth. He rubbed and patted her back, scraping wet strands of hair from her face.

I must warm her. He forced his stiff muscles to move, turning to scan the riverbank upstream. *Surely Tam or Ned will come soon.*

He struggled to his feet, juddering with the cold, stripped off his wet jacket and shirt, picked up his discarded greatcoat and rubbed it briskly over his chest and arms. Then he fell to his knees next to Grace and pulled her into a sitting position. He must warm her and he could not do that whilst she was clad in soaking wet clothes. Her cloak had already gone. She moaned as he struggled to remove her dress.

'What...?'

'Help me, my love.' He placed his cheek against hers and rubbed skin against skin. 'We need to get you warm.'

She scrabbled at his arm with weak fingers. 'Clara!'

'Hush. She is safe. The men are with her.'

Her entire body was shaking as he tugged again at her dress.

'Wha...no! You...you...'

Her words were slurred and weak, but still she managed to struggle as he worked the sopping woollen dress up her body and over her head.

'Miss Bertram!'

She stilled momentarily at his command, then thrashed her head from side to side. 'No, no. *Noooo...*'

Grimly, Nathaniel continued to disrobe her, until she was clad only in her shift. He lifted her to his lap and reached for his greatcoat, wrapping it around her, pulling her wet hair out from the collar. He rubbed her with brisk movements, praying the friction would warm her, talking to her to keep her awake.

'Stay with me, my darling. Don't leave me. Think of Clara.'

The welcome thud of hooves eventually sounded and Tam appeared. He slid to the ground.

'Thank God, milord.'

'Miss Clara?'

'Ned's driving the gig back to the Hall. Is Miss Bertram...?' He paused and peered more closely. 'I don't like her colour, milord. We need to get her home.'

'We do, Tam. I'll take Miss Bertram on Sammy and you can ride Zephyr to the Hall.' The stallion would never tolerate a double burden. 'Tell Mrs Sharp what's happened and to heat plenty of water ready for us.'

He wrapped his coat more securely around Grace and handed her up to Tam before regaining his feet and pulling on his boots. It took him two attempts to mount Sammy. His legs were about as much use as lengths of string and agonising pain ripped through the muscles of his right arm and shoulder as he dragged himself into the saddle.

'Where's Brack?' Tam asked.

A hard lump lodged in Nathaniel's throat. 'I've not seen him since he went into the water after Miss Bertram.'

Tam hoisted Grace up in front of Nathaniel, then he stripped off his own heavy coat.

'Here, milord. No good you coming down with the ague on top of all else. We'll come back out and search for the dog once Miss Clara's safe and I've spoken to Mrs Sharp.'

He swung up on to Zephyr and galloped away. Nathaniel blinked back hot tears, then muttered yet another curse. He was getting soft. But... Brack had been with him a long time. A loyal companion.

Grace stirred and he wrenched his attention back to the matter in hand. He flung Tam's coat around his shoulders, blessing the immediate warmth as it blocked the chilly December air from his still-damp skin, and then shifted Grace into a more secure position on his lap.

She was so very delicate. How would she survive? He pressed his lips to her temple, willing her to keep fighting. Her shivers were ever more violent. He must warm her. He loosened the coat around Grace and pulled her close into his bare chest, skin to skin. They would warm each other. He rearranged the coats around them and nudged Sammy into a walk, leaving the reins lying slack on his neck. He could not risk going faster and cause either of the coats to slip off.

His arms encircled Grace beneath the tent of the coats and he rubbed her slender limbs in turn. The delicate bones of shoulders and hips, elbows and knees revealed the lack of flesh beneath her skin. She weighed little more than a child.

'Stay with me, my darling. We will soon be home.'

Home.

Her presence had changed the Hall into a home for him after nine long years of it being nothing more than a roof over his head. She belonged there, with Clara and with him, and yet he had done everything in the past fortnight to make her feel unwelcome and unwanted, using his anger to hide from reality. He had seen the pain in her eyes and he had ignored it, more concerned with protecting his own heart and peace of mind.

They settled into a rhythm, with Grace huddled against his chest, his chin resting on the top of her head, his thoughts ranging free. He had not failed this time, as he had with his father. He relived his terror when he had seen her tumble into the river. His muscles tightened without volition, nestling her closer into him, willing the heat of his skin to warm her.

Cold killed. He saw it happen every spring, when an ewe lambed earlier than expected. If the weather was unkind and the lamb couldn't get dry and warm, it would soon succumb, the cold numbing it, slowing everything down until it sank into death.

He would not allow that to happen to Grace. That terror he had felt…he knew, with heart-stopping certainty, that it had been more than the horror he would have experienced had it been Tam or Ned who had fallen.

A low moan reached his ears and again his arms tightened reflexively. He could not lose her now. She felt so frail in his arms, but she had a strong will. She would survive.

She *must* survive.

For Clara's sake.

For his.

'Stay with me, my darling Grace. Stay with me.'

He had thought that by keeping her at bay his growing feelings might wither and die, but he had been wrong. They had continued to twine around his heart until he could no longer ignore the truth.

He was in love with Grace Bertram.

Fool that he was.

He needed to say the words. If the worst should happen, he needed her to know.

'I love you,' he whispered and pressed his lips to the cool skin of her forehead.

He had fallen in love with her, even though he knew she could never love a damaged soul such as he, and even though she deserved all the things in life he could not provide: friends, fun and laughter, parties and dancing.

It seemed the heart did not respond to logic.

He cringed at how he had treated her since his mother's visit.

God, please. Let her live, and I promise to change my ways. Even though I can never tell her how important she is to me, I will show her. I will make her happy. Every single day. I swear.

He rode right up to the back door. Everyone piled out, faces creased with worry, and Mrs Sharp and the other women carried Grace off to get her warm and dry.

'Tam's gone out to look for Brack,' Sharp said, as Ned took charge of Sammy.

'I must go, too. I need to find him.'

His legs buckled as he turned to follow Ned and he stumbled. Sharp was by his side in an instant, tugging Nathaniel's arm across his shoulders.

'Yer in no fit state to go anywhere, milord. There's a tub of warm water a-waiting in your chamber—best you get yourself warm and dry and some food inside you before you think about that. There's nothing you can do that Tam can't.'

'I'll go out, too, once I've settled Sammy, milord,' Ned called over his shoulder. 'Don't 'ee fret. We'll find 'im.'

Sharp helped strip Nathaniel, who could not even summon the energy to shield his scars as he normally would. Sharp took his wet clothing away, leaving Nathaniel to his thoughts. He closed his eyes and rested his head against the rim of his bathtub, feeling the heat of the water seep through his flesh and thaw his chilled bones. He had nearly lost her. Grace. She smiled in his imagination, her clear, soft skin radiant, her expressive gold-green eyes warm and sparkling, her blonde hair as fine and delicate as strands of silk. Then another picture took its place—river-drenched hair straggling across her face in dirty strands, lips blue and pinched, pale eyelids, fragile as a moth's wing, closed in utter exhaustion.

He exploded from the bathtub, unheeding of the water that sloshed on to the floor. A towel was draped over a chair near the fire, warming. He grabbed it and scrubbed at himself, then pulled the waiting shirt and trousers on to still-damp skin. He shrugged into his banyan and strode from the room towards the nursery wing.

He tapped at Grace's bedchamber door. Annie—Tam's wife—answered.

'How is she?'

'Sleeping, my lord. She—'

'Stand aside. I want to see her.'

He must see her. He needed reassurance. He needed to know she was safe. That she would survive.

'But—'

'You will be here the entire time. There can be no impropriety.'

He pushed the door wide, leaving Annie no choice

but to move out of his way. He crossed to the bed and stood staring down at her.

So small. So fragile. But her cheeks were pink, as were her lips, and her breathing was even and regular. The fear that had seized him loosened its hold and the tight band around his chest eased.

'Has the doctor been sent for?'

'No, my lord. She is bruised and battered, but Mrs Sharp is certain she will recover.'

He had faith in Mrs Sharp's experience in treating injuries and illnesses.

'She said Miss Bertram's chest sounds clear,' Annie continued, 'so she doesn't think she breathed in any water.'

'That is good. Has she regained consciousness at all?'

Nathaniel laid the backs of his fingers against the silken skin of her cheek. It was warm. As it should be.

Reassurance.

There was a graze on her forehead that had begun to swell, but otherwise she appeared unscathed.

'She came round when we bathed her, as she warmed up,' Annie said. 'But she didn't make much sense. She was gabbling about Miss Clara. And Brack.'

At her words, a crease appeared between Grace's eyebrows and her lips pursed. 'Brack.' Her voice sounded hoarse. 'Where's Brack?'

Annie came to stand beside Nathaniel. 'We told her Miss Clara was safe. Alice brought her before Miss Bertram went to sleep,' she whispered. 'But we didn't know about Brack.'

Grace's lids slitted open and she fixed her gaze on Nathaniel. She ran her tongue along her lips.

'Is he safe?' She pushed her bedcovers down and held her hand out to Nathaniel.

Annie tutted and pulled the sheet and blankets up, tucking them around Grace, but she resisted the woman's efforts to fold her arm back under the covers.

'Nath...my lord.' She spoke with urgency. 'He saved me. Brack.' Her lids drifted shut, then she sucked in a deep breath. He could see the effort it took to force her eyes open again. 'Tell me. Is he all right?'

He could not lie, not when those green eyes were fixed on him so beseechingly. He took her hand in both of his, resisting the urge to press his lips to her skin. Never, by word or deed, would he embarrass her by revealing the extent of his feelings for her.

'I do not know. Ned and Tam are out looking for him now.'

Her fingers clutched at his. 'He saved me. He pushed me towards the bank and I grabbed a branch, but he...he was swept away.'

She gulped, her eyes sheened with tears and her

anguish wrenched at his heart. He wanted nothing more than to protect her from anything and everything bad in this life. He stroked her hand, cursing the inadequacy of his efforts to comfort her. Unbidden, an image of Ralph Rendell arose in his mind's eye and a silent growl vibrated in his chest.

'I saw him…I could not…' Her voice trembled.

'Hush.' Nathaniel smoothed her forehead. 'We will find him.'

Somehow. Alive or dead, we will find him.

'You must sleep now. Please, do not worry.'

'You will tell me the truth?'

'I will.'

That image of Rendell would not go. Nathaniel knew he should only care about what was best for Grace, but still he hesitated. He did not want the man here. But…the curate had the right to know what had happened. He must set aside his feelings for Grace's sake.

'Shall I send for Mr Rendell?'

Her eyes widened. 'Am I dying?'

'No!' He gripped her hand. 'Of course you are not dying.'

'Then why…?'

'He is your…friend. I thought you might want to see him.'

Her lids lowered. 'No. There is no need.'

His spirits rose. Was she not as smitten as he thought?

Grace stifled a yawn. 'I am so very weary.'

'Sleep then. I shall see you later.'

After I have found Brack.

He headed for the door.

Chapter Eighteen

Nathaniel rode out on his bay hunter, Caesar, dread clogging his throat and that tight band once again clamped around his chest. He was afraid of what he might find but, at the same time, he could not rest until he knew what had happened to Brack.

The sun was low in the sky, the shadows lengthening and he reckoned he had an hour before it would become too dark to search. He aimed straight for the place where he had found Grace, and began to follow the course of the beck, scouring the bank and the undergrowth for any sign of his faithful dog. The failing light did not help his search. Brack's black-and-tan colouring would be easily camouflaged by the dark earth and fallen leaves under any bushes, unless he was out somewhere in the open. That was not likely. He would hole up somewhere, as long as he had an ounce of strength when he got out of the water. Nathaniel refused to accept the dog might not have succeeded in getting out.

After five minutes of riding Nathaniel muttered an oath, reined Caesar to a halt and slid from the saddle. He'd not been thinking straight. From a nearby hazel he cut a long, straight stick and, pulling the reins over the horse's head to lead him, he began to walk. His entire body ached, but he ignored the pain. There would be plenty of time to recuperate after he found Brack. He trudged on downriver, poking the stick into and under every bush, whistling and calling from time to time, ears straining for any reply.

He had searched maybe a quarter of a mile of bank when two figures on horseback materialised out of the gloom.

'Well?'

'Nothing, milord.' Ned touched his finger to his cap. 'Sorry.'

'We've ridden up and down this stretch twice, as far as the bridge, and we've seen no sign, milord.' Tam said. 'But we did meet Gil Brown from the Braithwaite estate and he promised to alert their men to keep an eye out. I doubt there's more we can do tonight.' He cast a meaningful look at the sky, darkening by the minute. 'It's going to be a cold one, by the looks of it.'

It felt hopeless, yet Nathaniel couldn't give up. Not yet. Not while there was still light to see by.

'You two get off home,' he said. 'I'll just walk on a bit further.'

The two men exchanged a look.

'We'll stay and help.' Tam started to dismount.

'No!'

Tam slowly swung his leg back over the saddle.

'Sorry. I did not mean to snap.' The men's stares burned into Nathaniel, shaming him. 'Thank you both for your efforts.'

He knew the men were concerned about him, but he needed to be alone. Hope had faded. If the worst *had* happened...he wanted to face that alone.

'You have ridden this stretch. I'll walk it, until it gets too dark. It will not take more than one of us to do that.'

Their hoofbeats faded into the distance and Nathaniel resumed his lonely search, praying silently even as he called Brack's name. He needed to know. He could not bear to imagine his faithful Brack injured and in pain. He would rather he was already dead than lying somewhere alone, hurt and slowly dying.

Finally, the night had drawn close all about him. He knew he must abandon the search. Heart a lead weight in his chest, throat aching with unshed tears, he flung the stick away into the darkness, threw the reins over Caesar's head and put his left foot in the stirrup. He had bent his right leg ready to propel himself into the saddle when Caesar threw up his head, his ears pricked as he stared at something off to their right, away from the river.

Probably a fox. Or a rabbit. He had nothing to lose, though, so he took his foot from the stirrup and walked towards whatever had caught the horse's attention. Caesar followed without hesitation. Nothing too strange then, or he would plant his hooves in the ground and refuse to move. Nathaniel swallowed, nerves playing havoc with his insides. *What if...?*

Feeling foolish for that sudden upwelling of hope, he called, 'Brack? Are you there, boy?'

He strained his ears. Nothing. He glanced round at Caesar, still on high alert, staring...staring...not wild-eyed, but focussed and intent. Nathaniel walked in the direction of Caesar's gaze. Ten yards. Fifteen. Caesar halted, snorting quietly, soft nostrils vibrating. Nathaniel stroked his nose, looking around, trying in vain to see...something.

He whistled.

The barest scuffle sounded from the undergrowth in front of them. He dare not drop the reins, for fear Caesar might finally take fright. He pulled the reins over the horse's head again and moved towards the sound. When his arm and the reins were at full stretch, he stopped, trying desperately to penetrate the darkness, wishing he had not discarded his stick.

Then he heard it. A low whimper. Heart in mouth, he cast around for somewhere to tie Caesar. If it was

Brack he would need the horse—well accustomed to carrying deer carcasses—to get him home. He tied Caesar to a sapling and then ran back to where he had heard that sound.

'Brack?'

A rustle. He honed in on it and moved forward with care. A bush loomed in front of him. Dropping to his knees, he felt beneath. His fingers met with damp, matted fur and another whimper.

'Thank you, God.'

With both hands, he felt along Brack's body, eliciting several whines. Hopefully they were bruises and not broken bones. He was horribly aware that Brack—stretched full-length on his side—had not even raised his head. He could not leave the dog here all night; he had no choice but to move him. He eased Brack from under the bush, closing his ears to his whines and one weak yelp. Dogs, unlike horses, were always vocal at the slightest hurt; he must trust that was the case this time. Nathaniel stripped off his coat and wrapped it around Brack, who was now panting in distress. Nathaniel's nerve almost failed him. What if he caused lasting damage?

I must. He can't survive out here. And I can't see to examine him properly.

'Sorry, old lad,' he muttered, 'but I've got no choice.'

He lifted Brack as gently as he could, then carried

him to Caesar. Mounting was awkward—he had to search for a fallen tree first, to make it possible—but they were soon on their way home, Brack's inert form lying across Nathaniel's lap.

He'd found Brack but would his faithful friend survive?

When Grace roused, the house was quiet and her room dark, just a residual glow from the banked fire to penetrate the gloom. She shivered, closed her eyes again and wriggled around, snuggling deeper under the covers, vaguely conscious of aches and pains in various parts of her body. Eyes still shut, she lay cocooned in the warmth, her mind scrambling its way from the depths of sleep, remembering her sense of achievement in harnessing Bill to the gig, and—she sat bolt upright, the covers falling unheeded to her waist.

Oh, dear God! Clara! She is safe...I'm certain she is safe. I saw her...they brought her in to see me.

Didn't they?

She threw back the covers and—*ouch*. What had started as a leap from her bed turned into a crawl. She had never felt so battered and bruised. She gritted her teeth against the pain and felt around for her slippers. She slipped them on and then found her chamber candle on her nightstand and took it to the fire to light it with a spill. Her shawl was draped at the end of the bed. She snatched it up, flung it around her shoulders—it was so large it almost reached the floor—and went to the door that connected her bed-chamber to Clara's. She raised the candle to light the room and her terror subsided at the tiny form sleeping peacefully. Her pulse steadied. A movement caught her eye and she realised someone else slept in there, on a truckle bed. It was Alice, presumably to attend to Clara if she woke, so Grace wouldn't be disturbed.

Grace stood watching her daughter, digging into her memory for what she could recall of the day be-fore. She remembered Mrs Sharp giving her a dose of laudanum to help her to sleep. She relived the mo-ment she had tipped backwards into the icy water and the unexpected strength of the flowing water that swamped her clothes and tumbled her along until she was beyond the ford and in the deeper water. She shivered, nausea squeezing her throat as she re-membered swallowing mouthful after mouthful of filthy water, desperately gasping for air every time her face broke the surface, and Brack...

She backed out of Clara's room. Had they found him? She frowned, the action prompting a pain in her temple. She touched her forehead, feeling the swell of a lump and the rough soreness of abraded skin. She should return to bed and yet, even as that thought crossed her mind, her stomach rumbled. She would give anything for a warm drink and something to eat.

She would go down to the kitchen—the range would have been banked for the night, but there would be enough heat to warm some chocolate and, besides, she could not sleep without discovering Brack's fate. If they had found him, he would be in the kitchen, where he slept every night.

Grace left her bedchamber and descended the stairs, wincing as she put her weight on her left leg. As she crossed the hall to the door that led to the servants' domain at the rear of house, the longcase clock struck two, making her jump, thereby setting the shadows cast by her candle to dance across the panelled walls. She shivered, pulling her shawl tighter around her.

She followed the passageway to the kitchen and lifted the latch, pushing the door open to reveal the soft glow of a single candle on the dresser. Stepping lightly, Grace rounded the table. There, stretched out on a folded blanket before the range, was Brack. His ear flicked and he thumped his tail gently against the floor, but did not lift his head, his neck being pinned down by a loudly purring Sweep, who was draped over it.

'What are you doing out of bed?'

The soft query came from the gloom at the far end of the kitchen. A tall form unfolded from Sharp's favourite overstuffed armchair, leaving a huddle of blanket behind. Nathaniel stepped into the light. The sight of him…the memory of what he had done for her… Grace shook her head, mutely, swallowing down the surge of emotion that threatened to overwhelm her.

'What is it, G… Miss Bertram? Are you unwell?'

He was by her side in an instant. Large, safe, comforting. Heat radiated from him and his scent—citrus soap with an undernote of warm male—invaded her senses. He slipped his arm around her waist, supporting her weight.

'You should not be down here. Come. Sit down.'

He urged her towards the chair. She resisted.

'No. I am well, I promise you, apart from a few bruises. It was only that I…' She turned within the circle of his arm and tilted her head, capturing his gaze. 'Thank you. From the bottom of my heart, I thank you.'

His eyes darkened as they searched hers. His lips parted as his head lowered, but then his shoulders jerked and he raised his head, breaking eye contact. She searched his expression. His lips were now a tight line. A frown creased his brow and a muscle bunched in his jaw.

'You have no need to thank me.' His voice was gruff as he removed his arm from her waist and shifted a fraction, putting space between them. 'Anyone would have done the same.'

She knelt by Brack, stroking him to cover the slap of humiliation.

'And you, handsome, steadfast Brack.' She leant over to press her lips to his domed head. Her eyes blurred with tears. 'Without you, I would certainly not be h-here.'

She gulped back a sob. Giving way to her emotions would achieve nothing other than to embarrass both her and Nathaniel. She would not have looked up at him so...so *invitingly*...but...had she imagined those tortured pleas? Those endearments? She brushed those unanswered questions aside. Whether she remembered truly or not could make no difference. She had acted without thought and Nathaniel's rejection was plain. And painful.

She would focus on the reality. She had survived. Her terror would fade and she would continue with her life. Much as she had after she had given up Clara. Grace had learned the value of resilience then and she would use that lesson now. She would survive Nathaniel's rejection.

Grace smoothed Brack's head, giving her time to compose herself. Sweep had by now roused, seeking some of her attention, and Grace tickled him under the chin.

'Is he injured? Will he recover?' she asked.

'We think that, like you, he is battered and bruised

and shocked, but nothing broken. He should be back to his old self within a few days.'

Sweep set himself to wash Brack's ear and then moved on to his eye. Brack seemed not to object. Grace patted him.

'Where did they find him?'

'About half a mile down river from where you were.'

'I am so relieved.'

Grace regained her feet, stumbling slightly. Nathaniel cupped her elbow—no supporting arm around her waist this time.

'I came down to find out if Brack was safe,' she said, keeping her gaze on the dog and the kitten, 'but I am a little hungry. Do you mind if I—?'

'Sit down and I will find something for you.' Nathaniel ushered her, again, towards the chair in the corner.

Weariness settling in her bones, Grace sank into the chair, folding her legs and tucking her feet under her as she snuggled into the still-warm, still-smelling-of-Nathaniel blanket. Nathaniel watched her until she was settled, an unfathomable expression in his dark eyes. She heard the vague noises of food preparation and soon found a plate with a slice of Mrs Sharp's fruit cake thrust into her hands.

'Thank you.' She nibbled at the cake, the plate balanced on her legs, until Nathaniel returned with a cup

of chocolate. She drank it gratefully, her lids growing heavy with the effort of trying to stay awake.
Vaguely she felt the bowl and plate being removed
and then she remembered no more.

'Ooh, miss! Such goings-on yesterday.'

Alice was wide-eyed as she lit the fire in Grace's
bedchamber. Grace winced at the protest of her sore
muscles as she rolled over.

'How is Miss Clara? Is she awake yet?'

'Not yet. She was awake in the night for a while,
so she is making up for it now.'

Which meant Alice, too, had been awake but she
was as cheerful as ever this morning, despite her disturbed sleep, as she cleaned her hands with a damp
cloth and dried them on her apron. Grace felt like
nothing more than snuggling back down and sleeping the day away, but it was time she got up. Clara
would wake soon, wanting something to eat... Grace
sat up abruptly, her hand to her mouth.

'What is it, miss? Have you got a pain?'

'No. No, I am all right. I had a recollection of something...' *Or was it a dream?* 'Alice. Did the men find
Brack yesterday?'

'No, miss.'

Oh, no. Poor—

'But his lordship did.'

'His lordship?'

He had brought her home and then gone out again for his dog? Her heart swelled with admiration for his loyalty and courage.

'Yes, miss. Half-dead he was. The dog, I mean, not his lordship, although he didn't look much better.' Alice bustled over to the bed and handed Grace her shawl. 'I've never seen him so...so...*anguished*. Nothing would do for him but to sit up all night in the kitchen in case Brack took a turn for the worse.'

So it wasn't a dream. She *had* gone down to the kitchen and talked to Nathaniel. And invited him—albeit wordlessly—to kiss her. An invitation he had refused. Nausea churned her stomach. But how had she got back to her bedchamber? She had no memory of anything after drinking that chocolate...

Alice walked to the door and opened it, then paused to look back at Grace. 'That's the trouble with animals, isn't it, miss? They can't tell you what hurts. Not like people.'

Not like people... Grace flopped back against her pillows. *But people can choose not to tell you what is wrong. And not all pain is physical.*

Nathaniel...

Alice was still speaking.

'I beg your pardon, Alice. I'm afraid I missed what you said.'

'I said, Mrs Sharp said you must stay in bed and she will bring you some breakfast directly.'

'But…' Grace levered herself up to a sitting position.

'Now, miss, you'd best do what Mrs Sharp says, or…' Alice rolled her eyes, then laughed. 'I'll look after Miss Clara. Mrs Sharp said to take her to the kitchen for her breakfast today.'

'Bring her in to see me first, Alice. Please? I need to see she is all right.'

'Oh, bless you. Miss Clara's bright as a button. It's you that needs looking after.' And with that Alice bustled from the room, shutting the door behind her.

Grace relaxed back into the pillows again, picking over the events of the day before, her thoughts circling and circling…avoiding…too afraid to confront the truth…too terrified to admit, even to herself, the awful thing that *could* have happened yesterday as a consequence of her actions when Bill had jibbed at the water's edge.

What if…?

The sound of the door opening dragged her from her thoughts. She plastered a smile on her face. But it was not Clara, or Alice, who appeared.

It was Nathaniel.

Chapter Nineteen

'Good morning, Miss Bertram.' His dark brown eyes were filled with concern. 'Alice said you were awake. How are you feeling this morning?'

'Sore.' Her burgeoning guilt forced her to admit, 'And ashamed.'

He came closer. 'Why ashamed?'

She sat up, hugging the covers to her chest. 'For the trouble I have caused. For the danger I p-put you in.' Her eyes swam as she finally confronted her worst fear. 'When I think…if you had not been there…what might have happened t-to…Clara…'

Her daughter's name strangled in her throat as she choked back a sob. This was the first time she dared to put that dread into thought, let alone words. Until this instant, it had remained a black spectre hovering around the edge of her consciousness. She had put her precious daughter in danger through her own stupidity. Tears burned her eyes and stung her nose.

Nathaniel perched one hip on the bed, facing her.

'You are not to worry about something that did not happen. It was an accident.'

'But she might have…she could have…' The tears spilled from her eyes, and she covered her face with trembling hands. 'I was so proud of myself,' she muttered through her fingers. 'Stupid! Stupid! I had proved I could harness Bill without any help and I did not want to turn back. My own pride almost cost my life. And yours. And Brack's. And Clara's…'

She ended on a wail. Strong arms came around her and she was hugged close to his solid chest, the steady thump of his heart in her ear as she cried out her guilt and her distress.

'Do not blame yourself. The fault was ours.' The rumble of his words vibrated through her, soothing her. How she wished she could stay cocooned in his arms always. 'We should have warned you the current is treacherous after heavy rain, even though the ford appears shallow enough to cross safely. We all know you are not used to country ways.' His hands cupped her shoulders and he moved her away, ducking his head to peer into her eyes. 'If it will make you feel better, Mrs Sharp is, even now, in her kitchen worrying herself sick that she had said nothing.'

'Mrs Sh-Sharp? B-but she does not even l-like me.'

A handkerchief was pushed into her hands.

'She is becoming accustomed to you.' There was a wry note in his voice. 'I thought you knew that.'

'I had begun to hope it was true.'

Grace dried her eyes and blew her nose, then tucked the handkerchief under her pillow.

'I might have need of it again,' she said in response to Nathaniel's raised brow.

'I can see I shall have to replenish my store of handkerchiefs. I recall you promised me at your interview that you would not succumb to your emotions again.'

Grace's heart lurched. 'You cannot…do you mean to send me away?'

'For crying? Or for depleting my stock of handkerchiefs? It was but a jest, Miss Bertram, albeit a poor one.'

I no longer even recognise a joke at my expense. I am useless.

The vague recollections that had plagued her since waking suddenly came into sharp focus. She could not contain the gasp that escaped her as she remembered Nathaniel carrying her from the river. Disrobing her…

'My dress.'

The words blurted out before she could stop them. Better she had waited to ask Alice, but it was too late and Nathaniel waited for her to expand that comment with raised brows.

'I…that is…I wondered…I remembered…' The

sick feeling in her stomach invaded her throat as she felt her face burn.

All the planes of his face seemed to harden. 'You remember correctly, Miss Bertram. Please understand that you were dangerously cold when I pulled you from the beck. You needed to be warmed and that was impossible with your clothing sodden with icy water.'

'Oh.' She plucked at the fringe of her shawl. 'I see. I do understand. Is… Did you… Are my clothes here? At the Hall?'

'Ah. No, they remain where I discarded them. On the riverbank.'

'But I will need—'

'You will not wear those garments again. Not whilst you are in my employ. I do not wish to be reminded of—'

He fell abruptly silent, a scowl upon his face, and Grace's heart sank. Of course he did not wish to be reminded of her stupidity and how it had almost killed him and Brack, not to mention the risk to Clara. But she needed her dress and her cloak.

'But I only have—'

'Enough.' He raised his hand, palm facing her. 'I will replace your clothing. There are lengths of fabric stored somewhere—you may choose whichever takes your fancy and make…or, no. Speak to Mrs Sharp. I believe there is a seamstress in the village who will make up some dresses for you. You will hardly have the time, with Clara to care for. And, for God's sake, do not choose brown or grey or any of those other dull colours you are wont to wear.'

Grace stared, flummoxed. 'But, my lord, I am a governess. I should wear clothing suitable to my—'

His gaze snapped to hers. 'And I, Miss Bertram, am your employer. If I choose to order my employee not to wear dresses that transform her into a drab, then I expect to be obeyed. Without question. Is that clear?'

The warmth in his voice belied his harsh words. Her heart lifted; he was not so very angry with her after all.

'Yes, my lord.'

She smiled tentatively. Truthfully, it would be no hardship to accept his offer. Dark colours always drained her complexion. She should not really care about her appearance, but she was woman enough to want to look her best, especially in front of Nathaniel.

'Thank you. And—and I am pleased Brack is safe. I did not know, last night, that it was you who found him.'

He raised a brow. 'Does it matter who found him?'

'I meant…that is…you went out again for a dog when you must have been as exhausted as me.'

'Not quite,' he said, with the glimmer of a smile. 'And Brack is not just *a* dog. He is *my* dog. I look after my own.'

'And you love him.'

'You think it strange that I care for my animals?'

'No! I think it admirable.'

It was not only his animals he cared for. He cared for Clara and for the people who worked for him too. For her.

'Thank you, again, for saving me yesterday, my lord. And for looking after me last night.'

His eyes crinkled at the corners. 'You are very welcome, Miss Bertram.'

A suspicion suddenly struck her. 'Did you put laudanum drops in my chocolate last night?'

A bubble of laughter rose inside her at the face he pulled, reminiscent of a small boy caught out in mischief.

'Guilty as charged. I apologise, but you needed to sleep, not lie awake fretting, so I thought you could use a little assistance.'

'No wonder I could not remember returning to my bed.' She willed her cheeks not to grow pink. 'I… Did you…?'

'I carried you upstairs, if that is what you are wondering. You did not stir. And you cannot—' he fleetingly brushed her cheek with one finger '—be embarrassed after the events of yesterday afternoon. I was the perfect gentleman, I can assure you.' A faint smile stretched his lips and was gone.

'I did not doubt it, my lord. Thank you.'

The bed rocked as he stood up. 'I am relieved to find you on the road to recovery and will leave you in peace. Mrs Sharp has prescribed rest for you today, so please ensure you do as she says.'

He turned on his heel and left the room, leaving Grace to ponder her growing feelings for a man who did not return them.

Or does he?

His mother had seen enough in his behaviour to prompt her to warn him off Grace and most success-fully, too, to judge by his behaviour since her visit. There was a definite softening in his attitude today, though, and she would swear she had not misremem-bered those frantic endearments when he rescued her.

But…her doubts about her own judgement were still powerful.

Look what happened last time I believed a man cared for me.

She conjured up the memory of the night before when she had gazed up at Nathaniel. He *had* been tempted to kiss her, but then he had ignored her si-lent invitation. He was her employer. A marquess.

Miss Fanworth's warning against dalliances with employers whispered in her memory. The teacher had joined the four friends as they waited in their shared bedroom for the carriage that would whisk Joanna away to her new life.

It never ends well, she had said. *Look at poor Ma-*

dame...and then she had blushed, pursed her lips and shaken her head when urged to tell the girls more.

Grace and her friends had often speculated about what had happened to Madame in the past. Rumours—passed down from each generation of schoolgirls to the next—told the tale of a newly qualified governess who had fallen in love with her high-ranking employer's heir. It was said that Madame had been paid off with the school in Salisbury, but that she had been left broken-hearted.

Grace struggled to believe the stern Frenchwoman had ever been so ill-disciplined as to allow her heart to rule her head—a trait of which she had accused Grace on more than one occasion—but then, the night before Rachel had finally left the school, she had discovered a little more of the truth. Unable to sleep, Rachel had gone downstairs and happened upon Madame reading a pile of old letters with tears in her eyes.

'Surtout, garder votre coeur,' Madame had said, before sending Rachel back to bed with a warm drink. *Above all, guard your heart.*

Rachel had told Isabel and Grace—Joanna had already left the school—and they had come to the conclusion the rumours about Madame's lost love must be true.

With a sigh, Grace wriggled down under the covers and rolled on to her side. Henceforth, she would make sure it was her head that ruled her heart. Madame had spoken wisely. At least she would still see Nathaniel every day. Perhaps now they could return to their chess games and their former, more comfortable relationship and forget the cold, unhappy atmosphere of the past fortnight.

She would encourage him to spend more time with Clara and she would focus on making them both happy.

It was four days since Grace's accident. Sunday morning. Everyone had gone to church, taking Clara with them, but Grace had declined to go, unable to face the inevitable questions about her ordeal.

As soon as the carriage disappeared from sight, Nathaniel said, 'Would you care to see the hawks today? The weather is perfect. We can fly one if you would like to.'

Grace beamed her pleasure, causing Nathaniel to burn with shame at the memory of his brusque rebuttal the last time she had asked to see the birds.

As they soon reached the top of the fell—the place where Grace had thought the eagle was attacking him—Nathaniel said, 'Are you certain this is not too much for you?'

Grace laughed, her eyes sparkling, her cheeks flushed with their walk. She wore an old black cloak of Mrs Sharp's—he had ordered her a new cloak, but it was yet to arrive—and a serviceable brown bonnet, but Nathaniel swore he had never seen any fine lady as beautiful as Grace Bertram.

'I am not tired. How could I be when you have walked up here at a snail's pace to accommodate my woefully short stride?'

He stopped anyway. 'Here is a good place. There is no need to go further.'

His kestrel, Woody, was on his arm. Next to the other birds of prey—the buzzard and the peregrine falcons—he was dainty and colourful and Grace had fallen in love with him, admiring the black-spotted, chestnut-brown plumage on his back and wings, and his slate-grey head and tail.

Nathaniel removed Woody's hood and set him free to fly. Grace watched, awe and delight on her up-turned face, and Nathaniel watched Grace.

'He is staying in one place now,' Grace said.

'He is hovering. It is how kestrels hunt. They have sharp eyesight and they watch for the movement of mice and voles, or for small birds. It is hard to see it, but if you watch very carefully you can see that his head stays perfectly still whilst his wings and his body absorb the currents of air.'

'Will he come back to you?'

'Yes, of course. I've had him from a chick. He could not survive out here on his own. Here, we will call him in.'

He stripped the gauntlet off his left hand and passed it to Grace. 'You are right-handed so you must wear the glove on your left so you can replace his hood and change his jesses over without fumbling.'

'What if I hurt him?'

Anxious eyes searched his and his heart flipped in his chest. How he resisted the impulse to take her in his arms there and then he did not know.

'Do not worry. I am here. I will do it.'

Her trusting smile set his blood on fire.

'Stand like this…' with his hands on her shoulders, he moved her so she stood sideways to where Woody flew '…hold your arm out in front of you, like so, with your fingers straight…' he raised her left arm '…and stay still.'

He stood close, his hand behind hers, holding a sliver of fresh meat. He let out a call to the bird, who, knowing there would be food as a reward, flew in, straight as an arrow, and landed on the side of Grace's hand. She gasped.

'I did not think I would feel him through the leather, but I can feel his grip.'

Nathaniel gave Woody his reward and folded Grace's fingers around the thin strip of leather— the jess—which was secured to the kestrel's anklet.

'There,' he said, Grace's lily-of-the-valley scent filling his senses, she was so close. 'Now you have control of when he flies again.'

They flew Woody several more times, then Nathaniel slipped on his hood and they started for home.

'Thank you, N...my lord,' Grace said.

He bit his tongue to stop himself from giving her permission to call him Nathaniel. How could that help in his efforts to keep her from his heart?

'I am pleased you enjoyed it, Miss Bertram.'

'Do you think...might I come with you again? I should like to see the bigger birds fly as well.'

As she spoke, she stumbled against him and he caught her, pulling her close. He looked down. She looked up. He was so tempted to succumb to the desire sizzling through his veins, but he could not. He stiffened his resolve and, with a pang of regret, he put her from him. She had accepted the scars on his face and his hand, but she was young ...naïve...she could not possibly realise the full extent of the damage that damnable fire had wrought. Imagining her horror at the sight of his naked body sent shudders of dread rippling through him. How could a beautiful woman like Grace ever accept—be intimate with— a ravaged man like him?

'Thank you for catching me,' Grace said, after a few seconds of uncomfortable silence. 'I should take more care.'

She sounded completely unconcerned and relief flooded Nathaniel that he hadn't followed his desire to kiss her.

'I should like to ask you about the Christmas decorations,' she then said.

'Yes?'

'I should like to cut some evergreens in the woods. Mrs Sharp said there is holly and ivy, and…and… well, some other trees, that I could use to make garlands to decorate the Hall.'

'You mean such as laurel and juniper?'

'Yes.' She didn't sound sure. 'I think she said those sorts.'

Nathaniel suppressed his smile, love filling him at the effort she was making to fit into this alien—for her—place.

'You do not need my permission to cut branches in the woods.'

'No. But I do need your permission to ask Ned or Tam to help cut them. And carry them home.'

Home. He liked the way she said home.

'Of course you may ask them. And I will help, too. When is it you wish to start?'

'A few days before Christmas. And then we shall make garlands and decorate the Hall on Christmas Eve. It would be nice…' her voice became wistful '…if we might have a Yule log, too. Do you think—?'

'The wood has all been cut for the winter. I doubt we have anything big enough.'

But he would move heaven and earth to find one, just for Grace.

Chapter Twenty

Two days later, Nathaniel appeared in the doorway of his book room as Grace descended the stairs carrying Clara—already dressed to go out—and her own new cloak and bonnet. She put Clara down when they reached the hall and the little girl ran straight to Nathaniel, arms aloft. Love, tinged with melancholy, laced her veins as she wished the three of them were a real family.

'You are going out?' Nathaniel swung Clara up and kissed her before putting her down again.

'Yes.' Grace avoided his gaze, draping her cloak over the newel post whilst she donned her bonnet. 'We are going into Shivercombe to consult with the seamstress and take her the fabric I have selected for my new gowns. I shall also visit Miss Dunn.'

'Are you sure about driving, so soon after your accident?'

Grace paused in the act of tying her bonnet ribbons under her chin. She adopted a light tone. Nathaniel didn't need to know the full extent of her nerves. 'I have to cross the beck again sometime, so why not today? I *must* replace my dress and I long to see Elizabeth.'

She had missed attending church on Sunday and Elizabeth had sent a very concerned note, via Mrs Sharp, enquiring after her health and inviting her to visit soon. Grace swung her new cloak around her shoulders and fastened the silver clasp at her neck.

She hesitated. She had already thanked Nathaniel for her new cloak, but this was the first time she had worn it. And she was very conscious of him watching her, his gaze sending shivers dancing across her skin.

'Thank you again for this beautiful cloak.' She stroked the fur trim.

'The colour suits you.'

His voice was gruff, as though he were embarrassed. The cloak was emerald-green velvet, lined with fur, and Grace had gasped with delight when she opened the package Ned had brought back from the village yesterday. It was the finest garment she had ever worn.

On impulse, she said, 'You could come with us, if you are worried.'

He stared. 'To the village?'

'Indeed. We will not stay above half an hour with Elizabeth and if it will set your mind—'

'Take one of the men.' He pivoted on his heel and shut the book room door firmly behind him.

Grace bit her lip. It had been a foolish thing to suggest. Of course he would refuse.

'Come, sweetie.' She took Clara's hand. 'Let us go.'

Her bravado lasted until the final part of the track that led down to the ford. As it came into view, her heart began to thump and she clenched the reins, inadvertently pulling Bill to a halt. How she wished Nathaniel was by her side, but no sooner had that thought surfaced than she quashed it. She glanced down at Clara, sitting quietly on the bench seat beside her. A pair of solemn green eyes gazed back at her, giving her the strength to overcome her nerves and drive on. The water was back to its normal level and flow and Bill did not hesitate to plod across the ford, but still Grace held her breath the whole way and only breathed easily again once they were safely through.

She called upon Mrs Campbell, the seamstress, and was measured for two round gowns, before calling at the rectory where a grand fuss was made of her. All the Dunns were present, as was Mr Rendell, and they demanded every detail of her accident, exclaiming with horror at her ordeal.

'I am grateful for your concern,' she said, finally, after the Reverend and Mrs Dunn had left the room.

'But I wish now to put it behind me. I know now not to attempt the ford when there has been heavy rainfall, so it was a valuable lesson.'

'A lesson? My dearest Grace, you have no need to put on a brave face for us.' Elizabeth reached down to pluck Clara from the floor and sat her on her knee. 'Your Miss Bertram is *very* brave, is she not, Clara?'

Mr Rendell flashed a sympathetic smile at Grace. 'Eliz...er... Miss Dunn, I believe Miss Bertram means to convey the message that she does not wish to be continually reminded of her ordeal.

'Let us instead discuss Christmastide, for it is a week tomorrow, and I have traversed the length and breadth of Langthrop Wood this morning in order to discover where the best holly berries grow, only to return somewhat disheartened.'

'It is a little early to cut greenery.' Elizabeth spoke somewhat absently, engrossed by now in a game of pat-a-cake with Clara. 'We do not decorate the church until Christmas Eve as a rule.'

'I know, but last year it took us so long to locate the best berries, we were decorating the church until well after dark, if you remember. I thought to save us time on the day if I knew their location, but now it looks as though we shall have to be content with nothing brighter than green leaves.'

'But I noticed an abundance of berries on my drive

into the village today,' Grace said. 'I may not recognise many trees, but I do know holly.'

An image flashed through her mind of Isabel, the previous Christmas, a sprig of holly with bright berries tucked into the red ribbon she had tied around her best bonnet. A wave of nostalgia hit her. How different this Christmas would be from last.

'But that is Shiverstone Woods, Grace. It is on Lord Ravenwell's land, and we could not...he does not...' Elizabeth's voice drifted into silence.

'I shall ask his lordship for permission,' Grace said. 'He may choose not to attend church, but the rest of us do and I am sure he will not object—'

'I do not need you to petition his lordship on my behalf,' Mr Rendell said, firmly. 'I shall ask him myself. In fact, with your permission, Miss Bertram, I shall accompany you back to Shiverstone Hall today in order to settle the matter.'

'But Ralph... Mr Rendell...what if Lord Ravenwell is angered?' Elizabeth's voice rang with fear. 'Why do you not allow Grace to—?'

'Hush, Elizabeth.' He leaned over and patted her hand. 'There is no need to upset yourself. The village rumours are built on fear of the unknown. His lordship was perfectly civil when last I called at the Hall and I have no fear of him. It is only right, as it is for the church, that I ask him myself. He can only refuse, but I hope he will find it harder to refuse me face to face than through the medium of an employee.'

Ralph? Elizabeth? Grace barely paid attention to their words—she was too busy speculating over the meaning of her two friends calling one another by their given names. How romantic it would be if they were in love, and they married, and had a baby...

She came back to the present with a start, her own name having penetrated her thoughts.

'I beg your pardon?'

'I said, I shall saddle my mare and then, when you are ready to leave, I shall ride back to the Hall with you. You can point out the hollies on the way. I am aware this must seem a trivial matter to you, but it is important to our congregation that the church be festively decorated to celebrate Our Lord's birth day. And, traditionally, the villagers use any leftover greenery to decorate their cottages.'

'I do not think it trivial, Mr Rendell, and I shall welcome your company on the journey home.'

'That is settled then.' Mr Rendell rose to his feet. 'I shall leave you ladies to your gossip and I shall be ready whenever you are, Miss Bertram.'

He bowed and left the room. Elizabeth's gaze followed him, lingering on the closed door as though he were still in sight until, with a visible start, she appeared to recall her visitors. She glanced at Grace, a becoming flush colouring her face, and then she ducked her head, burying her face in Clara's curls.

'Mr Rendell is a very pleasant young man, is he not, Elizabeth?'

'Oh, he is. He is so...oh! I simply must tell someone, but I must swear you to secrecy, Grace, for Ralph has yet to speak to Papa, but...we have an *understanding.*'

Grace clasped Elizabeth's hands. 'I am so happy for you. I hope...do you believe your father will give his permission?'

Elizabeth beamed, her dark eyes sparkling. 'I do hope so.' Then her smile faltered. 'But until Ralph gets a living of his own, we will have to remain here. It would be so wonderful to have a home of our own,' she concluded in a wistful tone.

'I am sure it will not be long before he is able to progress.'

'You will not tell Ralph—or anyone—that I told you? We did agree we must keep our love to ourselves until he speaks to Papa. I only hope it may be soon.'

'I will not breathe a word, Elizabeth, but I am delighted for you.'

'Ralph.' Clara looked from Elizabeth to Grace and back again. 'Ralph.'

'He is Mr Rendell to you, sweetie.' Grace tickled

Clara under the chin, then held out her arms. 'Come, Clara. It is time to go home.'

'You call that place home, Grace, but does it truly feel like home to you? I heard it was—oh! I am sorry, that was most indiscreet of me.'

Grace did not need to think about it. Despite the occasional longing for her old friends, she could not imagine living anywhere else.

'Yes, it does feel like home. I make no doubt Mr Rendell told you the house is sparsely furnished and dark, but his lordship has allowed me to make a few changes and I think it is an improvement.'

'Well, I think you are very brave, living there.'

Anger stirred. 'Lord Ravenwell is not an ogre and I have no need of bravery, I can assure you.'

'I did not mean—'

'And I did not mean to snap at you.' Elizabeth's stricken expression roused Grace's remorse—she was only reacting to the stories that circulated about Nathaniel. 'His lordship is kind to me and he loves Clara; how can people say such cruel things about him?'

'They tell their stories to fit the facts as they see them, Grace. If his lordship came into the village on occasion, they would base their opinions on what they see, not what their imaginations conjure forth.'

'If only they knew him as I do—'

Grace bit her tongue, her cheeks scorching as understanding dawned in Elizabeth's eyes.

'Oh, *Grace*...I did not suspect you had developed feelings for him. Please, do take care. You are a lovely young woman, but even if he did return your...your *affection* you surely would not wish to spend the rest of your life in such an isolated spot, cut off from everyone.'

'I have no expectations beyond my present position.' Grace stood up, preparing to depart.

'Now I have angered you. I am sorry for speaking so bluntly. It was unforgivable in me.'

Grace had no wish to leave Elizabeth on bad terms. 'No, it is I who must apologise. You spoke out of concern for me. And I truly have no expectations, Elizabeth, but...people can change, can they not?'

'Only if they truly want to, my dear. Do not forget, his lordship has lived his chosen life for several years now and therefore must be content. If he did crave a more sociable existence, do you not think he would have shown some signs of change by now?'

Grace hesitated. How could she put into words what she wished for, deep in her heart? She longed to cry: *Love can conquer all*, but she knew such a sentiment would worry Elizabeth and embarrass them both. No, she would keep her own counsel. And hope she was right and Elizabeth wrong.

'We must go now, Elizabeth. Goodbye.'

* * *

It was pleasant to have Mr Rendell's company on the drive home. He tied his horse to the back of the gig—much to the delight of Clara, who spent the entire journey on her knees, facing backwards, and chattering to the animal—and rode in the gig with Grace and Clara. They pulled up in the stable yard, handed the horses over into Ned's care and walked to the house.

'I will go and find his lordship,' Grace said, showing Mr Rendell into the drawing room.

'This room is much improved since my last visit.' He turned a circle. 'Is that your doing, Miss Bertram? You have an eye for colour, I see.'

Grace felt her cheeks heat with pleasure at his compliment.

'She certainly does.'

Grace spun round. Her heart gave a tiny lurch at the sight of Nathaniel, his brown hair windswept, filling the open doorway.

Nathaniel scowled. That delicate blush told its own tale. Her beau had escorted her home and Grace could not disguise her pleasure.

'I was up on the fells and I saw you driving up the track.' The eruption of jealousy when he had seen them had threatened to overwhelm him. It was contemptible. He must learn to be pleased for her—for them both. 'Good of you to see Miss Bertram safely home, Rendell.'

'It was my pleasure.' Rendell strode over to Nathaniel, his right hand thrust out.

From the corner of his eye, Nathaniel noticed Grace's gaze drop to his hand. It was gloveless and her expression revealed her qualms as clearly as if she spoke.

She is afraid I will snub him.

As she lifted her gaze to his, he raised a brow, stepped forward and clasped Mr Rendell's proffered hand, conscious of the whisper of relief that escaped her lips as he did so. When had she become such an important part of his life he was constantly aware of her and what she was feeling?

His instincts urged him to leave now, but his pride forced him to stay.

'I have asked Mrs Sharp to send in refreshments. You will take tea with us before you leave, Rendell?'

Nathaniel gestured towards the cluster of seating around the fireplace. 'Please, take a seat.'

He followed the curate across the room, but did not sit. Instead, he poked at the fire, stirring the flames into life. Mrs Sharp carried in the tea tray and departed again. Grace then poured the tea whilst Rendell made a fuss of Sweep—who had jumped on his lap—exclaiming over how big he'd become. Nathaniel accepted a cup from Grace and finally sat down.

The minute he did so, Rendell spoke, as though he had waited for the right moment. 'I had an ulterior motive in escorting Miss Bertram home, for I have a request to make of you, my lord.'

Random thoughts and suspicions darted through Nathaniel's head. Chief amongst them was that Rendell meant to ask his permission to court Grace.

Nonsense. Why would he need my permission? I am not her father.

But there was Clara. Nathaniel swallowed. Hard.

What if he knows the truth? What if he wants them both? What if...?

He slammed a door in his mind against those increasingly frantic conjectures.

'Go ahead.'

Clara bustled over to Rendell. 'Ralph,' she said, gazing up at him. ''n Sweep.'

A punch to the gut could not have stolen Nathaniel's breath more effectively. *Ralph?* He stole a glance at Grace, who was struggling not to laugh.

'Clara! This is Mr Rendell. You must not call him anything else. Can you say Mr Rendell for me?'

'Mr Wendell.'

'Good girl. That is better. I apologise, Mr Rendell, I fear Clara must have overheard something she should not have done.'

The curate's cheeks had bloomed red. 'It is of no matter, Miss Bertram,' he said hurriedly. 'Now, your lordship, if I might move on to the purpose of my visit—I am here to request permission for myself and some of the villagers to gather holly in Shiverstone Woods.'

'*Holly?*'

'Er...yes. I have searched the woods on the other side of the village, and the holly there has barely any berries and—'

'And the berried holly is needed to decorate the church for the Christmas services,' Grace said. 'You should blame me if Mr Rendell's request has angered you, for it was I who told him of the abundance of berries in Shiverstone Woods.'

Nathaniel hastily smoothed his frown away. If only he could admit to them it had been incredulity that creased his brow, not anger. Holly...he had worked himself into a panic, and all Rendell wished to discuss was holly? Although there was still the small matter of Clara calling him by his first name. She had heard that somewhere.

'Yes. You have my permission.'

Grace beamed. 'Thank you.'

'We will gather it over the next few days,' Rendell said. 'And we will then decorate the church on the afternoon of Christmas Eve. It is quite an occasion. Most of the village helps and then we have a short service, with carols.'

'It sounds magical.' Grace's eyes shone with enthusiasm. 'Might we… It would be lovely to take Clara, if you will allow it, my lord?'

'Your entire household would be welcome to come along, my lord.'

'I understood it was your intention to decorate the Hall on Christmas Eve, Miss Bertram?' She had told him of her plans over dinner the night before.

'It is, but we shall collect the greenery in advance, to give us time to make garlands, and then all we need do on Christmas Eve is bring them indoors and decorate the rooms. We should be finished in time to help at the church.'

He could not resist the plea in her eyes. He had sworn not to stand in the way of her having friends in the village, even if those friends did include the handsome curate.

'Of course you may attend. I am sure Clara will enjoy it.'

She beamed again—a smile that tore at his heart. If only she might always smile at him like so. He did not want to lose her, even though it seemed inevitable. His mind shied away from the complication of Clara. He would not let her go. But could he part mother and daughter? Clara, he knew, could be the means to keeping Grace at Shiverstone Hall even if she fell in love with another, such as Rendell. But… could he be so cruel? So selfish?

Loving Grace meant he wanted her to be happy. Always.

Impatiently, he thrust aside his conjectures. He would deal with these issues if...when...they arose. In the meantime, he would do everything in his power to keep Grace and Clara happy and content. And if that meant throwing himself into preparations for a Christmas he saw little point in celebrating this year, then so be it.

Chapter Twenty-One

'Not one, but two letters, Miss Bertram. You *are* popular.'

It was four days before Christmas and Ned had been to the village as usual to collect the post. Spying them on the table in the hall, Nathaniel used them as an excuse to pay a visit to his niece and her governess in the nursery.

'Two?'

Grace held out her hand and he gave her the letters before swinging a clamouring Clara up into his arms and spinning around with her.

'Oh, how lovely.'

Grace's cheeks were pink with pleasure and Nathaniel found his thoughts wandering in a completely inappropriate direction: Grace…hair wild and unrestrained…beneath him…pink with a completely different kind of pleasure. He forced his attention from Grace and to Clara, bending to tickle her face with his hair.

'They are from Joanna and Isabel,' Grace said. 'Is it not kind of them to write again, even though I have not yet replied to their letters?'

Her pleasure from something so simple humbled him. She had been through a difficult childhood, a heartbreaking experience, and she was in effect all alone in the world—he had not failed to notice her uncle had not replied to her letter—and yet still she saw the good in people and remained full of positivity. Was that due to her youth? Would she, like him, grow more cynical over time? Or was it simply in her nature to see the goodness and kindness in everything? Her attitude was contagious. It had changed his household, and for the better. Even Mrs Sharp had shed her misgivings about Grace.

Grace placed the letters, unopened, on the mantelshelf.

'Are you not going to read them?'

She shook her head, her blonde hair escaping from her pins in delightful tendrils that caressed her neck. 'I shall wait until I may give them my full attention, when Clara is asleep.'

'Read them. I shall play with Clara, so you will not be distracted nor feel you are neglecting her.' He sat on the floor next to his niece and began to stack brightly painted wooden blocks one on the other.

Grace smiled her thanks and reached for the first letter. From the corner of his eye he watched the expressions chase across her face. When she had finished, she looked thoughtful.

'I hope it did not contain bad news?'

'I beg your...? No. No, not bad news. It was from Isabel. Do you recall...my friend who married William Balfour, Viscount Langford's son?'

Clara, crowing in delight, dashed Nathaniel's tower of blocks to the floor.

'Indeed, I do.' Nathaniel scooped the scattered blocks into a heap. 'You were worried about her, I remember.'

And we disagreed about the need for love in marriage.

'I need worry no more, it seems. They have been to stay with Joanna and her new husband, Luke, at his family home in Hertfordshire. Isabel seems much happier than last time she wrote. Indeed, she talks of her husband in glowing terms...and, yet, still it feels as though there is something she is hiding. Oh, how I wish I could see her face to face and know that everything is all right.'

'If the other letter is from Joanna, could that shed some light?'

Nathaniel grabbed Clara and tickled her. She squirmed, giggling. When he released her, she scrambled to her feet and ran to the other side of the nursery. Nathaniel promptly started to rebuild the tower.

After a silence whilst Grace read Joanna's letter

and during which Clara charged at Nathaniel and demolished the tower once more, Grace set the second letter aside with a sigh and a look of longing on her face.

'You miss your friends, don't you?'

She started. 'Yes. But it is not that. It is…they have both moved on with their lives. That, somehow, more than anything, brings it home to me that there is no going back. Our childhood is over and two of the four of us are already wed. And Joanna is so very happy, I—'

She fell into silence. Had her thoughts drifted to Rendell? Was she envious of her friends' happiness? Did she hope…wish…the curate would speak and give her the same joy?

'Again! Again!' Clara hopped from foot to foot and Nathaniel began to gather the blocks once more.

'Joanna says Isabel and William have settled into their marriage,' Grace continued after her pause, 'and they are happier than they were at first.'

'See. I told you a successful marriage has no need of love or romance.'

She frowned, lips pursed. 'She *also* believes that Isabel has fallen in love with William, but not he with her. Or, at least, he is denying his feelings.'

Nathaniel found he could not hold her gaze and he focussed on Clara.

'Now, Miss Bertram, I shall build my tower again

and, this time, woe betide any young lady who tries to knock it down.' He wagged his finger at Clara, who squealed excitedly from the far side of the room.

Miss Bertram, it appeared, was not to be deflected. 'I cannot believe that will make a happy life for Isabel.' Her lids lowered, as did her voice, and he had to strain to catch her final words. 'Unrequited love, surely, must be the most painful cross of all to bear.'

This conversation needed to end. It was drifting too close to reality for Nathaniel's comfort.

'There is nothing you can do about it,' he said, 'so I suggest you put it from your mind.

'Whoooooaaaaa!' Clara had launched herself across the nursery, straight at Nathaniel, landing with full force on his chest, knocking him backwards. He used her momentum to lie on his back and swing her up above him, face down. 'Clara is flying, like a bird.'

He happened to glance across at Grace and he caught her watching them with that same look of longing. If it wasn't for Rendell, he might think... but no. To complete that thought would lead to madness. He had only to look at her and then at himself in the mirror. No, that yearning expression was no doubt a wish that it was Clara's father playing with her. Not him.

He sat up, standing Clara on her own two feet, and then stood up, brushing his hands over his breeches and coat. Again, Grace watched him, following the movement of his hands and Nathaniel's pulse quickened, stirring his blood. If only...

'I must go,' he said.

Grace also rose. 'We are due down in the kitchen,' she said. 'I said I would help Mrs Sharp make mince pies and gingerbread, and I promised Clara she might play with Sweep.'

'Sweep? Play Sweep?'

'Yes.' Grace picked Clara up and kissed her cheek. 'We shall go and see Sweep now. He has taken to staying in the kitchen,' she added to Nathaniel. 'I suspect Sharp feeds him titbits and Mrs Sharp is happy, now he is keeping the mice at bay. But Clara is not so happy, because she wants to play with him.'

'Let us hope her new toys at Christmas will help take her mind off the cat,' Nathaniel said as they left the nursery, side by side.

Tam had made Clara a wooden Noah's Ark and he and Ned were busy whittling animals to go inside it. Grace, too, had been busy making gifts. Some—her knitting and embroidery—he had seen, for she had taken to bringing it to the drawing room after dinner and working on it whilst he read aloud. But her painting, for the nursery wall, she said, was allowed to be seen by no one until Christmas Day. Her busyness had prompted him to set aside a little of his indifference for Christmastide and to purchase gifts for Clara and for Grace. In accordance with custom, the servants would receive their Christmas boxes on Boxing Day.

They were at the head of the staircase. 'Here, let me carry her downstairs. She is getting heavy; I have the bruising on my chest to prove it.'

He reached to take Clara and his hand brushed against Grace's. A faint gasp reached his ears, even as they jerked apart, Grace quickly relinquishing her hold on the child. Nathaniel's heart pounded and heat flooded his veins even as the hair on his arms and the nape of his neck stood to attention.

Grace's cheeks had taken on a tinge of colour. He saw her swallow as she raised both hands to lift her hair and repin it. Then she smoothed her hands down the skirt of her gown and finally she looked at him, with a strained smile.

'Thank you.'

Nathaniel rode Caesar into Shiverstone Woods and yelled Tam's name.

A faint shout came from deep within the trees and he turned the horse in that direction. Five minutes later he rode into a small clearing and reined Caesar to a halt with a vicious but silent curse.

There were others here. Strangers.

Tam, Ned and Grace were watching him and all he wanted to do was wheel the horse about and gallop away. He regretted riding Caesar. Had he been on Zephyr, he could have excused himself on the grounds the stallion would not wait quietly whilst he helped to cut and gather branches for Grace's garlands. As it was, he had no excuse.

Caesar sidled beneath him, tossing his head, reacting to Nathaniel's tension. He could not leave, not with Grace's eyes upon him as she walked towards him with such a welcoming smile. He gathered his courage and dismounted. How many others were here? How many eyes to gawp? How many fingers to point? How—

'Thank you for coming to help.'

She was by his side. She laid a tentative hand on his sleeve. He resisted the urge to shake her off.

'The villagers are here today to gather decorations for the church as well.'

'So I see.' What else could he say? It mattered what Grace thought of him.

He scanned the clearing and the nearby trees. Most of the people continued with cutting and bundling holly, ivy and other evergreens. There were a few surreptitious glances but, in the main, the villagers were getting on with the task in hand.

His heartbeat slowed. It would take an hour or so of his life. He could do that for Grace. He need not speak to anyone else and, if he did not speak, he knew they would leave him alone.

'Where do you want me to start?'

* * *

Christmas Eve dawned bright and cold. Clara woke Grace early, so she took her down to the kitchen for her breakfast. It would be warmer there. She went in, Clara on her hip, to find Sharp in his chair, sucking on his pipe, Sweep curled on his knee. Mrs Sharp was nowhere to be seen.

'Good morning, Sharp. Do you think it will snow?'

Sharp removed his pipe. 'Don't 'ee go wishing for snow, missy. It makes life very hard way up here.'

Grace sighed, knowing Sharp was probably right, but today she did not wish to be practical. She wished today and tomorrow to be fun-filled and romantic and beautiful, and a covering of snow would be perfect. It had snowed last Christmas in Salisbury. It had covered the ground and painted the rooftops and the bare branches of the trees glistening white, turning the school and its surroundings into a magical place for the four friends who had remained at the school for the Christmas holidays—their last Christmas as schoolgirls and their last Christmas together.

Grace pushed down her memories and the yearning that arose in their wake. She was here now. She had Clara. Surely she was worth any sacrifice? And if her love for Nathaniel must remain unrequited, then she must learn to accept it.

Madame had survived *her* lost love,

Isabel's recent letter, in addition to writing about

her marriage, had also contained extraordinary news about Madame who, sadly, was gravely ill with pneumonia. During a conversation about girls' education with the Duke of Wakefield, Isabel happened to mention Madame Dubois's School for Young Ladies, and the Duke had been quite overcome. The tale that emerged was of two young people who had fallen in love but, out of duty to his poverty-stricken estates and his family, the Duke had put aside his own desires and married for money. He did finance the school—just as those old rumours had always claimed—but he told Isabel he had made sure he was never told its location.

The Duke had then rushed away, to travel to Salisbury and visit Madame in her sickbed.

Poor Madame. Grace hoped she would recover and that she and the Duke were now reunited. No wonder she had warned her pupils against forgetting their station and falling for the seductive wiles of employers, or employers' sons. But Madame had never mentioned the danger of falling in love. Grace did not even have the excuse of being seduced. She had succumbed to the man himself—not to whispered compliments, adoring looks or tempting kisses.

'You are very quiet, missy.'

Grace started. She had pulled out a chair and sat at the kitchen table as though in a dream, a still-sleepy Clara on her lap.

'Sorry. I was thinking about decorating the rooms. The garlands—'

'The missus and Alice have already fetched them indoors.' With Mrs Sharp adamant that not one sprig of greenery should cross the threshold until Christmas Eve, they had made up the garlands in the barn, with a brazier to keep them warm. 'They're in the dining room, ready to be hung up after breakfast.'

Later that morning, a shadow fell across Grace as she placed the final candle in the garland that swathed the huge carved stone fireplace in the hall.

'The house looks very festive. Well done, Miss Bertram.'

She smiled at Nathaniel, the little leap of her heart at the sight of him now so customary as to barely register. 'Thank you. I have enjoyed it, but it has been a joint effort.'

'I know. Come…' he crooked his arm '…I have a surprise for you. Outside.'

He led her to the front door, which was rarely used. They stepped out into the porch and Grace gasped. Bill stood stolidly in front of the house, a massive log attached with rope and chains to his harness.

'A Yule log?' She beamed up at Nathaniel. 'But… you said…'

'It would not have been a surprise if I had told you my plan, would it? And there is something else.'

He pointed to the side of the porch. There, on the ground, lay a bundle of green, forked branches festooned with white berries.

'Mistletoe!' Grace felt a blush build in her cheeks. She could make a kissing bough. Would Nathaniel...? She covered her sudden embarrassment by saying, 'Where does that grow? I could not see any in the wood.'

'There is a lime tree in the park at Ravenwell. I sent Ned over a few days ago to fetch some.'

'He certainly brought a large bundle.'

With lots of berries...that is a lot of kisses. Grace knew all about the tradition of kissing beneath the mistletoe and plucking off a berry for each kiss. A swirl of anticipation tightened her stomach. *Will he kiss me? If I stand beneath the mistletoe, later, when there is no one else there, will he kiss me?*

She sneaked a look at Nathaniel as he directed Ned and Tam in unchaining the log. The three men heaved the log off the ground, but Grace had eyes for no one but Nathaniel as his shoulders bulged with the effort and his strong thigh muscles, clearly outlined by his breeches, flexed.

In no time, the log was positioned in the huge, open fireplace and Tam and Ned left, closing the front door behind them, leaving Grace and Nathaniel alone.

Grace had carried in the bundle of mistletoe. Nathaniel turned and she saw his eyes smoulder, like a

banked fire, and she felt again that tug of anticipation deep inside her. Her blood quickened and, certain she must be blushing, she moved away, putting
the mistletoe on to the floor by the round mahogany
table that now graced the centre of the large hall.

Then Sharp came into the hall, followed by Mrs
Sharp, Alice and Clara.

'I've brought the kindling, milord.'

Sharp set to work laying the small, dry twigs and
split logs around the Yule log whilst Nathaniel disappeared towards the kitchen. He soon emerged again
with a smoking lump of charred wood on a shovel.

They all gathered round as he placed the wood
on to the twigs already laid and piled more on top.
They soon caught and flames began to lick around
the Yule log. There was a cheer, and then the Sharps
and Alice—with Clara, who wanted to play with
Sweep—retreated to the kitchen, leaving Grace and
Nathaniel alone again.

Chapter Twenty-Two

'Why did you light the fire that way?' Grace asked Nathaniel.

'It is tradition,' Nathaniel said. 'Every year, a piece of the Yule log is saved and then, the following year, it is used to light the new one. That was a piece we saved from last year.'

'I thought you never celebrated Christmas?'

Grace felt absurdly let down. Nathaniel had shown no enthusiasm for Christmas and she had congratulated herself on changing his mind about celebrating this year.

'I do not,' he said. 'Not since…well…' He touched his cheek, fleetingly. It was the very first time he had ever referred to his scars and Grace was touched by this evidence of his trust. 'Then my family came to Shiverstone for Christmas last year and it was almost like old times. But…this year…I've been dreading… the memories…without Hannah and David…it did not seem...' His voice faded into silence, a muscle bunching in his jaw.

Poor Nathaniel. Any festivities would be bound to raise painful comparisons with last year.

'This Christmastide will not be the same, but I hope you will enjoy it in a different way.' Grace silently vowed that she and Clara would help him make new happy memories.

'I will. You have helped me see the importance of enjoying the Christmas season, for Clara's sake.' He indicated the mistletoe. 'Where shall I hang this?'

Grace eyed the mass of green. 'In here?' She indicated the hall. 'I shall tie a bunch with red ribbon. I doubt we will need all of it, however.'

She looked up and their gazes fused, sending heat spiralling once again through her body, making her skin tingle. Then, because it was nearly Christmas, and because she had offered a kiss—more than once—and been resisted, and just because she felt a little like the rebellious Grace Bertram of old, she bent, snapped off a branch and then straightened, holding the sprig of mistletoe above her head.

He stilled. Not a muscle twitched as he looked deep into her eyes. No smile. No frown. He could not refuse this time. Could he?

His eyes flared and then, with a heartfelt groan, he crushed her to him, his mouth covering hers: hot, hard, demanding. Her lips parted and he took possession, exploring every inch of her mouth. She clung to his shoulders as their tongues entwined, shivers of desire racing through her as she pressed close, the evidence of his arousal hard against her. Even as she melted into him, however, she sensed his change: like someone slowly awakening, as though his brain was catching up with the actions of his body.

He lifted his mouth from hers. She clung closer, but it was no use. Gently, he eased her back, then took her hand—the one that still clutched the mistletoe—and plucked a berry, holding it up between thumb and forefinger.

'You are right,' he said. 'Such a large bundle will be wasted here. Tell Mrs Sharp and Annie they may take what they need before you dispose of the rest.'

Grace loathed this confusion of emotions. How could he kiss her as though his soul depended on it, then dismiss her as easily as he would the leftovers of a meal once his hunger was assuaged?

'I shall take what is left over to the church this afternoon. I am sure there are plenty of men in the village who will be pleased to make use of it.'

Goading him was a risk, but she was cross and she *wanted* to provoke a reaction.

He scowled. 'You still intend to help decorate the church?'

'I do.' She raised her chin. 'You should come too. It would not hurt you and Clara would be thrilled.'

His eyes narrowed as a low growl rumbled deep in his chest. 'I never said it would hurt. Be ready at two.' And he stalked into his book room and slammed the door.

He did not want to go into the village, but that challenge was a provocation too far after that kiss. Until then, he had successfully carried the moment: breaking their kiss, despite the insistent clamour of his body for more, and faking a detachment so far from the truth it was ludicrous. He had goaded her. And she had goaded him right back. And then his pride stopped him backing down. Now, as the carriage rumbled across the ford and followed the lane to the village, it was too late to change his mind. He would not appear a coward in her eyes.

He could not believe it when she had snapped off that mistletoe and tempted him to kiss her. It was tradition: a bit of fun, a quick kiss under the mistletoe. And he, poor deluded fool that he was, had lost control and kissed her like a starving man at a feast. But…she *had* kissed him back. He had not imagined that. And now, he was more confused than ever. He thought her heart belonged to Rendell, but then why would she return his kiss with such…*passion*?

Grace sat opposite him, with Clara. She was beautiful, wearing her emerald cloak and, beneath that, the new blue-sprigged muslin dress that Mrs Campbell had made for her. Her eyes had shone when Ned had brought her two new gowns back from the village. She made the best of the hand life had dealt her. Unlike him. Her courage humbled him: she had travelled hundreds of miles to find Clara, for no reward other than to ensure her daughter was happy and loved.

Was *that* why she kissed him in return? Was her love for her daughter the motive for everything she did? Was she acting a role, intent on securing her future with Clara?

They walked up the cobbled path to the church door, the murmur of voices within getting louder with every step. As they entered, there was a sudden hush from the occupants. Nathaniel stiffened as he felt every eye upon him, but took courage from Clara's tiny hand in his. A symphony of whispers reached his ears, but how could he blame them for their curiosity when it was he who had fostered his own reputation?

A familiar figure emerged from the throng. Ralph Rendell strode down the aisle, hand outstretched.

'My lord, Miss Bertram—how good of you both to come. And little Miss Clara too.'

Despite that kiss, Grace showed no trace of awkwardness on greeting the curate, who appeared unsurprised by Nathaniel's presence. The villagers, one or two of whom Nathaniel recognised from collecting greenery, soon returned to their tasks. Such an enormous step for him seemed of scant importance to everyone else.

Nathaniel's head ached.

'Good afternoon, Rendell.' He made himself smile. 'We had some greenery left over from decorating the Hall: holly, mistletoe and so forth. We thought you might find a use for it.'

They were joined by a fleshy, older man, dressed in black with a white stock, and an attractive, dark-haired young woman.

'Thank you, that is most generous,' Ralph said. 'Now, Lord Ravenwell, might I introduce the Reverend Dunn and his daughter, Miss Elizabeth Dunn?'

Nathaniel shook hands with the clergyman and bowed to his daughter, who dropped a curtsy, tensing under the latter's open appraisal.

'The additional greenery is most appreciated, my lord,' Reverend Dunn said, 'but I must request that you do not bring mistletoe into the church.'

Nathaniel raised a brow. 'You have some objection to mistletoe, sir? I recollect seeing it in York Minster in the past.'

'That is an old tradition and the Dean there might do as he pleases. *I* do not believe it has any place in the House of God, with its links to the druids and paganism. However, it will prove most welcome in the Rectory.'

The vicar grinned and Nathaniel relaxed somewhat.

'Papa! May I tell Grace our news?'

'Rendell?' The vicar looked to his curate, who smiled.

'I have no objection.'

Elizabeth took Grace's hands. 'I am bursting with happiness.' Her cheeks bloomed pink as her dark eyes sparkled. 'You must be the first to know. Mr Rendell has spoken to Papa and he has given his consent. Our betrothal will be announced tomorrow.'

Shock reverberated through Nathaniel. His gaze flew to Grace, but she revealed no hint of distress as she hugged her friend and congratulated the curate. When the others at last moved away, Nathaniel placed his hand briefly at the small of her back. She stiffened. He dipped his head.

'That was unexpected. Are you all right? We can leave if you wish.'

Her puzzled frown seemed genuine. 'I was not surprised, for Elizabeth confided in me on my last visit. Come, let us fetch the greenery from the carriage.'

They brought in the branches of holly and ivy, laurel and juniper, and helped to decorate the church. Then the Reverend Dunn donned his vestments and read a short service before leading the congregation in singing carols. Clara, too young to know the words, warbled away happily and Grace's sweet voice rang out.

Hark the Herald Angels Sing… Nathaniel sang by rote as his mind wandered.

Not by a single word or look had Grace shown anything other than pure delight for her friends, but she *had* been forewarned. She'd had time to prepare for the announcement. Grace was resilient and self-reliant, but Rendell's choice of another woman must surely open the wounds from her unwanted and un-loved childhood, and from Clara's father's rejection. Nathaniel recalled his own despair when, despite the understanding between them, Lady Sarah Reece had accepted another man's proposal after Nathaniel's disfigurement.

He knew the pain of rejection.

Without volition, he rubbed at his right cheek. Two women—Sarah and Miss Havers—had rejected him on the strength of his facial scars alone. He'd never had the courage to reveal the rest of the damage wrought by the fire. He'd spent his life since then alone, apart from his servants and his family.

Until now. He looked around the congregation: happily singing, the odd few meeting his eyes with a smile. They already seemed to accept his appear-ance. Had his experiences as a young man—newly injured and facing the shocked stares and unkind remarks of strangers and the avoidance of former friends—driven him to wrongly believe all people would react in the same way?

He turned his gaze to Grace. She glanced up, smiling, her eyes warm. There was no one he would rather be beside, he realised, but that insight terrified him. He could never expose himself to rejection again. Those past memories were too strong; they still held the power to hurt. As, no doubt, Grace's memories of her lonely, unloved childhood could still hurt her.

Had Rendell's betrothal to Miss Dunn revived those childhood insecurities? Could that be why she had returned his kiss under the mistletoe? Had she been seeking comfort? Did she crave assurance that she belonged and was capable of being loved? Was that why she had fallen so readily for Clara's father's sweet words?

Well, he could offer comfort, he could provide a home. He could offer no more and, sooner or later, a woman such as Grace would want more. He had seen her pleasure as she interacted with the Dunns and the rest of the villagers and, although the danger posed by Rendell had passed, there would be other men.

She needed people around her, and happiness and laughter, and that he could not offer.

The singing ended.

'My lord. Miss Bertram. Would you care to join us for a bite of supper?' The Reverend Dunn stood before them. 'It will not be very grand, but I know Elizabeth and Ralph would welcome the opportunity to celebrate with their friends.'

'I am not sure,' Nathaniel said. 'It will be dark soon...'

From the corner of his eye, he saw Grace's smile fade and he was helpless to resist.

'...but...on the other hand, the sky is clear and, although not a full moon, there should be enough light to see us home.'

Ralph Rendell joined them. 'It would mean a lot to us if you can stay a while.'

'Very well. We shall accept. Thank you.'

Grace looked thrilled. And he was happy to make her happy.

Chapter Twenty-Three

It was late by the time they arrived home. Ned drove the carriage away from the front of the Hall with a rattle and a clatter of hooves, and then there was silence. The landscape was frosted, sparkling like a hundred thousand diamonds in the moonlight. The night air was still, scented with wood smoke, and Grace—pleasantly light-headed from the combined effects of the mulled wine, the infectious joy of the newly betrothed couple and the intimacy of that slow carriage ride in the dark, with Nathaniel and Clara, like a proper family—was convinced there was magic in the air.

It was a night when anything seemed possible. Nathaniel had visited the village and met his neighbours for the first time in nine years. He had helped decorate the church and he had accepted the vicar's invitation to supper at the rectory. He had already begun to change, thanks to her. How much further might he change, with her help?

Her future suddenly seemed full of promise and boundless possibilities and, for the first time, settled.

She had found a place to call home: a place where she belonged and a home where she was not only wanted, but where she was valued and valuable.

Clara was already asleep, cradled in Nathaniel's arms, and Grace opened the front door to allow him to carry her through. Brack, tail whipping back and forth, was there to greet them, as was Sharp. Grace put her finger to her lips and pointed to Clara.

Sharp nodded, sliding the bolts home quietly as he secured the front door.

'Will you be needing me for anything else tonight, milord?'

'No. You may go to bed, Sharp. Thank you.'

Sharp disappeared towards the back of the house. Nathaniel turned to Grace and her stomach flipped. Surely she was not imagining the heat in his gaze.

'I will carry Clara to bed,' he whispered.

Clara barely stirred as Grace undressed her and put her in her nightgown, then tucked her into her ready-warmed bed, after removing the warming pan with its load of hot coals. She kissed her little girl's forehead, smoothing her unruly curls, and then Nathaniel, too, kissed her goodnight. They left the room, Nathaniel holding the door for Grace and then closing it softly behind her.

Nathaniel hesitated. 'Shall you retire immediately?'

She shook her head, mute. She wanted to be with him. She longed to surround him with her love and to heal him and to help him return to the life he should be living.

If only he would take me in his arms.

She felt emboldened—by the night, by the hush of the house around them, by the wine—but not so emboldened that she could take the first step towards the intimacy she craved. She was sure the desire that smouldered deep in his eyes every time he looked at her was not mere wishful thinking on her part, but still she could not risk making the first move.

She played a little game in her head: *If he does not care for me, he will send me to my room. But...if he does care...*

'I am not tired,' she said, 'but if you do not wish for company, I shall retire to my sitting room.'

He half-bowed. 'I shall enjoy your company.'

They walked downstairs side by side, Grace's stomach dancing with butterflies. Was she wilfully allowing her imagination to lead her into the wrong decisions? Was it just because she longed for him that she imagined he felt the same? She, of all people, knew what the outcome of this night might be. She had Clara to prove it. And yet, her heart was so full of love for Nathaniel, so full of the yearning to take him in her arms and soothe away the years of hurt and loneliness, that she would face that risk with her eyes wide open and no regrets.

In the drawing room, the fire was still alight. Grace sat on the sofa whilst Nathaniel poured two glasses of wine from a decanter. He sat on a chair. Grace stared at the crystal wine glass in her hand, fiercely concentrating on the play of firelight through the ruby red of the wine, quelling her disappointment. She had been so sure he would sit by her side. Doubts now dominated, where only moments before she had been so full of hope. She sipped the wine, the spicy, fruity tang teasing tongue and throat, and cautioned herself not to get this wrong…not to make a fool of herself.

Her lips tingled with the effects of the wine. She glanced up as she soothed them, saw his gaze follow the movement of her tongue and her pulse leapt in response.

She had to break the silence—had to say something, no matter how inane, before she blurted out the truth she held in her heart.

'Thank you for coming with us today.'

He lifted his glass in salute, but said nothing.

'It must have been hard for you.'

A faint line etched between his brows and then was gone. If she hadn't been watching so closely, she would have missed it. He placed his glass on the side table and leaned forward, reaching to capture her hands. She stilled, her heart racing as their gazes locked. Her head whirled. She could drown in the brown depths of those beautiful eyes.

'It *was* hard, but not as hard as I anticipated.' His fingers firmed around hers. 'And I have you to thank for that. You have helped me face my fears.

'Before today I would have let the stares and the whispers of those strangers bother me and I would have walked away from those that stared. I have allowed my fear to dictate my life, but you have taught me to give others the chance to accept me for myself and not judge me by how I look.

'You have taught me there are more important things in life, such as Clara's future.' He hauled in a breath. His eyes darkened. 'I owe you so much, Grace.'

Grace turned her hands within his grasp and curved her fingers around his.

'You owe me nothing. Allowing me to stay here with Clara is reward enough. I am happy here. This is my home, now, for as long as you will allow me to stay.'

'Then that will be for ever, for I have promised you I will never part you from Clara.'

'Thank you. I cannot tell you how much that means to me.'

She willed him to kiss her, striving to communicate her love and her desire by a look alone, but that smouldering heat still did not flare into passion.

Why does he hesitate? Does he fear I will reject him?

Could she, by loving him, banish the pain of the past and show him the way to a brighter future? She could not be mistaken...this lost soul in front of her needed her. She had it in her power to heal his hurts and to restore his pride. She must find the courage to take the first step...

'Grace...I...'

'Hush.' Holding his gaze, Grace slid from the sofa to her knees before Nathaniel. She placed her fingertips to his lips, then slowly, gently, she stroked her hand over his face, caressing his damaged cheek, registering the uneven texture, as though knotted pieces of rope lay beneath the surface of his skin: tangible evidence of the fire that had changed his life for ever.

He stilled, every muscle tense, his eyes haunted.

She could not put into words how proud she was of him, for facing the villagers and for his willingness to change; such words would surely injure his masculine pride. No, she could not tell him, but she could *show* him all those things, and she could show him, by her actions, that in her eyes he was both beautiful and lovable.

She leaned into him, pressing her body between his muscled thighs as she placed her lips on his.

It was akin to kissing a statue. Hard lips, rigid jaw. She pressed closer still, raising her other hand so she cradled his face, her lips soft as they moved against his mouth. Every muscle appeared to wind a notch tighter, if that was possible, until, with a groan and a gasp, he took her in his arms, moulding her to him, as he angled his head, his lips softening and moving under hers. His mouth opened and their tongues met, igniting a fire deep inside.

She poured her heart and her soul into that kiss, molten fire sizzling through her veins until she could no longer tell where she ended and he began. Her body had melted, sinking into him like honey on warm toast. A strange ache spread through her, rendering arms and legs heavy with need.

She wound her arms around his neck, pulling his head closer, fingers threaded through his hair, losing all sense of place and time. He slid to the rug, holding Grace close to his chest as he lay on his back, hands roaming freely over her back, bottom and thighs, stoking her passion.

She fumbled at the knot in his neckcloth. His hands covered hers in a vice-like grip. Grace raised her head, studying his tight expression.

'What is wrong?'

'I…I cannot…'

She covered his lips with hers. 'Yes, you can,' she whispered. 'For me.'

His grip tightened momentarily, and then, with a growl, he released her wrists to tear the cloth from around his neck and cast it aside. Grace had no need to see his neck to understand his sudden doubt. Her fingertips, and then her lips, discovered the same bumpy texture as on his cheek and she feathered the entire surface of his neck and jawline with tiny, butterfly kisses: the soft, lightly stubbled undamaged side as well as the tight, uneven, stubble-free area that bore the scars of the fire.

She pulled away, raising her upper body by bracing her hands on his chest.

'Can you feel my lips on your neck?'

His hands tightened at her waist. 'No. Your touch is too gentle.'

He groaned then, as she lowered her body to his once more and pressed her lips more firmly to his neck.

'Can you feel that?'

'Yes, but only as pressure. It is like eating food without being able to detect the nuances of taste.'

She arched her upper body away from his again, capturing his gaze. 'Then tell me what gives you pleasure.'

A wicked light crept into his eyes. Large hands stroked over the globes of her bottom and squeezed as he rocked his hips, pushing the hard ridge of his erection against her.

'This.' He rocked again. 'This gives me pleasure.'

He raised his head from the floor and captured her lips again in a slow, drugging kiss. 'Infinite pleasure.'

In one swift movement that wrung a gasp from her, he rolled her on to her back and settled on top. His weight on her sent delicious swirls of anticipation throughout her body and her thighs parted of their own volition, the sensitive flesh between a yearning, hollow ache. She sighed, closing her eyes, succumbing to pleasure as gentle hands skimmed her neck and body and questing lips followed. She clutched his shoulders with urgent fingers, arching beneath him as he nibbled the exquisitely sensitive bud of her nipple through her muslin gown.

A hand skimmed up her leg, then pushed her stocking and garter down to caress her bare flesh even as he seized her lips in another scorching kiss. In feverish anticipation, Grace reached for the buttons of his waistcoat, then slid her hands inside, stroking his broad back, revelling in the play of honed muscles through the fine linen of his shirt. He was so big, so male...*all* male...and she wanted him with an urgency she could barely contain. She squirmed beneath him, vaguely aware that she moaned as she did so, and then his weight was no more. Her eyes flew open. He had propped himself up on his arms.

'Are you sure, Grace? You will not be...my appearance...' His uncertainty was tangible.

'Hush.' She pressed her fingertips to his lips. 'I am sure.'

She dared not say more. More words might turn into a plea, she wanted him so much.

He rose to his feet in one fluid motion and then gathered her into his arms, carrying her much as he had Clara earlier. He hugged her tight to his chest.

'I will not take you on the floor,' he said, before taking her lips again.

He strode for the door and they were up the stairs and in Grace's bedchamber in a flash. He placed her on the bed and immediately followed her down, pushing the neckline of her dress low to free one breast. He drew her beaded nipple into his mouth, sucking and nibbling until she was on fire.

Their clothes were gone—she barely noticed how and when—and finally they were flesh to flesh and he was moving over her and inside her, and she was arching to meet him, the urgency building, digging frantic fingers into his back…snatching at the sheet beneath her…clutching his hair as he dipped his head again to her breasts—striving for—reaching for—and then finally…finally…she was there and soaring free, her body pulsing with pleasure as Nathaniel withdrew and, with a heartfelt groan, spilled his seed.

Panting, Nathaniel drew her close to his chest and

hooked the blankets up to cover them. He pressed his lips to the top of her head and—happy, contented and replete—Grace sank into a satisfied sleep.

Chapter Twenty-Four

Grace opened her eyes to the vague awareness that a new day had dawned and there was a moment when she could not fathom what was different. Her mind felt—not unpleasantly—fuzzy and she lay still, warmly cocooned, fleeting images of the day before darting through her memory, like butterflies flitting in and out of patches of sunlight.

The day before… Christmas Eve…which meant today was—her idle thoughts stuttered to an abrupt halt. Those wavering memories steadied and co-alesced as she became conscious of a slight soreness between her thighs and the presence of a large, warm body in her bed, nestled into her back. Panic flowed and then ebbed and her lips relaxed and stretched in a spontaneous smile. Nathaniel. Her dream had come true. Carefully, she wriggled around until she faced him. She watched him sleep in the dim light of the early morning, love flooding her heart.

They could be a proper family now. Her and Nathaniel and Clara. And even, in the future, maybe they could have more children. Brothers and sisters for Clara. And he would no longer feel the need to isolate himself here at Shiverstone Hall. And—

Nathaniel's eyes opened. He blinked and she leant over and kissed him, tracing the sculpted muscles of his hair-roughened chest. She breathed deeply. He smelled wonderful and she snuggled closer. He smoothed her hair away from her face and kissed her, a wonderful, slow, drugging kiss. His hand skimmed her breast, then settled, and the flesh between her legs leapt in response.

'Good morning, Grace,' he murmured as he bent his head.

He circled her nipple with his tongue, then drew it deep into his mouth. She gasped and bit his shoulder.

'Do you like that?'

A wicked smile hovered on his lips and then he trailed his tongue down her body to the apex of her thighs. She sighed her pleasure, opening for him, giving herself up to the wonderful sensations spiralling through her body as Nathaniel loved her.

'We will be so happy, the three of us as a family,' she murmured later, as Nathaniel rolled off her and lay on his back.

He stared up at the ceiling, a deep line grooved between his brows. 'Family?'

'Why...yes. You and me and Clara...' Grace

propped herself up on one elbow, and traced his lips with her fingertip. 'Just think how she will benefit as she grows up. You will no longer have to bury yourself here at Shiver—'

He turned his head to stare at her. 'I *like* it here at Shiverstone.'

'Well, yes, of course. I know that. But, with me by your side, it will be different. We could live some of the time at Ravenwell; we could invite friends to stay—'

'I *have* no friends.' He sat up, scrubbing his hands through sleep-tousled hair.

Grace's spirits floundered for a moment before she rallied. If only she could make him see how much better his life could be. How much happier.

'Maybe not, at the moment, but you will love Joanna and Isabel when you meet them and I am sure their husbands are—'

'*No!*'

He leapt out of bed, keeping his scarred side facing away from her. He snatched his discarded shirt from the floor and tugged it over his head.

'But… I will help you. You must not fear—'

He stared at her, his eyes cold. 'I do not need your help. Nor your pity. I must go. Clara must not see me here.'

'No, of course not, but…she will know eventually,

w-won't she?' She could not prevent disquiet threading through her voice.

'Know that we slept together? That would hardly be appropriate for a two-year-old. Last night should never have happened.'

Instinct leapt to the fore; Grace knew intuitively what he was doing. He was retreating into himself. He was so used to protecting himself he did not see he no longer need do so. Grace flung the covers back and rushed to him, heedless of her nakedness.

'Nathaniel.' She grabbed his arms. 'Do not say so. Last night was...do you not see? We can be a family now. Think of Clara, how lovely it will be for her to have a new papa and mama.'

With every word she said, his expression hardened. How could she get through to him? Make him see how wonderful their future could be?

'With us by your side, you can take up your rightful place in society again.'

He shook her hands from him. 'I do not want to take my rightful place in society again. Last night was a mistake. We were both under the influence of too much wine. We were two lonely people seeking comfort. Nothing more.'

Grace snatched her shawl from a chair and flung it around her.

'It was *not* just the wine. That was not the only reason you made love to me.' Tears crowded her throat, choking her voice, and she kept swallowing in an attempt to contain them.

'I never offered anything other than comfort. I cannot be what you want me to be. I have no wish to change my life. I want you to go.'

The breath left Grace's lungs in a whoosh and her legs went to jelly. 'Go? What do you mean?'

'Leave. I don't want you here. I cannot bear to see you or to have you under my roof.' He tugged on his breeches, gathered the rest of his clothing and stalked to the door.

'But…you cannot mean that. Nathaniel…my lord… you *promised* you would never send me away.'

He spun to face her, his lips curled in a snarl. 'I do not want you here. I want you gone. Today.'

'But…I have nowhere to go.' Grace hauled in a ragged breath. She must stand up to him. This could not be happening. 'No. I won't go. I will not leave you and I will not leave Clara.'

He stilled, his brown eyes hard as they raked her. 'Go to Ravenwell. Take Clara. It is her you really want and, God knows, you have more right to her than I.'

Hot tears scalded her eyes. 'But—'

'Take her. I do not want you here. You presume too much, Miss Bertram.'

Fury now rose up, overwhelming her misery. 'Presume?' She all but spat the word. '*I* presume too much? And you, my lord? What of your presumption? Did you presume that, because I made a mistake once, I would be content for my body to be used to slake your lust? Do you now presume that your two-year-old niece's needs are of no account when they do not happen to coincide with your own whims?'

'I will never neglect Clara's needs. I will provide you with a house on the estate at Ravenwell and an income. Neither of you will ever want for anything.' He opened the door.

'Except love!' Grace tried one last time. 'What about my heart? How can I be happy without you?'

'Love? You already know my view on that, Miss Bertram.' His bitter laugh was cut short as he slammed the door behind him.

Grace's anger sustained her all through the soul-destroying packing of her belongings and the leave-taking of the staff, telling them she was taking Clara on a previously arranged visit to her grandmother. There was no way on earth Grace would leave her daughter with that heartless monster.

Nathaniel was conspicuous by his absence—riding out on Zephyr over the fells, according to Sharp, who handed Grace a pouch containing coins.

'His lordship said to take it to cover your expenses.'

Grace resisted the urge to throw it in Sharp's face. This was none of it Sharp's fault. Besides, she would have need of the money. A plan, born of desperation and fury, had begun to form in her mind. Her heart was in pieces, but she hid every hint of despair, concentrating instead on efficiency and practicality as she packed Clara's clothes and a few toys in a bag, including all the presents Grace had so lovingly made for her. She distributed her gifts to the servants and received some lovely scented soap from the Sharps and Alice in return, and then—the very last thing before she left—she went to the empty guest bedchamber where she had concealed the picture of Clara and Brack she had painted for Nathaniel. Her first impulse was to burn it, but she carried it to Nathaniel's bedchamber and left it lying on the bed. She hoped he would suffer every time he looked upon it. She had poured her heart and soul into making love with him and he had flung it back in her face.

She had been taken for a fool. Again.

Ned had agreed to drive Grace and Clara to Ravenwell and by eleven they were on their way, a lengthy drive ahead of them. Grace waited until both Shivercombe village and the Hall were behind them, then called to Ned to stop.

'Yes, miss?'

'There has been a change of plan, Ned. Please drive me to Lancaster.'

'Lancaster? But, miss, I were told—'

'Who told you, Ned? His lordship?'

'Why, no, miss. You did.'

'I instructed you to drive to Ravenwell, Ned, and

now I am instructing you to drive to Lancaster instead. It is quite all right. I have merely changed my mind about visiting Ravenwell...that is all.'

They would stay tonight in Lancaster and then head south. She felt guilty hoodwinking poor Ned, but she flatly refused to be sent off to Nathaniel's disapproving mother. With the money in the pouch she had calculated there would be just enough to get her and Clara to Salisbury. She did not much care what might happen to her after that, but what she needed now was a familiar place and a friendly face.

Miss Fanworth would know what to do.

Four days later, after a tortuous journey of jam-packed, rackety coaches and of further overnight stops at dubious coaching inns in Manchester, Birmingham and Bristol, Grace and Clara were set down in Cathedral Close, outside the stately façade of Madame Dubois's School for Young Ladies. Grace gazed at the familiar surroundings with a painful lump in her throat. Here were such memories. She had not expected to return so soon, nor under such circumstances.

The sheer obstinacy that had kept her going through the last four days faltered. Miss Fanworth might well be sympathetic, but she would not condone what Grace had done. As much as she had told herself Nathaniel deserved to lose Clara, she knew, deep down, she was wrong to bring her here without his knowledge or permission. And what of Madame? Her heart sank at the likely reception she would have from the formidable principal of the school.

A whimper from Clara triggered renewed resolve. They had come this far. They were both exhausted. She tightened her hold on Clara's hand, picked up their bags with the other and mounted the front steps to knock on the door. Many of the pupils and staff would have gone home for the Christmas holiday, she knew, but she also knew some would remain. Neither Madame nor Miss Fanworth had any other home.

The door swung open, its hinges well-oiled as ever, to reveal the sombre features of Signor Bertolli. His eyes widened above his magnificent moustache.

'Miss Bertram!' He gestured for Grace to enter and to sit on one of the sturdy chairs set against the walls of the spacious, brightly lit entrance hall, with its classical cornices and stately staircase. 'I will tell Miss Fanworth you are 'ere.'

He hurried across the hall towards the closed door of Madame's office and a sudden fear hit Grace, remembering Isabel's last letter which had said Madame was ill.

'Wait! *Signor!*'

The art master paused, looking back over his shoulder.

'Where is Madame?'

'She 'as been unwell with the pneumonia, but she is getting better. Miss Fanworth 'as been running the school.'

Two waves of relief hit Grace, the first at the news of Madame's recovery and the second at the realisation she would not yet have to face Madame. Could she and Miss Fanworth, between them, concoct a story to explain Clara's presence? Her little girl's wan appearance tore at her heart. The journey had been tiring for Grace, let alone for a two-year-old who did not understand why she had once again been uprooted from familiar surroundings and taken from the people she loved. The guilt had nearly overwhelmed Grace at times during that interminable journey when Clara had asked for her *'Uncle Naffaniel'*, but it had been too late to turn back and, besides, Grace could not summon the courage to face him again.

Thus, by the time Signor Bertolli showed her into Madame's office, and there was Miss Fanworth—plump, motherly Miss Fanworth—coming towards her with hands outstretched and a kindly yet concerned smile...

Grace burst into tears. Clara wailed. Miss Fanworth fluffed around, like a mother hen.

'Ask Cook to send up tea,' she said to the art master. 'And close the door behind you, please.'

She bade Grace sit on a fireside chair and she sat in the other, picking Clara up and settling her on her lap. She waited until the maid had brought up the tea tray and poured each of them a cup of tea, and then said, 'Tell me all, my dear.'

Between sobs and hiccups, Grace poured out her heart, finally ending with, 'Please don't tell Madame. She'll send us away. Please let us stay for a few days until…until…oh, Miss Fanworth, what am I to do?'

Miss Fanworth shook her head, wisps of light brown hair escaping from her cap. 'I do not know, Grace, my dear. You ever were an impetuous girl, but I really thought *that business* had taught you more caution. Still, we do not have to decide now. Little Clara looks exhausted. You both do. Let us discuss it further in the morning. I am sure it will all seem brighter then. Would you like to sleep in your old room with Clara? It is empty for the holidays.'

'Thank you, yes. And you won't tell Madame?'

'I won't say anything other than to tell her you are here, but you must examine your conscience as to how much *you* decide to tell her. She is not an ogre, you know. She cares very much for all her pupils, past and present.'

Suitably chastised, Grace hung her head. Miss Fanworth stood, lifting a now-sleepy Clara, who whinged at being moved. 'Come. I shall send a light supper for you both up to your room. You will feel much better after a good night's sleep and I am certain you will soon see the right road to follow.'

* * *

Nathaniel sat on Zephyr on the high fell by Shiver Crag, staring unseeingly over the land that stretched below him. He was dry-eyed, but there was a hollow inside him as big as the dale. Not just his heart had shrivelled and died, but every last cell had withered until all that remained was an empty, ugly husk.

Why had he sent her away? To punish her? To punish himself? He had told himself he did it for her own good—to set her free, as he had set the eagle free—but the truth was that her vision of their future had completely unnerved him. He had convinced himself he could never make her happy and that she would, sooner or later, reject him.

Their final exchange still haunted him.

'Neither of you will ever want for anything.'

'Except love! What about my heart? How can I be happy without you?'

'Love? You already know my view on that, Miss Bertram.'

She had said nothing about love until then. Did she mean it? *Could* she love a man such as him?

The answer was as clear as the view before him. Yes. She could and she did. She looked at him and she did not see his scars. She saw *him*. She loved *him*. Her unflinching courage humbled him.

He had been a fool.

An utter fool.

Stubborn. Heartless. Cruel.

A coward. And, shamefully, he knew that last to be the truest of all. He had been panicked by her expectations and too afraid to expose the truth in his heart in case she rejected his love.

He had been scared of losing her, so he had sent her away.

Could any man have got it all so very wrong?

He turned Zephyr's head for home.

The following morning dawned grey and cold. Clara—heavy-eyed and snuffling and asking for Uncle Naffaniel—could not be placated and by early afternoon, when Madame sent for Grace, she was almost relieved to hand the care of her beautiful little girl to Miss Fanworth.

What kind of mother am I?

Heartache, guilt and inadequacy plagued her as she climbed the stairs to Madame's bedchamber, her steps slowing as she neared the door. How could she face the all-seeing, all-knowing Madame when her thoughts and emotions were so utterly confused and raw? She tapped on the door.

'Come.'

That familiar voice was as imperious as ever. Heart in mouth, Grace entered, shutting the door behind her.

Chapter Twenty-Five

Grace had never before seen the inside of Madame's bedchamber. It was as graceful and tasteful as expected, furnished in elegant rosewood, the walls papered in rose and ivory stripes.

Madame reclined on a rose-coloured *chaise longue* set before a window, her dark, silver-streaked hair draping, loosely plaited, over one shoulder. Madame herself was pale, but her grey eyes were as sharp as ever under her dark brows and as Grace approached her the familiar apprehension fluttered deep in the pit of her stomach.

There was something different about Madame, though—something Grace could not quite pinpoint: a gentler cast to her features that was not solely due to the absence of her customary tightly scraped bun. There was a softening in the lines around her eyes and mouth that made her appear less harsh.

Madame beckoned, indicating a chair near the *chaise longue*. 'Come, Miss Bertram. Sit here and tell me why you have returned, for I cannot think it is because you pine so very much for your old school.'

Grace sat down and haltingly confessed to Madame all that had happened, omitting only the fact that Clara was her natural child.

'This man. This Marquess. He sounds an unhappy man. He is, I think, scared. He rejects you before you reject him.'

'But...I would not reject him. I love him.'

'And you tell him this?'

'He does not believe in love.'

Madame shrugged. 'He says he does not believe in love, but he is a man. He wants to feel loved. He wants to be the centre of your world. He is more complex than many men, but at heart that is what he needs, even if he does not see it.'

Grace cast her mind back to Christmas morning. 'But...I told him we could be a family. I tried to make him see how happy we could be: how Clara would benefit, how we could have friends come to visit, how he could take his rightful place in society again.'

'Ah. And did you pause to consider he might not wish to change his life? That your Marquess— who has cut himself off from everyone for so many years—might need time to adjust to a new future?'

'No.' Grace bit her lip as she confessed, cheeks burning as she realised for the first time how thoughtless she had been.

'I thought not. You have not changed, Miss Bertram, you are as impetuous as ever, never stopping to think about consequences. But...still...I find I do not understand the role of this Clara. Have you grown so fond of her in such a very short time?'

'She is easy to love. Everyone at Shiverstone Hall loves her.'

'But her uncle—he sends her away with you. Why did he do so? Does he not love her? Is he not a man of honour? Is *he* not the child's guardian?'

'He adores her! And she adores him.' Grace felt her face flame at the passion in her reply.

'And yet he is prepared to lose her. And you take her from the man you profess to love, even though you know he will miss her.' Her voice grew stern. 'Tell me the whole truth, Miss Bertram, for how can I help you otherwise?'

Tears prickled. 'She is my daughter.'

'So...' Madame's tone gentled '...*this* is what happened to your baby. I did wonder but, of course, I could not ask.'

Grace's head spun. 'You *knew* about my baby?'

'But of course. I know everything that goes on in my school. Did you doubt it?'

'But...' Grace stared at Madame, and everything she thought she understood about the Frenchwoman shifted, re-forming into a very different picture.

'But...why did you never—?'

She fell silent as Madame raised an imperious hand. 'My position was such that, had I acknowledged your foolishness, I should be forced to take an action I did not wish to take. And so I chose to turn the blind eye.'

Grace hung her head, ashamed her stupidity had forced Madame to compromise her principles.

'You will bring Clara to visit me,' Madame said, 'but I find I am weary now. We shall talk again.'

Grace descended the stairs, her mind whirling. Madame's words helped her view Nathaniel's actions in a different light; she had much to think about.

Below her, Miss Fanworth had just admitted a distinguished, broad-shouldered gentleman. He removed his hat to reveal thick, silvery hair, there was a murmured exchange, and then he headed for the stairs, nodding to Grace in passing.

She reached the entrance hall. Clara ran to her, crying, the minute she saw her.

'She has been very fretful,' Miss Fanworth said. 'I think she fears you will leave her.'

Those words hit Grace with the force of a lightning bolt. What had she done to her daughter?

'And she keeps talking of a sweep, or I think that is what she said.'

'Sweep is her kitten.'

'Sweep? Brack?' Clara's sorrowful plea wrenched at Grace's heart.

Grace did not know how to console Clara. She could not promise she would see Sweep and Brack again. She did not know what the future held. She hugged her daughter tight.

'Who was that gentleman?' she asked, in an effort to distract herself.

'That is the Duke.'

'The Duke?'

'Of Wakefield. He visits Madame every afternoon at three o'clock.'

Grace gazed up the stairs, but the Duke had already vanished from sight. 'Is it true what Isabel wrote to me about him? He told her that he and Madame... well, that they had been in love, many years ago.'

'Yes, it is true. And now they have found one another again. Oh, it is so romantic.' Miss Fanworth's eyes misted over. 'His visits have done her the power of good; the change in her is astounding. And he has vowed to come every day until she is fully recovered.' Miss Fanworth sighed, one hand pressed to her ample bosom. 'Such devotion. Would that I might so inspire a man.'

Would that I might, also.

Nathaniel. Just thinking his name turned Grace's knees to jelly and set up a wanting, deep down inside, that gave her no respite. Madame's voice repeated through her head and the conviction grew that she must go back.

The very thought terrified her, but how could she not? She must face up to the mess she had made of her life. And of Clara's.

On New Year's Eve Grace was reading a story to Clara in the library when Miss Fanworth bustled in, waving two letters.

'They are from dearest Rachel,' she said. 'One for each of us. I dare say she had not received my letter with your address in it by the time she sent these. That is fortunate, is it not?'

She sat opposite Grace and they opened their letters at the same time. Grace read the joyful announcement of Rachel's betrothal to her employer, Sheikh Malik bin Jalal Al-Mahrouky and of their plans to marry in the spring, then stared unseeingly out of the window.

'Well…what splendid news.'

Grace started. 'Yes, indeed. I am thrilled for Rachel.'

Then why was her heart leaden with self-pity? What kind of person envied a friend's happiness? Her three friends were now settled and she was truly happy for them, but…

I am the only one alone and unloved. As I always have been.

Even as a child she had been unlovable. Tears scalded her eyes, and she stood abruptly.

'Would you mind…could you finish Clara's story for her? I will not be long.'

She ran from the room and up the stairs, unsure of where she was going until she found herself outside Madame's door. She did not allow second thoughts. She knocked.

'Well, Miss Bertram? Have you made your decision?

'No. I do not know what to do.'

'Listen to your heart. It will tell you what to do for the best.'

The best for me? Or for Nathaniel? Or for Clara?

Grace thought of the Duke, with his silver hair and his dignity. Madame had faced heartbreak.

All those years apart.

'Did you listen to your heart, Madame?'

'Ah.' Madame closed her eyes, lost in thought.

'Non, ma chère,' she said, eventually. 'I listened to my conscience. I gave him up without a fight, because I loved him and because I could offer him nothing. I ignored my heart, believing it was for the best. Perhaps, if he had come after me…if he had tried to persuade me…but he did not. He is honourable, and he put his duty first.

'I have regretted it every day of my life. Now, we have another chance and we both know that love, it does not die. It hides away. It bides its time, until it may shine again.

'You have the chance I did not have: to fight for your love, to reassure your Marquess that what he can offer is enough and that you will be content. He is afraid he will be unable to make you happy. If you are sure he can, go back and tell him what is in your heart. That is my advice. What is the worst that can happen?'

'He might reject me again.'

'He might. You must learn to accept that you cannot mould others' lives to suit your own purposes. And if he does…you are a strong woman; you will survive. Would you be any unhappier than you are now?'

Madame's words haunted Grace as she returned to the library and to Miss Fanworth and Clara, whose woebegone face lit up when she saw Grace.

'I think,' Miss Fanworth said, 'that Clara is scared you will vanish too. She needs a great deal of reassurance.'

My little girl is unhappy and it is my fault.

Could she risk returning to Shiverstone? If Nathaniel did not love her…if he sent her away…she would lose Clara too.

But she is no longer mine. I gave her away and I cannot support her on my own. Whatever the risk, I must return her to Nathaniel. He loves her and he will care for her whatever comes of him and me.

'Miss Fanworth.'

'Yes, my dear?'

'Please, will you look after Clara? I am going to buy a ticket. To go home.'

The teacher's kindly face wreathed in smiles. 'I am so pleased, but I will miss you, and Clara. When will you leave?'

'The day after tomorrow,' Grace called, as she rushed out of the door.

New Year's Day, 1812

Grace was in her bedroom with Clara, packing in preparation for their journey the next day, when she heard a carriage draw up outside the school. It must be three. She peered out of the window for one last look at Madame's Duke.

The carriage outside was mud-spattered. The horses' breath clouded in the chill air and the driver was... *Ned*! Joy erupted through her. She snatched Clara from the bed.

'He's here, Clara. Uncle Nathaniel is here.'

Nathaniel tapped his foot as he waited on the doorstep of Madame Dubois's School for Young Ladies. The door finally opened to reveal a matronly woman with kind eyes and a welcoming smile.

'Good afternoon. May I help you?'

'Miss Grace Bertram,' he said. 'I have come for her and for my niece.'

Her smile faded and she made no move to allow him entry.

'This is a school for young ladies, sir. Might I enquire as to your purpose in seeking Miss Bertram?'

She reminded him of nothing more than a mother hen fluffing up to protect its chicks and, despite his irritation, he warmed to her.

'I have come to take them home.'

She visibly subsided and opened the door wider. 'They are upstairs. Please, come in.'

Nathaniel strode towards the stairs. At the foot, he became aware of several whispering and giggling girls staring at him over the balustrade. He had faced worse on the journey south, but soon discovered that if he ignored people's reactions, they quickly lost interest. A few silly girls would not stop him.

Nothing mattered more than finding Grace and Clara.

He ran up the stairs and there they were. What could he say? What words would heal the hurt and mend the chasm between them? But words were not needed. Her smile shone out and she ran to him, and then his arms were full.

Grace and Clara.

Back in his arms, where they belonged.

They parted, Clara now in Nathaniel's arms, her pudgy arms locked tight around his neck.

'Uncle Naffaniel.' She kissed his cheek.

'Did you miss me, poppet? I missed you. And so does Sweep.'

While he talked to Clara, his eyes were on Grace, devouring every inch of her, oblivious to their audience.

'How did you know where to find us?'

'Ned heard you enquire about a stagecoach to Salisbury when he dropped you off in Lancaster.'

The mother hen arrived at the top of the stairs, puffing. 'Girls! Go to the common room immediately.'

The girls scurried down the stairs and out of sight.

'My lord, this is Miss Fanworth,' Grace said. 'Miss Fanworth, the Marquess of Ravenwell.'

Even Nathaniel, with all his personal misgivings, could hear the pride in Grace's voice and his heart swelled with hope.

'Shall I take Clara whilst you talk?'

Miss Fanworth reached for Clara, who tightened her hold on Nathaniel's neck. Only when she had possession of Nathaniel's hat would she consent to go with Miss Fanworth, satisfied her Uncle Naffaniel would never leave without his hat.

'She has been miserable without you,' Grace said. 'I am so sorry.'

'You have nothing to be sorry for. It was I who sent you away. And I have regretted it every day since. I missed you so much.'

He must say the words out loud. He would not continue to live in fear of rejection. 'I love you, Grace Bertram.'

Grace stepped close, gazing up at him, her green-gold gaze intense. 'I love you too, Nathaniel. And I *am* sorry because you were right. I did presume too much. I never questioned whether the life I *thought* would make you happy was what you truly wanted.'

'With you by my side, sweetheart, I can change. I *will* change.' He brushed her lips with his, stroking a tendril of hair from her face.

She leant into his hand, turning her head to press a kiss to his palm. 'There is no need to change: it is *you* I want, Nathaniel, not the life you can provide. As long as we are together, I will be happy.'

'But I *want* to change. I have had time to think… to adjust…and I no longer wish to hide myself away at Shiverstone. You have helped me to accept myself, scars and all. You have given me the courage I lacked. With you by my side, I can face the world again.'

Her familiar lily-of-the-valley scent weaved through his senses and he crushed her to him, taking her lips in a scorching kiss, losing all sense of time and place as their tongues tangled and he caressed her curves, aching with need.

The bang of a door downstairs roused him.

'Is there somewhere we can go?' he whispered against her lips.

'My bedchamber.' She took his hand and led him to a room containing four beds and a half-packed portmanteau. 'This is my old room: the one I shared with my friends,' she said. 'It no longer feels the same, despite the memories. We have all moved on.'

Nathaniel took her in his arms. 'You have moved on to make new memories. The old ones are still there, to be treasured, but you cannot go back in time.'

'I no longer have any desire to go back in time. All I desire now is a future with you, however you will have me.'

Gentle fingertips stroked his face. He captured her hand and kissed those fingertips, one by one.

'I am sorry I doubted you,' he said. 'I loved you and I wanted you, but I was afraid and I fought my feelings for you with every ounce of my strength.'

'Shh, my love. No more apologies, no explanations.' Her breath whispered across his skin as she pressed her soft curves against him. 'We have no need of words. Come.'

She urged him to a bed. He sank on to the mattress and she settled on his lap, cradling his face as she kissed him. He stroked her lips with his tongue and she opened to him. Silence reigned for several minutes as lips, tongues and hands expressed their love.

Nathaniel wrenched his lips from hers. 'I could never believe a beautiful girl like you would look at an ugly monster like me.' He feathered kisses over her face and neck, the blood pooling hot and heavy in his groin.

She touched his cheek. 'You are so very far from being ugly or a monster. You are a beautiful man, inside and out.'

His vision blurred and he blinked as he forced a laugh. 'Beautiful? Now that is coming it too strong, even for you, my darling.'

She shook her head, loose wisps of blonde hair framing her face. 'Beauty means nothing.' She placed her hand over his heart. 'It is what is in here that counts. Always.'

With a groan, he tilted his head and nuzzled her neck. She squirmed and giggled, fuelling his blood all the more, and he lifted her, laying her back on the narrow bed, crushing her lips with his as he covered her with his body. She was warm and pliant beneath him as she returned his kiss, reaching beneath his jacket to pull his shirt free. Warm hands slid under his shirt, over his bare chest and a quiet sound of satisfaction hummed deep in her throat.

She reached for the fall of his breeches, desire burning in her eyes as her fingers closed around him. The last vestiges of his restraint flew away. He tugged at the hem of her gown. She raised her hips to assist him. He skimmed her satin thighs to play amongst the soft folds between, his touch eliciting a breathy, *'Yes'.* She writhed beneath him, widening her legs, urging him on.

He settled between her legs and pushed into her slick, welcoming heat, then stilled, savouring the sensation as she tightened around him. He took her lips in another searing kiss as he slowly withdrew. Then he thrust, hard. She gasped into his mouth even as her hips rose to meet his and then they were moving together in glorious rhythm.

He knew instinctively when she was ready: he felt the tension build within her, felt her teeter on the edge. He drove into her again, sending them together into a starburst of ecstasy.

Some minutes later, Nathaniel cranked open one eyelid and took in their surroundings. He looked at Grace, still lying beneath him, eyes closed, a satisfied smile curving her lips. She was utterly beautiful. He longed to pull her into his arms and drift into sated sleep, but they could not take that risk. Not here. Not now. He forced himself to his feet, tucking his shirt into his breeches as he crossed the room to peer out of the window.

'Nathaniel?'

The worry in that one word had him whirling to face her. The uncertainty in her eyes near unmanned him. *Hell and damnation!* He reached the bed in two strides, pulled her to her feet, and folded her into his arms.

'I am here,' he murmured. 'I will never let you go again.'

Her tension dissolved and she relaxed into him. She fitted against him perfectly. He rested his chin on the top of her head, content for the first time in nine long, lonely years.

'I love you, Nathaniel.'

He lifted her chin with one finger. 'And I love you, Grace, very, very much.'

There was something he must do. A question to ask. But…first…he lowered his head and kissed her again, tenderly, worshipfully, the smooth perfection of her lips soothing his soul.

A tap at the door had them springing apart. Miss Fanworth peered in, her cheeks pink.

'Clara started to get upset so I thought I should bring her up to you.'

Nathaniel took Clara from the kindly teacher, thanking her, then ushered her from the room, shutting the door behind her. He turned to Grace and, still holding Clara, heart pounding, he dropped to one knee. Grace's eyes widened.

'It seems fitting Clara should be a part of this,' he said. 'Grace Bertram, I bless the day you came into my life. You have unlocked my heart and my soul and I love you more every day.

'Please, will you do me the honour of becoming my wife?'

'Yes! Oh, yes!' Grace fell to her knees and wrapped her arms around Nathaniel and Clara.

'Me too, Uncle Naffaniel?'

Nathaniel and Grace laughed as one and Nathaniel hugged Clara a little tighter.

'You too, Clara, poppet, you too. We will be a proper family, and you will be our adopted daughter. But we will never forget Hannah and David.'

'No, we will never forget Hannah and David,' Grace said. 'Even though I never met them, they will always hold a very special place in my heart.'

Nathaniel bowed his head, the memories of his sister and her husband still painful, but no longer as raw.

'When they died, I railed against the Fates for taking away my only friends and for forcing my life along a different path. But love and hope and a new future have sprung from that tragedy and I bless the day you both came into my life, my beautiful Clara, and my dearest, darling Grace.'

'Me too, Uncle Naffaniel.'

Epilogue

Ravenwell Manor—23rd December 1812

'Milady!' Alice rushed into the drawing room, her plump cheeks quivering. 'Milady!' She skidded to a halt, hand pressed to heaving bosom. 'There's carriages a-coming. *Three* of them.'

'All three together? How wonderful.'

Grace jumped to her feet, then froze, her hand to her mouth. Alice reached her side in an instant.

'Oh, milady. Again?'

'No.' Grace shook her head. 'No, it is not the sickness. I rose too quickly and felt light-headed, that is all. Now, come. We have visitors to greet.' She cast a swift glance around the room. All was neat and gleaming. 'Will you ask Fish to tell his lordship—?'

'I am here.'

The deep voice came from the doorway and Grace pivoted to face Nathaniel: handsome, inherently masculine, *hers*. Her heart gave its customary somersault and then melted at the sight of Clara, holding his hand. She was growing so tall, her soft brown curls falling down her back in ringlets. Grace could not wait to introduce her new family to her friends.

'Alice, will you alert Cook that we shall require luncheon in an hour, please? Are all the bedchambers prepared? And the servants' quarters?'

'Yes, milady. Shall I take Miss Clara now?'

'No. She will come with us to greet our guests.'

Alice, who had moved back to Ravenwell Manor with Nathaniel and Grace after their marriage, scurried from the room. The Sharps had elected to stay at Shiverstone Hall as caretakers and Ned, Tam and Annie had also stayed behind, to care for the animals and Nathaniel's beloved hawks. Every few weeks, Nathaniel rode over to the Hall to fly his birds and stay the night and, in the spring, they planned to return as a family for a longer visit.

If I am able to. Grace smoothed her hand over her gently rounded stomach, and a warm glow of contentment suffused her.

Nathaniel's gaze tracked the movement of her hand, then lifted to her face and she saw the heat banked in his eyes. Anticipation tugged deep within her, but there was no time to dally.

'How are Ralph and Elizabeth? Have they settled into the vicarage?' she asked, to distract him.

Nathaniel and Clara had been to visit the newly

married Rendells in their new home, taking with them a bunch of freshly gathered mistletoe. The elderly incumbent of the local church, St Thomas's, had recently retired and Nathaniel had gifted the living to Ralph Rendell.

'They have and they are as happy a pair of lovebirds as ever I did see—except for us, my darling, irresistible wife.'

He cradled Grace's face and brushed a kiss to her lips. Then his eyes darkened and he lowered his head again, and kissed her until her insides were molten. But, this time, she must resist and, hands on his chest, she pushed him away.

'Nathaniel! Our visitors will be here any minute.'

He chuckled and kissed her again. 'It is precisely because their arrival is imminent that I am taking advantage whilst I may. You must not begrudge me a little sustenance to see me through the next few hours.'

'Papa! Mama!' Clara tugged at Nathaniel's sleeve for attention.

Grace's heart swelled. Clara might never discover that Grace was her natural mother but, once she and Nathaniel had wed, they had agreed Clara would be their adopted daughter and they would be her father and mother from that day forward.

Nathaniel scooped Clara high. He put his lips to her cheek and blew, making a rude noise that had Clara giggling and squirming in his arms as they all made their way to the front door. Their servants were beginning to congregate in the hall, ready to conduct the visitors to their bedchambers.

'The Reverend Rendell was most appreciative of the mistletoe,' Nathaniel said, with a grin, as they reached the double entrance door, standing wide in readiness. 'In fact...' he tipped his head towards Grace, lowering his voice '...nothing would do for our new vicar than to test it out with his bride. I don't know...' he shook his head, his brown eyes brimming with merriment '...if that is the way a man of the cloth sees fit to behave in full view of his benefactor, what hope is there for society?

'They send their pleased acceptance of our invitation to join us for Christmas dinner, by the way.'

'How lovely it will be to have our friends all here,' Grace said. 'Mother is delighted at the prospect of seeing a full dining table at the Manor once again.'

Nathaniel's mother—after a distrustful start with her new daughter-in-law—had soon accepted Grace and they were now firm friends. She now lived in the Dower House on the estate, but she visited almost every day.

The rumble of the carriage wheels and the hoof-beats of eighteen horses—three teams of four, plus six outriders—grew ever louder as they reached the end of the long, straight carriageway that led from the road and negotiated the turning circle that would bring them to the front steps of the Manor.

The sky was uniformly white, with not a hint of grey, and the air was still—almost as though it held its breath in anticipation. Nathaniel had predicted snow and Grace breathed a silent thank you that it had held off until the travellers arrived.

The carriages halted and the silence—punctuated only by the occasional jingle of a bit or stamp of a hoof—was deafening in its own way. A sudden attack of nerves assailed Grace. It had been almost a year and a half since she had seen her beloved friends.

Will they be different? What will they think of me? What will their husbands be like? What if—?

She felt Nathaniel's hand at the small of her back, large and reassuring. She glanced up at him.

'Don't be nervous. You will be fine. You'll see.'

His eyes met hers, steady and confident with no sign of apprehension, and Grace marvelled at the change in him since the day they met. And then there was no more time to worry, for carriage doors were being flung wide and there they were.

Joanna. Rachel. Isabel. Three dear, familiar faces.

Tears blurred Grace's vision and she blinked rapidly, so as not to appear an emotional fool and yet...

They came together in a rush: hugging, kissing and exclaiming.

And tearful—even Joanna, who had never, ever been seen to cry before.

All four of them, in a laughing circle, with tears rolling unashamedly down their cheeks.

Isabel peered out of the window. 'Now that we are safely arrived, I declare it may snow to its heart's content.'

They were gathered in the drawing room after a delicious luncheon.

Grace joined her. 'I believe you will get your wish.' She lowered her voice. 'You will tell me if there is anything you need, will you not, Isabel?'

'Thank you, Grace, darling, but you must not worry about me. I feel exceedingly well. Blossoming, you might say.' Isabel smiled, and placed her hands either side of her swollen belly with a sigh of contentment.

It was chilly by the window and they moved nearer to the warmth of the fire.

'Do you really think it will snow, Lady Ravenwell?'

Grace smiled at the handsome young boy's serious expression. Rachel's stepson, Aahil, had never seen snow in his life. Neither had his younger sister and brother, Ameera and Hakim, who both sprawled on the floor next to Clara, playing with her Noah's Ark.

'I think it will, Aahil. And then...' Grace eyed each of her friends in turn '...we will build a snowman. Do you remember—?'

'The Christmas before last!' Isabel's blue eyes sparkled. 'We all stayed at school and we built the *biggest* snowman...'

Joanna, sitting on the sofa, newly born Edward cradled in her arms, smiled. 'That was such a happy Christmas.'

'This one will be better.' Rachel sat next to Joanna and leaned over to admire the babe. 'He is *soooo* sweet, Joanna.' There was a note of longing in her voice. 'May I hold him?'

'Of course.' Joanna passed her son to Rachel, who crooned softly until he settled again.

'Our snowman will be bigger and better.' Hakim, hopping from foot to foot in his excitement, joined Aahil. 'Will it snow, Lady Ravenwell? Will it snow, do you think?'

Hakim had seemed timid on first arrival, but had soon lost his shyness with all these new people. His father, Malik—exotically dark and impossibly handsome, with piercing eyes—broke off his discussion with Nathaniel about hawking, a popular means of hunting in his beloved Huria.

'Calm down, Hakim, or I shall send you to the nursery,' he said. 'If the Fates smile upon us, it will snow. Bombarding her ladyship with questions will change nothing.'

'He is excited, Malik. And full of energy after

spending so many days cooped up in the carriage,' Rachel said, as she cradled Edward.

'As am I.' Luke, Joanna's husband, stood up and stretched. 'I beg your pardon, ladies, but I need to work off some of this energy. Ravenwell, I believe you mentioned a couple of new hunters? Any chance of putting them through their paces?'

All four men perked up and Grace found herself exchanging knowing looks of amusement with her three friends.

'Indeed. However, before that...' Nathaniel turned to Aahil. 'How would you like to help us bring home the Yule log, young man?' He cocked a brow at Malik. 'I don't know if you're familiar with the tradition, Al-Mahrouky, but the Yule log is specially selected to burn the full twelve days of Christmastide. It is brought indoors on Christmas Eve and lit and then, if possible, a piece is saved on Twelfth Night to light the following year's Yule log.'

'But it is not Christmas Eve until tomorrow,' Joanna said, from her seat on the sofa. 'Will that not bring bad luck?'

'We will not tempt fate by bringing it indoors until tomorrow, but we must drag the log closer to the house before it snows. We can leave it in one of the outbuildings overnight. What do you say, Aahil? Are you feeling strong?'

'May I, Father?'

'Very well, son.'

'Me too!' Hakim bounced up and down.

'May I come too?' Ameera stood up.

'Me, me, me!' Clara shouted, scrambling to her feet, lining up with Ameera and Hakim in front of Nathaniel. 'Papa. Papa. Pleeease.'

'Clara, I do not think—'

'*Pleeeaaase*, Papa.' She turned beseeching eyes to Grace. 'Mama, please.'

Grace raised her brows at Nathaniel. She saw him bite back his smile and she knew he would be helpless to refuse those three pleading faces.

'Al-Mahrouky?' Nathaniel directed his question at the Sheikh, who nodded.

'Very well,' Nathaniel said to the three. 'If you promise faithfully to do exactly as you are told, you may come.'

'Thank you,' they chorused.

Ameera, tugging Clara with her, moved closer to Nathaniel. 'Does that hurt?' She pointed to Nathaniel's scarred cheek.

There was the sound of indrawn breath and Rachel straightened as though to remonstrate with Ameera, but Grace caught her eye and shook her head.

Nathaniel smiled down at Ameera. 'No. Not now,' he said. Then he crouched down before the three youngest children. 'But it hurt a great deal at the time and that is the reason you must always be very careful with fire.'

'I am pleased it doesn't hurt,' Ameera announced. 'May we go outside now, please, Lord Ravenwell?'

Nathaniel laughed as he stood up. 'Yes, Ameera, we will go now.' He winked at Grace. 'We'll take a couple of footmen to help with the children. It will give you ladies a chance to catch up with the gossip.'

William, his light brown eyes creased with amusement, said, 'Judging by the non-stop chatter since our arrival, I cannot credit there is any subject still uncovered. They already appear to have catalogued the happenings of every single day since last they met.'

'You, Mr Balfour, are a tease.' Isabel slapped her husband playfully on the arm. 'Run along and play, you men, and leave your womenfolk in peace. We still have many important matters to discuss.'

'Important matters! Ha!' Luke stooped to kiss Joanna on the cheek. 'Children and babies, I'll be bound.'

'Are you suggesting that children and babies are *not* important, my dear?' Joanna regarded her husband quizzically.

He laughed. 'You have me there, my sweet. Children and babies are, of course, the most important of all things. I stand corrected.' He reached out and tickled Edward's pudgy cheek with a gentle finger. 'I fear you must wait a year or two to join us, my son, but at least you shall stay nice and snug indoors whilst we men brave the elements.'

After the men and children had gone, Edward's nursemaid whisked him off to the nursery and the four girls were left together.

'Ravenwell Manor is wonderful, Grace. It is so modern, so beautifully appointed, and this room is exquisite,' Isabel said.

Rachel and Joanna nodded their agreement.

'It was completely rebuilt after the fire.' Grace gazed around the drawing room, her favourite room in the house, decorated in shades of green and cream. 'Nathaniel's mother planned the décor.'

'Is that the fire that injured Nathaniel?' Joanna asked in her soft voice.

'Yes. He went back inside to rescue his father, but he was too late.'

Pride swelled at his bravery and at his courage in facing a full life once again, for her sake and for Clara's, and now…she placed her hand against her stomach…for their future family as well.

Grace looked up and found Rachel watching her, an unfathomable expression on her face.

'Are you quite well, Rachel?'

Pink suffused Rachel's cheeks. 'Are you…are you increasing, Grace?'

Isabel's head jerked up, her copper curls bouncing.

'Really? Are you, Grace? Why have you not told us? How exciting. We shall all be mothers together.'

'Isabel! Really. Calm down,' Joanna said, with a laugh. 'Grace has not answered Rachel yet and you are already three jumps ahead of us. You do not change.'

They all laughed.

'I'm sorry, Grace. But…is it true?'

'Yes! We will have a brother or a sister for Clara by the early summer, God willing.'

Then she recalled Rachel's expression. Would her news upset her friend? There had been something… that longing in her voice, earlier, and the look in her eyes when she held baby Edward…

Hoping and praying there was nothing amiss, she said, 'Your time will come, Rachel. You have only been wed nine months and—'

'I think I am with child.' Rachel blurted out her news with a blush.

The gasps were audible, then they all spoke at once.

'Are you sure?'

'How do you know?'

'But you never wanted children.'

'A lady can change her mind,' she said primly, in reply to that last comment from Isabel, and then she burst out laughing. 'I am not certain, but I'm fairly sure. I haven't even told Malik yet…I did not dare, for fear he would stop me journeying here for Christmas.'

A contented glow suffused Rachel's face as she added, 'He is very protective.'

'So we will truly all be mothers. With children by the men we love. How glorious is that?' Isabel stood, flinging her arms wide, and then twirled in a circle. 'Two years ago, we were all dreading our futures as put-upon drudges and now…look at us. Married ladies all and with children we never expected to bear.'

'Except for Grace,' Joanna said. 'Do you know, Grace, for all it was such a terrifying ordeal for you, in a way I envied you. You would be the only one of us to be a mother. Even though you had to give Clara away, still you had experienced the most wonderful thing that can ever happen to a woman.'

Grace clasped Joanna's hands, understanding the pain of her childhood with no family to love her. They had that in common.

'I never knew you felt that way, Joanna. I never believed anyone could envy what happened to me. But I see, in a way, what you mean. I always knew that somewhere in this world there was a part of me. I bless the day Miss Fanworth told me the names of Clara's adopted parents.'

'We have both found true families now, Grace. Although…' Joanna paused, her brow wrinkled with thought '…I eventually came to realise that Madame Dubois did love me, in her own way. She and the rest of the teachers were a kind of family to me, but I was too busy envying the other girls and their conventional families to realise it.'

Rachel laughed. 'No one could ever accuse *my* family of being conventional but, speaking of Madame, it is fortunate she never found out about the baby, Grace, or your life might have turned out very differently.'

'Ah, now that is where you are mistaken,' Grace said. She told them what Madame had told her the previous Christmas. 'She turned a blind eye because she knew my uncle would cast me out.'

'So the sly old thing knew all the time. Well, well.' Isabel subsided into an armchair.

'Talking of Madame,' Joanna said, 'I have some *marvellous* news about her and also about the school and Miss Fanworth.' She paused for effect, a mischievous glint in her eyes.

'Hurry up and tell us.'

'Stop teasing, Joanna.'

'Tell us quickly before I burst!'

'We-e-e-ll...' Joanna eked out the moment, clearly enjoying being the news bearer.

'Joanna!' Isabel, sitting next to Joanna on the sofa, nudged her. 'Tell us. I am in a delicate condition, don't you know, and I must not be stressed.'

Joanna laughed. 'Oh, very well. Do you remember the Duke of Wakefield?'

'Yes, of course. *I* told *you* about him at that soirée

last Christmas Eve and I wrote to Grace and Rachel about him.'

'And he visited Madame last Christmastide, when Clara and I were there,' Grace said, 'and Madame told me her tragic love story. I wrote to all of you about that. And I do know Madame fully recovered from her illness, for Miss Fanworth wrote and told me so.'

'Yes, she has recovered. In fact, she has so far recovered that she wed her Duke last week, and Madame Dubois is henceforth to be addressed as her Grace the Duchess of Wakefield.'

'A *duchess*?'

'How do you know?'

'Why did you not say before?'

'Yes, a duchess. And I know because Luke and I attended the wedding. And I did not say before because we had so much else to share.'

'So Madame has her happy-ever-after as well,' Rachel said. 'I am so pleased for her.'

'And the school?' Grace asked. 'You said you had news about the school.'

'She has gifted it to Miss Fanworth, who is now the principal.'

'So, we four and Madame get our handsome princes, and poor Miss Fanworth gets a pile of bricks and mortar.'

'Isabel!'

'Anyway,' Grace said, with a sly glance around her friends, 'there is always Signor Bertolli.'

She mimicked his Italian accent and twirled an imaginary moustache and the others burst into fits of giggles. They had long speculated over the Italian art master and his apparent liking for the plump, motherly Miss Fanworth.

Without Madame and her iron discipline at the school, who knew what that feisty Italian gentleman might get up to?

Christmas Eve

Grace awoke the following morning and rolled over to face Nathaniel. He still slept, warm and tousled and *delicious*. Stealthily, she leaned over and kissed his lips. He stirred and reached for her, eyes still shut.

'You are insatiable, woman,' he grumbled as he drew her close.

She snuggled against him, reaching between them as his hand delved for the hem of her nightdress and trailed up her bare leg.

When they eventually surfaced, they discovered a world transformed. The expected snow had fallen— so much snow it shrouded the land as far as the eye could see, thickly distorting every familiar feature. The sun shone in a cloudless sky, and the snow-covered landscape glistened and glimmered invitingly.

* * *

Somehow—and Grace was not sure quite how it happened—it was arranged that the men would take the excited children outside to build a snowman before bringing in the Yule log, whilst the women stayed indoors to decorate the house with the garlands Grace and the servants had crafted over the past week.

Hmmph! Stay indoors where it's nice and warm, indeed.

She did not voice her frustration to her friends, however. After all, they were not children any more and Isabel, in particular, might not wish to risk going outdoors in her condition.

They had finished decorating the dining room and were about to start on the drawing room when the door flew open to reveal Isabel, clad in her sky-blue velvet fur-lined cloak and twirling a matching bonnet in her hands. Grace had not even realised she had disappeared.

'Why should the men have all the fun?' Isabel said. 'I want to go outside in the snow. We can finish decorating the house later. Grace has done all the hard work already. What do you say, girls? Will any of you join me?'

Grace, Rachel and Joanna, as one, dropped their garlands and chorused, 'Yes!'

Grace rang the bell and sent maids to fetch their cloaks, hats and gloves. Whilst they waited, Isabel continued to twirl her bonnet until, with a sudden ex-clamation, she stopped, plucked out the short plume tucked into the hatband and discarded it. She then broke a forked branch of mistletoe from a kissing bough and put it in place of the plume.

'There.' She grinned saucily. 'Three berries, as well. I *shall* have fun in the snow.'

They tumbled out into the garden, where Luke and William were rolling a snowball for the body of the snowman and Nathaniel—with Brack by his side—was helping the three smallest children roll another for the head. Malik and Aahil stood aside, watching.

Rachel tutted. 'Aahil needs to play. He tries to em-ulate Malik, but he is nine years old. If he cannot be a child now, when can he?'

And, with that, she scooped a handful of snow and threw it straight at Malik, hitting his head and knocking off his hat. He spun around, his dark eyes flashing with an anger that soon melted when he saw Rachel.

Luke, meanwhile, had seen what happened. 'Come on, men,' he yelled. 'War is declared!' And he grabbed a handful of snow and lobbed it at Joanna.

Malik's aloofness lasted all of ten seconds. With a sudden laugh, he joined in, and then they were all throwing snowballs, laughing and shouting, whilst Brack gambolled around, barking and snatching at mouthfuls of snow.

A truce was called only after Joanna slipped flat on her face in a snowdrift. Luke was by her side in an instant.

'Enough,' he panted, grinning widely as he lifted her up. 'You, my beautiful lady wife, are coming indoors right now to get changed out of these wet clothes.' He strode towards the house, carrying Joanna.

'Can we finish the snowman?' Aahil gazed up at Nathaniel, dark eyes wide, hair sprinkled with snow.

Nathaniel patted his shoulder. 'Of course we can. You fetch the head whilst we set up the body.'

Malik helped Nathaniel manoeuvre the larger of the two balls into place outside the drawing-room windows and Ameera scampered through the snow to help Aahil whilst Clara and Hakim chased Brack.

Grace, Rachel and Isabel were content to watch, catching their breath after so much laughter. William joined them, his brows raised suggestively as he looked his wife up and down.

'New bonnet, my dear?'

Isabel preened a little. 'Oh, this old thing? I have merely retrimmed it, Husband.'

He wrapped his arms around her and kissed her soundly, then plucked a berry from the mistletoe. 'Only two more? You disappoint me.' He kissed her twice more, removing a berry after each kiss. 'That is better, for no one else gets to kiss *my* wife.'

The snowman was soon completed and Aahil, as the eldest and tallest of the children, crowned him with an old hat of Nathaniel's. Ameera wound a scarf around his neck and, together, they made his face with coal for eyes, a carrot for a nose and a row of hazelnuts to mark his mouth whilst Hakim and Clara stuck lumps of coal in a crooked line down his body, for buttons. An old clay pipe completed the transformation.

The children stood back, eyes and smiles wide.

'Is he magic?' Hakim whispered. 'Will he come alive and have adventures when it is dark and we can't see him?'

Rachel crouched by his side and hugged him. 'He will if you believe in him, Hakim.'

They were all warm and dry, congregated in the drawing room, when Luke and Joanna eventually reappeared.

'At last,' Isabel cried. 'We are waiting to light the Yule log.'

Two of the footmen had brought the log indoors earlier, setting it in the drawing room grate—only just big enough to accommodate it.

'Sorry.' Luke looked entirely unrepentant.

'We were playing with Edward,' Joanna said, with a blush and a stifled giggle.

'We're all here now,' William said, with a merry glance. 'I have been looking forward to this.'

The fire was lit, using a blackened lump of wood saved by Sharp—bless him—from last year's Yule log, and then all the adults helped drape garlands around the room, adding candles, whilst the children played with Sweep, who was fascinated by all the greenery. Isabel fashioned a dainty headdress for Ameera, using sprigs of juniper, interwoven with red ribbon and tiny fir cones. Clara and Hakim then wanted their own headdresses, so she made two more whilst a delighted Ameera danced around the room.

Finally, all that was left was to hang the kissing bough. After some dispute amongst the men as to who was the tallest—Malik won, by an inch, over Nathaniel's six foot two—the bough was hung from the chandelier in the centre of the room, just high enough that Malik could stand beneath without it brushing against it.

Then the maids brought in mulled wine and fruit punch and warm mince pies, and cleared away the remaining greenery.

Isabel, her rich copper hair shining in the candlelight, sang a carol, filling the room with her exquisite voice. And then they were all singing, their voices rising and falling in a rich blend, and Grace found herself blinking back tears. Nathaniel, next to her on the sofa, hugged her close and before long, Clara clambered up to join them in a singing, laughing, loving heap.

As the singing came to an end, Malik held up his hand for silence.

'I thank you for inviting myself and my family to join in celebrating Christmas at your home,' he said.

He stood straight and solemn, but Grace was sure she detected a twinkle in his eyes.

'I have found enjoyment in all of your traditions,' he continued, 'but the one I most appreciate—' he grabbed Rachel's hand and tugged her to stand beneath the kissing bough '—is this one.'

He bent his head to kiss Rachel, who wound her arms around his neck and kissed him back enthusiastically.

Malik plucked a berry from the bough and then kissed Rachel once more. There was a moment's stunned silence as the rest of the room watched and then William, with a wink at Isabel, stood up.

'I say, Al-Mahrouky. Leave some for the rest of us to enjoy.'

Malik lifted his dark head. 'You had your fair share of berries in the garden, Balfour. Do not think it went unnoticed,' he said, to a round of laughter.

Nathaniel then stood, raising his glass, and a sudden hush fell over the room. One by one, those still seated rose to their feet.

'I should like to propose a toast.'

Nathaniel's deep voice sent a *frisson* of desire chasing up Grace's spine. As if sensing her reaction, he captured her gaze with his, the faintest of smiles tugging at the corner of his mouth. The angle he stood, next to the fire, highlighted his damaged cheek, but Grace barely noticed it now. It was a part of him and loved and adored by her as much as, or even more than, every other inch of him.

'To Christmastide—a time for friends and for family and a time of joy—to beloved friends from our past and to firm friends in our future, and to happy families, those who are present and—' his fiery gaze lowered to Grace's belly, leaving a scorching trail of desire in its wake '—those we have yet to meet.'

From the corner of her eye Grace saw Malik place his hand, fleetingly, on Rachel's belly. Rachel's gaze jerked to his. He nodded, then slipped his arm around her waist and hugged her close into his side.

So he does *know.* Grace caught Rachel's eye and they shared a contented smile.

Luke and Joanna stood close together, with eyes only for one another as they drank their toast.

'And, last but not least,' Nathaniel continued, 'to the newly wed Duchess of Wakefield, whose discretion and whose sage advice is greatly appreciated by *this* husband at least.'

'And by this one,' Luke said, raising his glass again as he smiled into Joanna's eyes.

'To Madame, for all she has done for me and for sending me away. She was wise, indeed, for if she had granted my wish of staying at the school to teach, I should never have met you, darling Luke.'

'And to Miss Fanworth,' Grace added, 'for if it was not for her, I should never have found Clara, nor you, my dearest love.'

'Yes. To Miss Fanworth, without whom I would never have travelled to Huria and met Malik and my beautiful stepchildren,' Rachel said.

'To Madame, Miss Fanworth, and their School for Young Ladies,' Isabel cried, raising her glass high as William snaked his arm around her waist.

A quiet bubble of contentment swelled inside Grace. 'To us, to friendship everlasting, to happy memories, and to the brightest of futures,' she said as she raised her glass for the final time.

'We all have so very much to be thankful for.'

* * * * *

If you enjoyed Grace's story,
you won't want to miss the first three
THE GOVERNESS TALES *stories*

THE CINDERELLA GOVERNESS
by Georgie Lee
GOVERNESS TO THE SHEIKH
by Laura Martin
THE RUNAWAY GOVERNESS
by Liz Tyner

MILLS & BOON®
Large Print – April 2017

ROMANCE

A Di Sione for the Greek's Pleasure	Kate Hewitt
The Prince's Pregnant Mistress	Maisey Yates
The Greek's Christmas Bride	Lynne Graham
The Guardian's Virgin Ward	Caitlin Crews
A Royal Vow of Convenience	Sharon Kendrick
The Desert King's Secret Heir	Annie West
Married for the Sheikh's Duty	Tara Pammi
Winter Wedding for the Prince	Barbara Wallace
Christmas in the Boss's Castle	Scarlet Wilson
Her Festive Doorstep Baby	Kate Hardy
Holiday with the Mystery Italian	Éllie Darkins

HISTORICAL

Bound by a Scandalous Secret	Diane Gaston
The Governess's Secret Baby	Janice Preston
Married for His Convenience	Eleanor Webster
The Saxon Outlaw's Revenge	Elisabeth Hobbes
In Debt to the Enemy Lord	Nicole Locke

MEDICAL

Waking Up to Dr Gorgeous	Emily Forbes
Swept Away by the Seductive Stranger	Amy Andrews
One Kiss in Tokyo...	Scarlet Wilson
The Courage to Love Her Army Doc	Karin Baine
Reawakened by the Surgeon's Touch	Jennifer Taylor
Second Chance with Lord Branscombe	Joanna Neil

0317 GEN STD LP